A Foggy Sunrise

A True Story

David Kimel

A Foggy Sunrise

A True Story
Copyright © 2014 David Kimel.
All rights reserved. No part of this book may be used or reproduced by any means, graphic, electronic, or mechanical, including photocopying, recording, taping or by any information storage retrieval system without the written permission of the publisher except in the case of brief quotations embodied in critical articles and reviews.

First printed by iUniverse LLC, 10/15/2014

Published by: Paramount Book Publishing

Printed in the USA
Second Edition, 2025

To you, my father, for being the guiding light in my path.

Contents

Foreword

David Kimel has written an autobiography rich in emotion and sentiment, which he titled **A Foggy Sunrise**. At first, he intended it solely for his family — as a keepsake for his children and grandchildren. But books have lives and destinies of their own, and this one outgrew the limits set by its author. What was meant to be an intimate testament has ultimately revealed itself as a vivid documentary-fresco of an era, as seen through the eyes and soul of the child and adolescent he once was.

As it happens, David Kimel and I are of the same age — children of the same generation, which I have often called the wasted generation. We both grew up and came of age — unaware of each other — in close proximity, during one of the darkest periods in history and in one of the world's most contested and manipulated geographical spaces.

This, because we had the misfortune of being born in the last century on the eastern edge of Europe, right in that fateful decade when Hitler rose to power, imposing his version of German socialism, while Stalin strained every nerve to spread the Soviet version across the globe. Both *isms* turned politics into dogma, dictatorship into secular messianism, and social life into a kind of terrorist slavery, where order was maintained through mass surveillance, genocide, and extermination camps. The free world, still suffering from the lingering aftereffects of the Great War's psychoses, was haunted by undercurrents of unconscious sympathy for the two *isms* — one promising some the millennial Walhalla of a superior race, and the other offering the proletariat its vision of paradise.

While the Nazis and the Bolsheviks were perfecting hells far easier to construct than their demagogic heavens, democratically elected Western politicians chose to look the other way, complicit, and accepted the most extravagant demands of the two dictators in the naïve hope that doing so would indefinitely defuse potential conflict.

As a result, Austria and Czechoslovakia disappeared, Finland lost Karelia and Petsamo, and Romania was brutally stripped of half of Transylvania, the Cadrilater, Bessarabia, and half of Bukovina. But in September 1939, when Poland was divided and occupied by Germany and Soviet Russia under the terms of the Hitler-Stalin agreement — known as the Molotov–Ribbentrop Pact — confrontation could no longer be avoided. And so, the Second World War began.

Romania — the country where David Kimel and I were born, just a few months apart — never had imperialist ambitions. But on the eve of the Second World War, it was the fourth-largest oil producer in the world, the breadbasket of Europe, and easy prey. A dangerous and unfortunate combination made worse by the fact that in the years immediately preceding the conflagration, Romania was ruled by King Carol II — who had already abdicated three times, usurped his son's throne in 1930, and in February 1938 established a quasi-fascist personal dictatorship with no political platform beyond the cult of his own personality. He skillfully used the state budget to line his own pockets, while neglecting the proper equipping and arming of the military. At the same time, due to his inept policy of distancing Romania from France and Britain (whose guarantees he officially renounced in July 1940) and aligning instead with Germany — a move that failed to yield the expected results — the Kingdom of Romania found itself, by September 1940, isolated, defenseless, and without external support. In that critical moment, Carol II abdicated for the fourth time, having transferred absolute power the day before to General Ion Antonescu, on the condition that his son, Mihai, be recognized as king.

General Antonescu, a man of integrity and a fine military leader, lacked a political party, had no real political training, and was not well-liked by career politicians.

The only political group willing to support him at that time was the Iron Guard — a nationalist organization with fascist and Nazi sympathies. Though its history and agenda go beyond our current scope, it's worth noting that under Carol's dictatorship, the Guard had been persecuted and its leaders assassinated. Determined to seek revenge, the Iron Guard — after a brief period of collaboration with Antonescu — attempted to overthrow him in January 1941 through an armed rebellion. The anti-state action — joined by criminal and underworld elements — though short-lived, was bloody. Before being crushed by the army, it was marked by the assassination of Romanian cultural and political figures, acts of vandalism, and the monstrous massacre of Jewish civilians.

The calm that followed was fleeting, for on June 22, 1941, Germany turned on its former partners in territorial plunder by invading Soviet Russia. Romania was forced into the war without consulting its population, and many Romanians held onto the hope that, once the provinces recently seized by the Soviets were liberated, the Romanian army would withdraw from the fighting. That hope proved to be an illusion — and, given the complex circumstances of the time, an impossibility. For Romania, the war was a catastrophe. Bucharest suffered the unenviable distinction of being bombed clumsily by the Soviets, extensively, efficiently, and destructively by the Anglo-Americans, and finally — briefly but with precision and devastating force — by the Germans. Beyond the more than one million Romanian soldiers who perished in the fighting on both eastern and western fronts, tens of thousands of innocent civilians were killed during the war, and over a million lost their homes and life savings. During one of the American bombing raids, the Kimel family too paid dearly — through no fault of their own. The father, in a desperate attempt to salvage the family's modest belongings, nearly lost his life. He suffered serious wounds and burns but had the strange fortune of being identified as German. In a final twist of irony, he received exemplary care in the German military hospital in Giuleşti.

Before long, Germany's great and lightning-fast early victories had turned into "strategic withdrawals to pre-established positions"—a general staff euphemism for defeat. Following the entry of the United States into the war alongside Britain, France, and the Soviet Union, and thanks to massive American support in troops, food, and weaponry, German setbacks multiplied and turned into disasters on every front.

In August 1944, the Red Army crossed the Dniester River, and the front line stabilized temporarily on Romanian territory, not far from Iaşi, as Antonescu began negotiations with the Soviets for a possible armistice. On August 23rd, urged on by a court clique hostile to the country's leader, King Michael I had Antonescu arrested. Believing—wrongly—that this would save his throne, he signed a humiliating armistice with the Soviet Union through Communist representatives. It was the first and only time in history that a monarch at war arrested his own head of the military and handed him over as a prisoner to the enemy.

From that moment until 1989, Romania remained—

sometimes more, sometimes less—but without interruption under Soviet occupation, exploitation, and control.

It is also true that the Nazis had used Romania's natural, human, and industrial resources—this being the only reason for their interest in such a small and seemingly insignificant country—but they paid in gold and top-quality technologies. The Soviets, by contrast, not only took everything they could to the point of exhaustion without paying a cent, but also confiscated the national treasury, including what the Germans had paid for, and in return exported to us a culture foreign to our Latin spirit and a gangster-style socio-political system.

Although Romania, in the final phase of the war, fought alongside the Allies against the Axis and suffered heavy losses in both lives and material, once peace was declared it remained territorially impoverished and became a captive satellite of the Soviet Union.

What not a single Romanian citizen knew for a very, very long time was that, on the evening of October 9, 1944, in the Kremlin, over a glass of vodka, Winston Churchill gifted Romania to his friend Joseph Stalin—in exchange for Greece. But it wasn't only the later misfortunes of the Romanian people and the other nations of Eastern Europe that stemmed, at least in part, from those unethical backroom agreements between the two "greats." The turmoil in today's world also traces some of its roots back to that same moment.

For 44 years, Romania went through sweeping and radical transformations, and our wasted generation—Kimel's and mine— was forced, willingly or not, to face the systematic destruction of Romania's intellectual and cultural life, the collapse of its agriculture, chronic food shortages, betrayals, infighting, and all the other perennial expressions of class struggle. But what stifled us the most—beyond all measure—was the lack of freedom, the suppression of personal initiative, and the uncertainty of tomorrow in a system ruled by the overzealous vigilance of the political police.

That David Kimel, a member of a minority group with a history spanning millennia of persecution and exile, did not feel at ease in Romania is hardly surprising. In fact, Socialist Romania— governed, at least on paper, by the "most worthy sons of the people," the members of the Communist Party—treated all other citizens as if they were part of an inferior minority. Honest and well-done work had no value, because only crafted rhetoric and empty slogans were truly prized. I myself, though Romanian by lineage going back centuries, felt like a stranger in my own country. Kimel had the chance to leave our unkind motherland earlier. When the opportunity finally came, I too leapt into the unknown. Once again, fate had it that we both passed through the same refugee camp in Greece, still without meeting each other. But as my father used to say, "a rolling stone gathers no moss"—and here again, **A Foggy Sunrise** stands as honest testimony.

What, who, or where one's homeland is? *Ubi bene, Ibi patria*—where it is good, there is the homeland, the Latins used to say. But today? That's a hard question, especially since there is no clean, sheltered, peaceful place left on this planet where truth reigns supreme and justice alone governs. Sadly, neither Kimel nor I have an answer.

Gabriel Watermiller

February 2019

PART 1

A GOOD DAY IS SEEN IN

THE MORNING

Preface

Life welcomes us as temporary guests. The world existed long before our arrival and will be there a long time after we leave. It's like jumping into a river, getting wet, playing and swimming a little, and then coming out on the beach to dry and rest under the sun. Then you leave, but the river remains undisturbed as before, passing its peaceful water toward the mighty sea.

As guests, we can see life with delightful eyes, seeing the wonders it has created around us, or displeasing aspects of life, if we are never pleased by her hospitality. People may look at the same picture but perceive it differently. I'm not entitled to judge anyone, but in my short passing, I have tried to capture like a camera, a few snapshots around me the way I found them, as a witness of facts and places from my past. The snapshots preserve memories just as documents do, leaving to our followers a proof that many of their paths still hold the warm imprints of our footsteps, and those of our forgotten ancestors.

Nothing could better reward my effort to describe my story than my sincere belief that it will be understood, judged with indulgence, and remembered by the ones who bring our blazing torch forward.

DAVID KIMEL

Chapter 1
At the Beginning There Was Light

I

The book of life writes itself. We only project on its blank pages our chosen paths, or the one given to us by fate. The book of life does not need sophisticated words or poetic metaphors to describe its stories; they are already there, following us everywhere and every time, like an unseen camera recording every action and word. From this book we solicit our memories and originate the whole history.

At my writing desk, I am facing this immaculate blank page that symbolizes my first moment of life, at the start of the day of January 20, 1934. I was the first born to my parents, who'd married only two years earlier. My 28-year-old father was a page setter typographer at a daily newspaper named *Dimineaţa* (*The Morning*). My mother, who came from Bulgaria and did not know the Romanian language, had just turned 29. My first home was located at 10 Sabinelor Street, which was close to King Carol Park behind the Metropolitan Seat hill; it wasn't far from the center of Bucharest. Our landlord's name was Mr. Tabacu.

I remember we had a small apartment with only two rooms.

The first room was a kitchen and a living room. A delicate floral curtain delicately printed over a yellowish fabric divided the room, leaving the stove and the kitchen table hidden back from the living area after the cooking was finished. Not far from the entrance door and by the wall was a massive cabinet of varnished black wood that supported an upper crystal display with two large crystal framed doors. On its mother had her best porcelains, beautifully encrusted glasses and painted plates that made her feel like a proud housewife. In the center, in front of the curtain, stood a large table that was always covered with a tablecloth embroidered by Mother and surrounded by four comfortable chairs. The second room was the bedroom.

The courtyard outside was square and paved entirely with cobblestones that left no place for trees or plants. It was bordered on three sides with whitewashed cottages that formed the square. A wrought-iron fence at the street enclosed the square. Every cottage was divided into small apartments like ours, with entrances atop of three cemented stairs because each place had a small, unfinished basement. There, in this dirt-floored basement, we stored winter firewood, a couple of barrels of pickled green tomatoes and cabbage, and fresh carrots buried deep in a sandy hole.

My very first recollection brings me into this courtyard. I see myself inside this round, milky-white, enameled steel basin in which Mother let the water warm up in the morning sun, down on the ground by the cemented stairs of our entrance. I had a little straw hat covering my head and was full of joy as I splashed the water around with my hands. Mother was sitting next to me on the steps, stitching or crocheting something. After a while, she would bring a large plush towel, hold me on her lap, and wrap me in it. Once I was covered in the towel and glued to her chest, she patted me softly on the back, making me hum out a long "a-a-a-a" with a tremulous sound, which made her laugh. Sometimes other ladies, our neighbours, came around and asked Mother questions, to which they'd laugh. Mother also laughed, embarrassed for not being able to understand the true sense of their wicked questions.

Apparently, I was quite mischievous from an early age, though I don't remember it myself. My family says that one time I was playing outside in the courtyard in a rolling walker. Apparently, I found the gate open, and I went out to explore the street on my own. When Mother saw that I'd disappeared, she was alarmed and went to wake my sleeping father for help. They both searched for me everywhere, the police station, hospitals, and even at the morgue—but I could not be found. In despair they asked everyone, but no one had seen me. Later that evening, the policeman who patrolled the neighborhood told them that he had found a child wandering on the street. He didn't know who I was, so he left me under the supervision of the tobacco merchant at the street corner. There I was found, sitting on top of the glass counter and eating candies.

Father usually worked every night at the newspaper. After the rotary printing press started shooting out the newspapers very early in the morning, he would arrive home tired and go straight to bed for a few hours of sleep. Mother and I left him alone each morning in the bedroom without disturbing him while he slept; both of us went in the kitchen. Here I played on the pine floor over which was laid a wide wool carpet. The kitchen table was covered with an oil cloth over which Mother prepared our meals. The wall-to-wall curtain was drawn open allowing sunlight to stream through our wooden-and-glass door. I had the entire room as a playground, but I chose to play most often under the table, pushing my toys closer to Mother's legs, from which she turned me away, pretending that she was sad. Many times, she chased me around, and when she caught me, she hugged me with her soft arms, and I had to fight her rain of kisses. Later when Father woke up, before he returned to work, we would have dinner around the front table, and Mother would tell him all the news from around the neighborhood.

One day is very vivid in my mind. I woke up from my sleep across the bed at the bottom of my father's feet. He had had an accident printing some business cards on a small press that automatically opened and closed its hungry jaw. As Father placed a card inside the open press, a coworker approached him with something important. For a short second, while he still held his hand inside, the press began closing its starving jaw over his right-hand fingers, crushing two of them. He never lamented, I remember, although his middle finger was cut off and the other one had to be reconstructed. Now he was resting in bed, holding his wrapped-up hand over his head and leaning against the headboard.

The late afternoon summer light filtered into the room through the window's lace curtains, which Mother had crocheted before her wedding. The entire home was filled with all kinds of handmade items and embroidered pieces of prestigious works that at the time made a good girl proud to have such a nice trousseau. Mother came in from the kitchen, undressed after a bath. Upon seeing me awake, she suddenly slid down behind the bed panel and said, "Look, Dorel is not sleeping."

II

Toward the end of November 1937, Father woke me, late at night. In his hurried movements, he dressed me for an unexpected trip outside. It was dark, cold, and damp as we moved quickly though the empty, silent streets. Father held Mother's arm, while I clung to the little suitcase handle, he carried. When I slowed down from fatigue, he lifted me effortlessly in his arm while holding the suitcase. We reached a large house with staircase leading up to the entrance which opened into a long, green corridor. Father helped Mother inside, handed her the small suitcase, and held her in a brief embrace. Once she down the corridor we turned back into the night. Only later did I learn that this was Caritas Hospital.

After some time, we reached the home of Aunt Raşela, my father's sister who was already waiting for us in her kitchen. She lived in a spacious cottage with several rooms, stretching all the way to the street where Uncle Aurel's tailor shop stood. The kitchen also served as a bedroom for Maria, the servant. Inside warmth filled the air, carrying the sweet scent of freshly baked pastries. Yet Father did not step in. He placed me gently into my aunt's arms and hurried back into the night.

Aunt Raşela was one of the twin sisters who were born after my father. In total, there were six children in the family, each enduring the hardships of childhood famine, illness, and the turmoil of World War I. The eldest, Uncle Herman, remained in their natal hometown of Piteşti, north-west of Bucharest. He took on responsibility of caring for their aging mother, who now lived alone in her modest home. The second brother, Pavel, married a renowned dressmaker in Bucharest named Fani, who gave birth to their son, Aurel. Tragically Uncle Pavel, whom I didn't know, passed away at a young age from tuberculosis, leaving his family behind.

The next child in line was my father, Avram. As a child, he was sent to apprentice at a printing shop, learning the trade from an early age. At just ten years old, he struggled with school, his lisps making him the target of cruel taunts from classmates. Over time, he overcomes the lisps by reading aloud, but this was not enough to keep him in school - after only two years, he needed to abandon school. During the war, food was scarce, and there were many young children to be helped. My grandfather, a quiet and kind – hearted man, was a roofer from the Galician province of Poland. After settling in Pitești and starting a family, he suffered a devastating fall from a high roof, unable to work. With his livelihood lost, his only remaining joy was gathering with others at the local tavern in evening, sipping a cinzeaca (50-millilitre glass) of țuică (plum brandy), while exchanging news and stories from around the world. Since my grandfather was unable to work, the heave burden of sustaining the family fell on my grandmother's shoulders. Determined and resourceful, she took up sewing for a few loyal clients in the neighborhood, ensuring there was bread on the table. A patient and pragmatic woman, she understood the realities of their situation. She encouraged her children to contribute as much as possible to support the household, especially now that the two youngest daughters were growing and needed additional care.

After the war, Father was drafted into the army and assigned to an airfield regiment near Bucharest, at Pipera. Having worked from a young age, he quickly found employment at a small printing shop nearby, laboring through the night to earn additional income. With his wages, he discretely compensates his superiors, allowing him to send money home to support his mother. Once his military service ended, Father secured a position at Socec-Lafayette Printing House in Bucharest. For a time, he lived with his late brother Pavel's family, sharing their modest apartment.

Uncle Pavel had rented a basement apartment near the bustling Central Railway Station, known as Gara de Nord. Father had his bed in the kitchen, sleeping on a couch draped with a worn blanket. Aunt Fani was always occupied with her clientele, assistants, and caring for her young son, Aurel. She also had a deep attachment to her elderly cat, which stubbornly insisted on sleeping atop Father's chest. Though he adored animals, he could never grow accustomed to this nightly disturbance. Each time the cat returned to his favor spot, Father gently placed it in the oven until morning. One day in a rush to leave for work, he forgot to release the poor creature. When he returned that night and discovered his mistake, he knew it was wiser to find another place to live.

Aunt Raşela and Aunt Sofi, the twin sisters, began their apprenticeships at a prestigious ladies' hat shop, where they perfected the craft of designing exquisite bonnets. Their creations soon rivaled those from Bucharest and even Paris. Both married outside of their hometown and settled into new lives with their husbands. Aunt Raşela wed a tailor from Bucharest, a two-time widower with two sons from previous marriages. Not long after their wedding, my aunt welcomed her own son, Benu.

Aunt Sofi, on the other hand, married a young man from Giurgiu who owned a haberdashery shop named La Degetar (At the Thimble). His shop stood near town's circular downtown plaza, known by locals as *Pe Farfurie* (On the Plate).

The youngest brother, Manole, was the spoiled one. What their mother and siblings had saved for the girls' trousseau, he regularly stole, prying open the cupboard door with a blade. Later, when he joined his friends in the city, he indulged in a carefree life. Eventually he met a girl from Ploieşti, married her, and started a second-hand clothing business in her city.

During the winter of 1932, Father received a note from Aunt Sofi saying that the Danube River had frozen over. At the time verbal messages were often delivered by travelling salesmen conducting business in Bucharest - faster and more reliable than the postal service. Aunt Sofi lived in Giurgiu, a small town on banks of Danube River, which formed the border between Romania and Bulgaria. In her message she mentioned a planned trip across the frozen river to visit friends and acquaintances in the Bulgarian town of Ruse, also known as Rusciuc. The journey across the solid ice-covered river – stretching about one kilometre – offered a rare opportunity for gathering and celebration. These visits always rewarded travellers with warm hospitability, lively reunions, and an abundance of laughter. Father joined them on the planned Sunday, and they went to see many friends the group that Sunday, eager to see a place beyond country's border.   That day, fate led him to my mother's house. A few months later, in June, they married happily. Their wedding celebration took place in the courtyard of 9 Crângaşi Road, where Aunt Raşela lived with her family.

After Father left me with Aunt Raşela, she put me to sleep in the guestroom – a dimly lit space, crowded with heavy furniture that loomed ominously in the shadows. The flickering silhouettes of branches, cast by the large tree outside, danced like ghosts across the ceiling, making me scared. In the morning, Father gently woke me, dressing me for the day. We ate our breakfast in the small kitchen at the back of the house before setting off on a bus to the Central Railway Station. The platform was lined with rows of trains, their towering carriages waiting in stillness. There Father met a familiar gentleman holding a large suitcase. They exchanged a few words before Father turned to me with a serious tone:

"You must behave properly," he said. "You're going on a trip to see Uncle Herman for a few days."

The gentleman took my hand, and I stood watching as my father disappeared into the bustling crowd. His lingering kiss on my cheek was still warm, and I held onto that moment as the station swirled with movement around me.

As the train started to move slowly leaving the busy platform behind, I stood glued near the window and watched people waving to us from there. Behind them, stationed, a long chain of wagons seemed to be moving backward with increasing speed. Some were black painted, but also, I seen blue wagons, green, and even red ones with golden inscriptions painted over the windows. Leaving the platform. we escaped the chaotic symphony of vendors, passengers, and the lively energy of the railway station. The gentleman kept me close throughout the journey, ensuring I stayed safe. When we arrived in Piteşti, he led me to a refined shoe shop on Main Street, where my uncle worked. At lunchtime, Uncle Herman closed the shop, and together we walked to his house.

Uncle Herman and his wife, Aunt Coca, had no children. Aunt Coca greeted me with warmth and excitement, ushering me into their elegant home. We settled into their stylish dining room in the center of the house, where she served us a delicious meal. As we ate, she asked me questions about my parents and our home. For dessert, she treated us to a plate of rich chocolate cream. When she asked how I liked it, I replied eagerly:

"I like it very much, but Mommy never make it such" My aunt and uncle exchanged amused glances and burst into laughter at my innocent phrasing.

After Uncle Herman returned to work, Aunt Coca finished her kitchen chores before retiring to her bedroom with a book in hand. She loved to read and often spoke about writing her own book once she completed her research. Reading was sacred to her—she didn't like being disturbed.

To keep an eye on me without distractions, she let me rest beside her as she read. If I couldn't fall asleep, she handed me her heavy gold bracelet, securely fastened to her left wrist, letting me play with it. When I showed signs of boredom, she would take her white, soft, round breast out of her blouse and turning over to face me, would let me play with that too.

I remember returning home with Uncle Herman and Aunt Coca on the Christmas Day afternoon. The house radiated with warmth and tranquility, filled with beauty of holiday season. As always, the curtains let in a soft, golden glow, bathing the room in light. Father greeted us with joy, lifting me high toward the ceiling with his strong arms. Mother lay peacefully cradling a tiny, sleeping baby in her arms, - my new little sister, Simona.

But the happiest surprise of all was waiting for me on one of the night tables – beautifully wrapped box adorned with a shiny red ribbon. Inside was a toy airplane with two wide wings and a coil-spring motor that could be wound up using a butterfly-shaped key. Father pulled the airplane from the box, turned the key one, two, three times, then let it run on the floor on its own. It was the most beautiful toy I had ever seen. Overcome with excitement, I hopped around the room, clapping my hands with joy.

The airplane rolled forward, the propeller spinning, until reached the wall and stopped. Unable to contain my delight, I begged Father to wind it up again and again. After a few joyful runs, the airplane slid under the wardrobe, out of reach. Determined to retrieve it, Father lay flat on the carpet and, with the help of fire tongs, carefully pulled it out.

III

It's fascinating how memory works. I was not even four years old when my little sister, Simona, was born, yet the vivid detail of that time is still scattered in my mind. I must have watched Mother feed Simona countless time, yet not a single image of those moments stays imprinted on the canvas of my mind. I don't recall whether Simona slept in one of the big beds with us or whether she had a cradle or a swing of her own. Her lullabies, too, have faded into oblivion.

What I do remember, however, is that my closest friend was a nine-year-old girl named Gabi Ionescu. Gabi lived in the same courtyard as us. She was neat and kind, nearly two times taller and older than I. She had a remarkable talent for crafting animals out of plaster molds – delicate figurines that she shaped with her fingers and pieced together with precision. Sometimes she mixed different colors to make her figurines look more lifelike. I admired her skill, though my own attempts resulted in nothing more than a long, slim, round sausage-shape that could pass for serpents at the best. The figurine I cherished most was a little mouse she made. It had a sharp mouth, whiskers, and a slender tail that tapered elegantly at the end.

Gabi's mother, madam Ionescu, was a woman of medium build, usually dressed in a flowing, floral house gown. She was often busy in the kitchen, sometimes offering us pastries or samples of her cooking. Their apartment was larger than ours, but even in the middle of the day, its rooms remained dim. Heavy curtains veiled the bedroom windows, and only the soft glow of nightstands fixtures illuminated the space. I never met Gabi's father, which made me wonder whether she had one. Whenever Mother let me outside to play and I felt bored or alone in that large courtyard, I would go to knock at Gabi's door for companionship. If Gaby wasn't home, her mother still welcomed me inside and allowed me to play with the delicate figurines displayed on her nightstand.

Sometime Madam Ionescu, brought me into the kitchen to chat as she worked around the stove, asking questions about my sister and my parents.

One day while Gabi was at school and I was playing with her little mouse, Madam Ionescu entered the bedroom, to change into a fresh gown. As she undressed, she asked me:

"W do you want to be when you grow up?

"An aviator," I answered without hesitation.

She smiled. "Why an aviator and not a doctor? Don't you like to heal people?"

She draped her clean gown over her shoulders and sat beside me on the edge of the bed, leaning in closer.

"Tell me; don't you rather be a doctor?"

Her voice softened as she took my hand, pulling me gently between her legs, which rose out from beneath her satin chemise.

"Do you know that I have a little hump that causes me pain. Wouldn't you like to help heal it?"

I nodded. Her expression turned serious, her locking onto mine. Holding my chin between her fingers, she whispered:

"But you must not tell a soul about this. Do you understand? Nobody must know! If I hear that you said a word, I'll be angry —

and I won't let you come here ever again. Understood?"

"Yes!" I said instantly.

Madam Ionescu studied me for a moment before lifting her chemise over her pale, rounded belly.

"Look, I'm hurt here, "she said, pointing to a small lump rising from the dark valley between her hips. "Do you see this little villain? It hurts here!" She placed her finger over it and pulled me closer. "Put your little tongue on it to make my pain go away!" she murmured pressing head toward the shadowed hollow.

After a while, when the pain disappeared, she sat up, tied her gown firmly around the waist, and gave me a spoonful of jam from a jar:

"Don't say anything about this, okay?" Then she led me to the door and let me go.

In the following days, though I knew Gabi was home, Madam Ionescu refused to let me in. A few mornings later, while I played in the courtyard, she called me over and invited me inside to play with Gabi's figurines again. I eagerly picked up the little mouse, shaping its tiny tail between my fingers, when Gaby's mother entered the bedroom and sat beside me on the bed, stroking my hair. She sighed.

"The villain is hurting me again," she said, reclined across the bed and uncovering her belly. "Can you heal me?"

I looked at her stomach, stretched and spilling slightly over the shits like dough, and a thought came to me.

"Where are the scissors?" I asked.

"What? What do you need scissors for?" she asked me frowned.

"To take the baby out!" I told her. Confusion flickered across her face:

"What baby? There is no baby," she answered.

But I insisted. I think I made the connection with the stories that Mother told me when she was pregnant with Simona, and the idea had settled deep in my mind.

"There is a baby in there. Give me the scissors to take the baby out!"

Madam Ionescu's expression darkened. She stood abruptly, pulling her gown around her, already "healed." Without a word, she ushered me toward the door and pushed me outside.

I never fully understood what happened, but I do remember that my mother eventually learned that I had seen Madam Ionescu naked. I don't know whether she spoke to Gabi's mother, but by the time spring arrived, Gabiand her family had moved out of our courtyard. I never heard from them again.

IV

That summer of 1938 brought more than the unbearable heat – it carried news of escalating war preparations, Hitler's rise to power in Germany, and recent order to annex Austria and Sudetenland. In Romania, the nationalistic policies of Octavian Goga's government fueled rising hostilities toward foreigners, particularly Jews. As a result, father - a Jewish man – was laid off from the newspaper. Debt quickly accumulated, and soon, our landlord, Mr. Tabacu, informed us that we have to vacate our home.

One sweltering summer day, Father took Mother, Simona, and me to the railway station and put us on a third-class train to Giurgiu. He lifted our old suitcase onto the rack above our heads near the window, kissed us goodbye, and stood on the platform, watching until we were swallowed by the distance. Our destination was Aunt Sofi's house. That heat was oppressive, and the train was packed with passengers. People were pressed so tightly against one another that some were nearly over us as we sat. We gasped for some fresh air from the open windows, but the scorching wind carried only the thick scent of train smoke.

When we arrived in Giurgiu, the station erupted into chaos. Crowds poured onto the platform, surging wildly in every direction. In the midst of the turmoil, Mother clutched Simona in her arms while I lingered beside her, weighed down by luggage. She scanned the faces around us, searching for someone familiar. But no one was there. The heat, dust, and deafening noise – voices shouting, carriers hauling heavy luggage to waiting horse carriages outside in the street – did not promise a peaceful stay. I watched the restless movement around us, feeling a ripple of fear.

Then, finally, Aunt Sofi appeared, waving a handkerchief hastily to catch our attention. She lived in an old house not far from the haberdashery shop in the town center.

The wagon-style home was large, with multiple rooms, its doors and windows flung open to invite the air. The house swarmed with children—Aunt Sofi had three sons and a baby daughter, Lola, born around the same time as Simona. A live-in maid, a petite woman with a perpetually frazzled expression, struggled to keep up with the endless demands. She never seemed to know whom to listen to first – the boys, who were constantly fighting, screaming, and jumping – or the parents, who rarely saw eye to eye. In her small baby bed, the newborn sister, Lola, wailed loudly. It wasn't long before Simona joined her in a chorus of cries.

Uncle Rubin remained at his shop while Aunt Sofi and Mother debated our sleeping arrangements. Eventually, they decided I would share a bed with my cousin Hermuş, who was two years older than me. Iancu, the oldest of the three, slept with Jackitu, the youngest. That first morning, I woke to humiliation – my bed was wet. Hermuş and his brothers erupted into laughter, bouncing on their beds and pointing at me.

"Pee-pee boy! Pee-pee boy! He peed in bed! He peed in bed!" they shouted gleefully, their taunts relentless. From that morning on, they teased me daily. I didn't remember ever wetting the bed before. Only Mother understood me. She pulled me into her arms and whispered gently:

"Soon we'll go home, and everything will be all right."

Two weeks later, on a Sunday afternoon, we returned to the railway station. This time the entire family – Aunt Sofi, Uncle Rubin, the boys, Lola, and even the maid (who helped with the luggage), came to see us off. Mother held Simona in one arm and clutched my hand with the other, absorbing the rush of the last-minute advice and farewells. Hugs and kisses were exchanged before she guided us into the train's wagon.

It hadn't been easy for her in Giurgiu. The constant chaos – the shouting of four boys, the shrill cries of two babies' girls competing for dominance – had weighed heavily on her. The endless jealousy fueling my aunt's daily breakdowns when Uncle Rubin returned late in the evening, smelling of alcohol and ready for a confrontation, only deepened her discontent. But worst of all,

Mother resented being treated as a second servant in the house, when all she had wanted was to lend a helping hand.

As our train rolled into Bucharest, Father was already waiting for us on the platform. He helped us off, embracing each of us warmly before gathering the luggage. We made our way to the streetcar station in front of the railway building, were Father shared news of our new home:

"You'll like It," he spoke. "It's on a quiet street," we were assured.

After only a few stops, we stepped off and cross Podul Grant (the Grant Bridge) on the wooden pedestrian boardwalk. It was separated from the bustling two-way road, allowing us to look down and watch the slow movement of trains gliding beneath us.

Finally, we arrived at our new home at 52 Eduard Grant Street. The house was smaller than our previous apartment on Sabinelor Street. The courtyard was unpaved, with a water outlet positioned toward the back. Two cottages faced each one another; one with smaller rental apartments. To the right stood the tallest and most spacious building, occupied by our new landlord, Mr. Dobre. Our home lay across from his, near the street, with other tenants settled behind us. We had only a kitchen and a bedroom. The bedroom, painted stark white, felt cramped compared to our previous home. A large, framed window, deeply set into a thick wall, let in the light.

Our furniture, made of solid varnished oak, barely fit, leaving, little space to walk. Mother took pride in keeping it polished, running soft cloth over its golden luster daily. A large jute carpet covered the floor, though much of it rested hidden beneath the beds and other furniture. The space between the window and the foot of our two beds formed the only open area, centered between two-night tables. The handmade curtains framed the window gently. In the corner, beside the kitchen door, stood the metallic cylindrical wood stove with black tubes stretching toward the ceiling, where a round elbow tube entered the wall. The kitchen was narrow, its dirt floor concealed by a large reed wall to wall mat, layered with rugs to keep our feet warm. There was no electricity.

Aunt Raşela lived only one street away, and I often saw her visiting us, accompanied by Maria, her maid, who carried a basket of food for us. Father was away most of the day, but in the evenings, he filled our home with stories after dinner. Sometimes, he told us old fairy tales; other times, he played with us, immersing us in games and laughter. One winter day, he began to assemble a galena radio receptor, carefully mounting it in the deep window niche of the bedroom. With headphones over his head, he adjusted the tiny brush encased in a glass tube, slowly maneuvering it to connect it to the yellow crystal at the other end. He spent the entire afternoon trying to capture a sound – any sound – but the radio remained silent. Eventually, he set aside, for another day, which never come. For me, however, the radio became my favorite toy. With the headphones snug over my ears, I sat on in front of the window, pretending to turn an imaginary wheel, humming the steady whir of an engine. I saw myself soaring the sky in an airplane, racing down the streets in a fast car, or standing victorious as a brave combatant – just like the heroes I had seen in movies.

Sometimes, Father took us to the theatre on Crângaşi Road. We'd wait for him in the cashier hall while he visited the director, carrying the daily paper to show off the beautiful advertisements he printed on its pages. This gesture often earned us free entry. After the movie, Mother would stop at the Greek pastry shop on the corner, picking up roasted pumpkin seeds or even some baked pumpkin squares. I loved those treats - especially the pumpkin with its caramelized blackened crust, its sweetness rich as honey.

A neighbor's boy, slightly older than me, introduced me to mischief one winter. He taught me how to whistle between his teeth, how to spit, and other nasty tricks. Across the street lived some young schoolgirls. One of them had a big steel sled and, on occasion, would pull me along the snow-covered sidewalk. When she turned it sharply, send me tumbling onto the dirty pavement. I would arrive home soaked, my coat packed with snow, my hands aching from the cold. But the worst pain came in the kitchen. When I stood near the stove, the tawing pain in my frozen fingers became unbearable, and I cried while as Mother struggled to remove the single-fingered wool gloves she had crocheted for me.

On a spring evening, just before sundown, a commotion spread through the neighborhood. People rushed down the street, shouting that the movie theatre was on fire. Mother quickly took Simona in her arms and ran outside to see what was happening. Left alone in the kitchen, I continued playing near the table, lost on my own world. On the white tablecloth sat a plate of warm pastries, dusted generously with powdered sugar. When Mother returned, she glanced at the plate, then at me, and asked:

"Dorel, did you take any of this?"

"No," I answered focused on my play. She pressed further:

"Tell the truth, and I will not punish you. Did you take any?"

"No!" I told her as I continued to play.

To her, my refusal to admit, wasn't just dishonesty - it was defiance. Anger flashed in her eyes as she reached for fire tongs, pulling me toward her:

"Do not lie to me! Understand? Do not lie to me!" she shouted, her voice sharp with frustration, as she struck me on the head tongs.

When she saw blood, her fury dissolved in panic. She took

me in her arms, kissing me, crying as she dressed my wound. That night she held me close to her chest until I fell asleep. Sadly, this incident would not be the last I was punished for telling the truth.

V

When Father came home, he told us been called back to the army. With unpaid rent piling up, our landlord, Mr. Dobre, informed him that we need to find another place to live.

This time, we moved to 29 Tabla Buţii Street, at Madam Stela's. The street sloped down from Giuleşti Road all the way to Piaţa Grant (Grant Market). At that time, the outer streets of Bucharest only partially asphalted - one sidewalk was smooth, while the other remained paved with cobblestones. Our home was on the asphalted side.

The property consisted of a single cottage, stretching along a narrow courtyard. Our apartment sat toward the far end, after Madam Stela's. As before, we had just two rooms, a bedroom and a kitchen. Madam Stela kept chickens, a proud rooster, and a lovely young pig that ran freely across the yard. Near the gate stood a deep well, iron pulley supporting a tin bucket that descended into its depth, for cool, fresh water. In the center of the courtyard, a water tap installation provided us with easy access to water for household needs.

Madam Stela, and her husband, Mr. Gică, had no children. In Romania, it is customary for younger people to address their elderly fellows by adding the word Aunt or Uncle, even without family ties. Uncle Gică was a quiet, kind man, always well dressed in light-colored suit and tie - except when tending to household chores. He was polite, handy, and let me watch him work, talking to me about what he does. He carried himself with neatness and precision, his black wavy hair combed carefully to one side. A thin moustache curved over his upper lip shaped so perfectly, it almost appeared painted on. One detail stood out starkly—his motionless right eye, always concealed behind a glass imitation. At home, Father called him "chiorul" (the one-eyed man).

Soon, Father began arriving home dressed in his military uniform - a green tunic with matching pants, shiny black boots wrapped with fabric gaiters, spiralling neatly up to his knees. His large officer's cap, adorned with a glossy black peak, cast shadow over his forehead. Father was already tall and thin, but the uniform made him appear even leaner. His visits were short – he was always in a hurry, heading straight to the regiment.

Aunt Raşela continued to come over almost daily always carrying a basket of goods. She rarely lingered - her husband, Uncle Aurel, was stingy and jealous, and never wanted to risk his displeasure. When she couldn't come herself, she sent Maria, her maid, in her place with something for us.

One day soon after Father was demobilized, he took me to the grocer's shop across the street to settle some debits. The countertop was lined with jars of colorful candies – some wrapped in gold and silver foil, others in shimmering colored paper, each one temptingly bright. Among them, large chocolate coins that look real, gleamed under the shop lights, their surface stamped with the effigy of King Carol II, his metallic helmet adorned with a plume of feathers. Seeing my fascination, Father bought two golden coins - one for me and one for Simona.

Behind our home, the neighbors had a wax cherry tree that stretched above our roof, its branches heavy with golden fruit. One day, Uncle Gică climbed onto the roof through the side attic door - and took me along. Branches spilled over the warm steel roof, laden with clusters of ripening cherries, glowing brightly in the sun. Sitting between Uncle Gică's legs, I reached out as he pulled the branches closer, helping me pluck the sweet, juicy fruit and pop them straight into my mouth. We filled a bucket with cherries, but more often than not, we ate them right there, unable to resist their golden sheen and irresistible flavor. When Mother saw me up there on the roof, she nearly fainted.

That fall, I registered for kindergarten, just down street, at the corner with Giuleşti Road. Father took me in the morning, dressed neatly in a new checkered blue-and-white uniform, starched white collar, and a bright red bow beneath my chin. Holding my hand, Father introduced me to a young lady teacher in the school courtyard, then left me standing there - tears welling in my eyes. I felt abandoned in a strange, foreign world. The teacher, slim and strikingly beautiful, moved through the courtyard like a mother hen, carefully gathered us, guiding us into the classroom. Inside, she seated us at small tables, each with two little chairs. She asked for our names, instruction us to sit with our hands behind our backs, before handling each of us a square of thick cloth, a needle, and a printed design on paper. We were taught to perforate the figures from the drawing, carefully pricking out the shapes. Beside me sat a restless little girl, constantly shifting, talking, and fidgeting. When the teacher wasn't looking, she pricked me under the table with her needle. Later the teacher moved her to the first row of tables, replacing her with a quiet boy.

At break time, before recess, the teacher lined us up two by two, instructing us to hold hands. We walked in silence down the corridor, stepping carefully into the schoolyard. We returned in the same orderly fashion.

Later that winter, after returning home from an evening visit Mother had a sudden craving for something sweet before bedtime. Still wearing her old blue gabardine coat, fastened with large wooden buttons, she hurried to open the beveled crystal glass doors of the upper showcase. Inside, she kept most prized possessions - fine crystal, chinaware, treasured wedding gifts, and delicate pieces from her mother's house. She was looking for her comfiture plates, decorated with a broad red border framing elegant handmade paintings. Father, still holding a sleeping Simona in his arm, stood near the entrance door with me at his side. As Mother opened the two thick crystal doors, the entire showcase lost its balance, tipping dangerously forward over her. Father released my hand and lunged forward to catch the falling cabinet just in time. But the contents inside – the exquisite plates, cups and goblets – slid out like an unstoppable waterfall, cascading over across the floor. Not a single piece remained intact.

The tragedy was indescribable. Mother's reaction was heart-wrenching. Her tears poured endlessly, as though she lost a dear loved one. Without her treasure of expensive plates and crystal, she felt poor, stripped of all pride. Anger and frustration followed. She blamed Father accusing him of negligence of never properly securing the showcase to the lower cabinet. She sobbed uncontrollably for hours. Father was angry too, but he never whispered a word. Growing impatient, seeing that there was no end to this, told her to go to bedroom to sleep. But Mother refused. She pushed him away, punching him on his chest with clenched fists, calling him names in her fury. And that's how the fight started.

Simona, now awake burst into tears. I also had tears silently streaming down my cheeks, helpless - not knowing whom to beg to stop. Mother collapsed into a chair, crying powerlessly, while Father, without his coat or hat, walked out into the darkness of the night.

The next morning, we woke fully dressed in our winter coats, the wrinkled sheets untouched beneath us. The room was cold; the floor littered with shards of broken porcelain and glass. Mother's face was swollen, her eyes red, her hair unusually disheveled. Father did not return. For days, my parents avoided each other, never speaking, never changing a glance. When Mother confided to Aunt Raşela explaining everything, my aunt finally told Mother the truth. Father had been unemployed for over a month. Each day he went to the Central Railway Station, carrying travellers' luggage to carriages and taxi cabs for small money. Sometimes commissioners from Giurgiu or Piteşti sent him to run errands, and so he brings home whatever money he could. Mother never knew how he had been earning an income until that moment. She sat in silent disbelief, tears pooling in her eyes.

That evening, when Father came home for dinner, Mother greeted him with a steaming hot meal and a large bouquet of flowers smiling softly in the middle of the table.

Chapter 2
Gathering Clouds

I

The summer of 1939 found Mother, Simona, and I in Ploiesti staying at Uncle Manole's house. He and his family resided in the vicinity of the city market, where they ran a second-hand clothing shop, offering a wide-ranging mix of suits, dresses, coats, shirts, and even shoes. Some could've been seen from the street hung around the door. A showcase window displayed garments around an old mannequin dressed in a plaid suit and a hat.

Uncle Manole spent his days smoking outside, seated on a chair near the entrance, watching pedestrians pass by. Sometimes he'd call out:

"Hello, mister! How about dressing up you nicely?"

If he saw the man hesitate, Uncle Manole sprang from his chair, gently grabbed the man's arm, and ushered him inside. Behind a counter stood Aunt Debora, always ready to greed newcomers. Cigarettes dangling from their lips, they spoke in perfect synchrony, guiding the man toward a tall, framed mirror leaned against a bookshelf brimming with merchandise. Jackets, pants, shirts

- even hats - were presented, touched and tried on the customer, weaving a constant stream of persuasion. Price negotiation stretched long, but in the end the handshake sealed the deal. As it was their tradition, they headed to the corner tavern together for a good luck drink.

My uncle and aunt were born merchants, unrelenting negotiators who thrived on haggling and persuasion. Once entered their place, no customer left empty-handed. They bargained endlessly, taking turns in their arguments, layering logic and charm, until their unsuspecting buyer—dizzy from too much talk— yielded, paid, and left. Truth is, they sold cheap, happy for a small profit.

"A penny sold is a penny gained" was their slogan.

On good days, they returned home laden with gifts and candies, filling the house with delight.

Uncle Manole and Aunt Debora had two children—Paula, a year younger than me, and Simon, about the same age as my sister, Simona. But Simon was different. At two years old, he could not stand, could not speak, could not move. Curled into a fetal position, he lay on the bed, moaning, his hollowed cheeks and enormous, vacant eyes rarely showing signs of recognition.

In the evenings, the whole family gathered around the large dining table, under a heavy crystal chandelier that bathed the room in golden light. Among us sat Aunt Debora's mother, a small yet commanding widow, with an intimidating, powerful energy that made everyone pay attention to her. Like her daughter, she was a proud chain smoker too.

The servant, a middle-aged woman from the countryside, joined us at the table as well. Dinner was noisy, the meal plenty, and glasses were never empty—red wine for adults, lemonade for children. I remember those reusable lemonade bottles, their porcelain hinged corks secured with a wire mechanism, clicking open with each use. Laughter filled the room as adults ate, drank, and smoked simultaneously. Simon lay watching from his bed, his moans soothed by a spoon of sugar wrapped in a cloth, fed to him by the servant. This kept him quiet and busy.

Simon, like my sister Simona, was named in Jewish tradition, honoring our grandfather, Simon the roofer, who had passed before our birth. I received my name, David, after Aunt Debora's father, who had also died before I was born. Yet my parents always called me Dorel, a poetic name chosen by Mother, meaning Dor-el (Longed dear). Paula, my cousin, was named after Uncle Pavel, my father's older brother.

Paula was bright and curious, already counting, adding, subtracting, and reading the newspaper with ease. Her grandmother made her read aloud daily, sharpening her skills. Each afternoon, Paula and I were sent to nap together, tucked under the same blanket. We never slept. Instead, we whispered, giggled, and played secretly. One day, in our muffled laughter, we discovered our "forbidden parts." When Mother walked in, we froze in terror and never been allowed to sleep together.

The holiest days in the Jewish calendar, Rosh Hashanah (New Year) and Yom Kippur (Day of Atonement), arrived in September. In preparation, two fat, white chickens were selected for the occasion. After dinner, with the table cleared, the servant brought the chickens, their legs tied and placed them by Aunt Debora's mother's feet. Weve been told to gather in a silent circle around her. With her head covered by a woolen scarf, she held a prayer book in her left hand while, with her right, she lifted each chicken above our heads, moving it in slow, ritualistic circles, murmuring ancient Hebrew prayers. As children, we kept our heads lowered, watching curiously, but understanding none of it. Mother told me that trough this prayer, our sins would pass to the chickens. In our own home, my parents honored the Jewish holidays, but never in this way.

At dawn, Aunt Debora's mother and the servant packed the chickens into reed baskets. Taking Paula and me, they led us to a place where ritual sacrifice of animals was performed. Arrived at a courtyard beside a large warehouse where at its end stood a metallic door. In front of it, people lined up clutching live chickens, waiting for their turn. Inside, an old man—a rabbi, with a long white beard, dressed in a black, shiny coat, glasses perched beneath a wide-brimmed hat—stood by a small window, its faint light filtering in. In the corner, a stainless-steel basin gleamed under the dim glow, its rounded bottom slick with water.

The rabbi inspected each bird carefully, stroking their feathers with his thumb. After declaring them kosher, he hung them on basin's wire hooks, crossing their wings neatly behind their backs. With a swift, practiced motion, he cleared their neck feathers, then took a sharp blade and made a small incision, murmuring a soft prayer as a thin stream of blood pooled into the basin below. Within seconds, the chickens lay still, their life slowly slipping away. A hose connected to a water tap washed away the blood, draining it into the canal. Once the birds ceased moving, the rabbi gently folded their heads under their wings, allowing us to pack them for home. Aunt Debora's mother paid the rabbi, and we made our way back.

II

We returned to Bucharest shortly after the holidays, only to find a new home waiting for us at the same address where Aunt Raşela lived, at 9 Crângaşi Road. But this house was unlike any we had lived in before. It was inside a shop, its large street-facing window shielded by heavy wooden shutters. Before we moved in, the space had housed a siphon bottle refilling shop, a thriving business at the time—since many people mixed their wine with soda water.

Each day, thick custom-made bottles were brought in, refilled, and sent back out. The bare cement floor was interrupted by a canal in the center, covered by a round steel grate, punctured with tiny holes like a strainer. The walls were lined with whitewashed water pipes. At the back, a small, narrow room with white walls reflected the daylight filtering through a wide, overhead window near the ceiling, allowing glimpses of the sky and the top of a towering acacia tree from the courtyard.

We entered through a secondary door, which led into a dark gangway, its arched ceiling resembling a tunnel, connecting the street to the courtyard. The main shop space was large, with electricity and water. A wood-burning stove sat near the canal mouth, while the cooking stove was installed in the smaller back room, leaving just enough space for our kitchen table and a few chairs. Against the middle wall in the main room, our beds lined up beneath the water pipes. Above them, two large, framed portraits of my grandparents stared down at us. Next to them, over the night tables, hung two sepia-toned photographs of my parents' wedding. The wide window facing the street disappeared behind Mother's lace curtains, but they allowed no light inside, blocked entirely by the shutters.

The washroom, built from bricks and cement, stood at the far end of the courtyard, designed in a Turkish style without a seat. It had a water installation, but in winter, the pipes froze if the door was left open.

A majestic old acacia tree dominated the square courtyard, casting its dense shade across the space. At its base, beside its sturdy trunk, stood a water tap, with a sewer grate covered in iron mesh.

Two parallel buildings ran from the back of the courtyard to the street, framing the space. Between them, the solid structure of the siphon shop offered privacy and security. The right-side older building, belonged to Uncle Aurel, a tailor who had lived there for years, earning a respected reputation in the neighborhood. Across from his was a newer, taller building, its façade finished in calcium-veccio, occupied by the Fridman family. The entire structure formed an L-shape, with the siphon shop. Atop siphon shop and part of Fridman building on the second floor, lived Dr. Perno's, the dentist, whose apartment entrance faced the back door of the siphon shop inside the gangway. Below, at the street side, stood Schmidt's Cleaner Shop on the far side of the gangway. The courtyard could be accessed through the gangway or via a narrow wooden gate between the siphon shop and Uncle Aurel's tailor shop.

Aunt Raşela had three children, but only the youngest, Benu, was hers. The elder two, Sergiu and Ticu, were Uncle Aurel's sons from previous marriages. His first wife had set herself on fire in a tragic act, suffering an agonizing death. His second wife passed away from natural causes. Uncle Aurel himself was bald, older, and somewhat withdrawn. He was not particularly social with us and took his daily naps undisturbed—strictly enforcing silence around the house. Yet, he was a dedicated family man, a skilled tailor, and a hard worker. He trained young apprentices from the countryside, teaching them his trade.

My cousin Sergiu, a tall, slim young man, had finished school and worked in an office. His slicked-back black hair made him seem arrogant, cool, and indifferent. Whenever he played with me, he'd tap my nose, bringing me to tears.

Ticu, the middle child, was kind and entertaining. He knew countless stories, always leaving me eager for more. Benu, a high school student, wore a gold-embroidered number on his sweater arm. Often, he took me to the corner sweets shop and buy me candies.

Crângaşi Road never slept. Buses, cars, and horse carts moved without pause, their presence constant, day and night. Elegant black carriages, their proud horses adorned in encrusted harnesses, carried passengers through the streets, guided by drivers in long, dark velvet coats. Much of the traffic streamed from Grivița Road, flowing endlessly over Podul Grant (the Grant Bridge). At the street corner, bus number 38 stopped, carrying passengers toward Gara de Nord (the Central Railway Station). One day, Benu walked me to the bus stop and whispered:

"Do not tell Mother I'm leaving. You know nothing!"

I blinked. "Where are you going?"

"To Sora, to buy something." (Sora was the nearest universal shopping center, across from Gara de Nord.)

I begged him: "Take me with you!"

"I can't! I'll bring you candies."

With that, he jumped onto the bus just as it halted and disappeared into the moving crowd.

Across Western Europe, Germany's war machine had begun sweeping through nation after nation. Romania, under mounting pressure from Germany, was forced to surrender territory—its eastern regions ceded to Russia, the southern to Bulgaria, and the northern to Hungary, all in an effort to avoid invasion. The Germans gained unrestricted access through Romanian land, advancing toward Russia. In response, Romania joined Germany's Russian campaign, eager to reclaim Bessarabia and Bucovina, territories lost in 1939.

By 1940, ominous changes had taken hold of the streets. Men dressed in green shirts with diagonal black leather straps—the uniform of the Legionnaires—became a common sight. Their presence mirrored the Storm Troopers of Nazi Germany, who wore brown shirts. The Legionnaires in Romania adopted their nationalist ideology directly from Hitler's *Mein Kampf*, portraying Jews as the source of all the world's problems, advocating for their elimination.

Shops owned by Jewish families across the city were forced to display banners in their windows—wide strips of paper with large black letters spelling "JIDAN" (the Jew), a derogatory slur. One evening, young men in green shirts entered Uncle Aurel's shop, plastering a Jidan banner onto his window. The following day, one of the same men returned, offering to remove the banner in exchange for a large sum of money. Uncle Aurel refused, turning him away without hesitation.

Newspapers launched a fierce campaign advocating for the recovery of Bessarabia and Bucovina, regions Romania had been forced to surrender.

"All lands taken from Russia," they proclaimed, "must be colonized by Romanians, who will receive these properties free of charge." Jews were not excluded from this process.

My cousin Sergiu, increasingly anxious, was desperate to

escape, insisting he would leave alone if necessary. Rumor was heard later that he befriended some legionaries and came with the idea of soliciting money in exchange for banners removal. When accused of stealing, frightened he wanted to run away.

Uncle Aurel, deeply shaken by the banner on his shop window, sold what he could, packed suitcases with clothes, valuables, and money, and took his entire family away. Before leaving, Aunt Raşela entrusted Father with letters written for Grandmother in Piteşti, asking him to send them at weekly intervals. She also left money, telling Father to mail small amounts monthly. Grandmother was not supposed to know they had fled far away.

Father now worked at a small typography behind the Telephone Palace, Bucharest's tallest tower. Mother knew that early in the afternoon, she had to bring us there to meet Father after work.

I remember watching the Number 6 streetcar arrive at its final stop in the center, behind the tall brick wall enclosing the back gardens of the Royal Palace. Curiously I watch the driver switching the rail track blade with an iron stick, then backed up the wagons into a side street before finally returning frontward, heading back to a new trip north

. Mother dressed us neatly, ensuring we behaved properly,

not wanting to embarrass Father in front of his colleagues. Inside his workshop, Father was preparing galleys. I watched intently as he picked up lead letters, arranging them one by one in a holder with closed ends, shaped like an L. The ink-blackened letters, stored in wooden boxes, were sorted meticulously from the wide drawer atop a tall cabinet—one of many, each lined against the walls. Father still had work to do, so he pulled open a cabinet drawer, hoisted me onto it, and let me play with the scattered lead letters inside. Mostly, I was mesmerized by his precision, watching his fingers—quick like a chicken pecking for seeds—as he selected and aligned each letter.

"This is how books are made," he told me.

I don't remember whether we went to a movie or a restaurant that night, but we arrived home late, darkness already settled. As we entered the gangway, a figure emerged from the shadows:

"Thank God you're here! I've been waiting for hours."

It was Grandmother from Piteşti. She stood shivering, wrapped in a thin black overcoat, her long silver hair tied in a loop, her head covered by a lace shawl. Father rushed forward embracing her:

"Mother, why didn't you send word that you were coming? I would have met you at the train," he told her.

We brought her inside. Mother lit the fire in the wood stove, preparing a warm meal. Simona, asleep in Father's arms, was gently laid to bed. Grandmother handed me a white handkerchief, bundled with candies from her purse.

"Save some for your sister," she whispered, patting my hair.

She had arrived before dark, sensing something was wrong in Bucharest—though no one had warned her. When she reached Uncle Aurel's shop, she saw the shutters drawn tight, the house sunken in darkness, lifeless inside. She collapsed, fainting on the street. Neighbors helped her, explaining that the family had gone to Transnistria. They offered to take her in the next door Iliescu's restaurant until we would retuned, but she refused. Instead, she sat alone on the small cement step of our side door in the gangway and waited.

The next morning, Grandmother asked Father to take her to the railway station—she wanted to go to Ploieşti, to see her son, Manole. Father pleaded with her to stay, at least for a few more days, but she wouldn't change her mind. By the end of the week, we received a telegram from Ploieşti:

Grandmother had passed away.

III

Father returned home from Ploieşti after two days. He looked exhausted, thinner than before, and his unshaven red facial hair made him appear strangely rugged. When he lifted me up for a kiss, his rough beard tickled my skin.

He told us that grandmother had fallen sick almost as soon as she arrived in Ploieşti—and never left her bed again. She had sensed that something terrible had happened in Bucharest—and when she learned the truth about Aunt Raşela, her heart broke. Her life ended within days, quietly—without a word, a sign, or even a moan.

Mother wept for Grandmother, though she had never been particularly close to her. When she married and moved to Romania, Father had asked Grandmother to stay with them in Bucharest, hoping her presence would bring Mother comfort. He knew his new wife was an orphan from the age of thirteen—believing that Grandmother's companionship would help fill the void. But strangely, things did not unfold this way. Mother waited all day for Father's arrival from work, dreaming of time together in intimate, uninterrupted and unshared moments with her husband. Yet, Grandmother also waited for him. When Father finally came home, Mother found herself frustrated— her time with him constantly divided, leaving little space for them to be alone except late at night, when all they could do was sleep.

Their first home stood across from Banu Manta City Hall, not far from the Șosea. Once, the Șosea had been Bucharest's grand promenade avenue, where the city's elite paraded driven in carriages or astride their finest horses, displaying wealth through elegant attire. Now, its wide sidewalks stretched beneath the cooling shade of towering chestnut trees, their dense foliage forming an arch, concealing the city's most opulent palaces. Named after Russian General Kiseleff, a figure instrumental in uniting Moldavia and Wallachia a century earlier, the Șosea remained Bucharest's most enchanting evening stroll, even today. Because it lay so close to home, Father often invited both Mother and Grandmother for a walk. Both accepted eagerly.

They would stroll up to the Arch of Triumph, then circle back, stopping at La Bufet (At the Buffet), one of the most renowned restaurants in the area. Its splendid summer garden, guarded by ancient trees, was famous for its sizzling mititei (Romanian spicy rolled burgers), their aroma drifting onto the street, irresistible to every passerby.

Each time Father asked them for a walk, Grandmother would immediately grab her bag and little hat, ready to leave at once. She would wait patiently in the courtyard. Mother, however, refused to leave before ensuring everything was perfect, checking her dress, carefully rolling her hair into a loop, scrutinizing every detail in the mirror. Grandmother's to go with them, began to irritate Mother, and one day, she refused to go altogether. Despite Father and

Grandmother's pleas, she stood firm. Grandmother realized she was no longer welcome and returned to her home in Pitești.

Leaving her family in Bulgaria had not been easy for Mother. She had left behind her father, three sisters, and a brother. Her mother had passed shortly after giving birth to their only son, having diabetes. With five young children demanding constant care, she had little time for her own health—until one day, her body swelled so dramatically, she was barely recognizable. Her death devastated the family—and my grandfather never remarried. Mother was the third daughter, followed by one more sister and her brother. They lived across the Danube, in Ruse.

The house was comfortable and prosperous, because my grandfather was famous for his exceptional skill in cutting fine crystal. His talent opened doors to the Royal Palace in Sofia, where he was hired as a master craftsman, working there for many years. Because of this, his daughters had the privilege of attending Notre Dame's Pension, a school run by nuns, where they were taught the refined etiquette of high society—learning to be proper housewives and ladies. But beyond that, they gained fluency in several foreign languages. Mother spoke Spanish, German, and French, reciting ballads and poems, translating them into Romanian, eager to share their meaning. Sometimes, Father playfully teased her stories—not to mock, but in gentle amusement.

Among the photographs in our family album, there was a card-sized picture where I sat on my grandfather's lap, taken when Mother brought me to Bulgaria a year after I was born. For that visit, Father took a second job, because Mother told him she couldn't go home empty-handed—she needed presents for everyone. Later, I learned that Grandfather had originally come from Vrancea, Romania, where he had mastered his craft under a German artisan. During the war of 1914, as the Romanian Army retreated to Iași, the situation grew desperate. Grandfather fled across the Danube, seeking refuge in Bulgaria. There, he fell in love with a beautiful blonde woman, married her, and had five children— but their years of happiness were short-lived.

The eldest of Mother's sisters, Anna, worked as a secretary in a lawyer's office. The lawyer proposed to her, and they soon had a daughter, Vizica, who was six years older than me. In that precious photo, where I sat on Grandfather's lap, Vizica stood beside him, hugging his shoulders. Sara, the second sister, had trained in stenography and worked for a large commercial firm. Eventually, she traveled to Palestine, where she married the owner of a shop in Haifa's port. Mother was the third sister. The next one, Șendy, married a good, kind man and had two children. But soon after, her husband passed away, and she never remarried. The youngest of them, Israel, the only boy, became a lawyer.

Mother had received many offers for work, but because her

sisters had their own families, she felt responsible for caring for Grandfather, her brother Israel, and the household. One such offer came from a relative in Bucharest, Uncle Marius, who represented Singer Sewing Machines. He owned a large showroom downtown, on Victoria's Way, and played a key role in my parents' wedding.

When Father crossed the frozen Danube into Bulgaria, every native from Giurgiu had a friend or relative on the other side, and it was customary to visit them. Some travelers from the group came along, and through these visits, Father eventually found himself inside Grandfather's home. Not knowing the language or anyone in the room, Father retreated to a corner, watching the lively gathering unfold. The house was full of guests, as the family hosted everyone with food, drinks, and warmth. Mother noticed the solitary young man, and as a good hostess, she approached him. She did not speak Romanian, but she tried to talk to him, nonetheless. With a few German words, but too few for a conversation, Father, struggled to respond politely, attempting to excuse himself. But where words failed, a smile, a glimpse of his blue eyes, and the unspoken language of fingers became their form of communication. They must have enjoyed themselves, because their conversation—wordless, yet full of expression—continued for the rest of the evening.

Not long after that visit, Grandmother in Pitești received an unexpected knock at the door. Standing there was a gentleman from

Bucharest, a representative of Singer Sewing Machines. Grandmother, a seamstress herself, answered him that her old sewing machine, works fine, and she didn't intend buying a new one. The gentleman at the door said that the machine he wanted to sell comes with a lifetime guarantee. Then, almost casually the gentlemen asked her if she knew that her son had visited Bulgaria.

"Sure, I know." Grandmother nodded. "My son keeps no secrets from me."

"And your son told you that he met a young lady there?" asked the gentleman smiling.

"Yes," answered Grandmother, a little intrigued while the gentleman took a step forward, his tone warm yet serious:

"That young lady is my niece. Can we talk?"

Grandmother paused for a moment, then gestured toward the doorway.

"Of course. Please come in."

A few months later, in the spring of 1932, in June, to be precise, my parents celebrated their wedding in the backyard, behind the siphon shop, beneath the towering acacia tree—the same acacia tree I now watch, as its branches sway gently in the wind.

IV

Cold days followed, but still without snow. Father had the keys to Aunt Raşela's house, and he tried to sell some of the belongings left behind. Across the street stood Mr. Gogu's barber shop, where he lived in the rooms behind his shop. One day, Mr. Gogu purchased a few items including the kitchen stove, for a thousand lei (Romanian pounds).

"I'm short on money now," he admitted, "but next week, I'll pay my debt in full."

Above the siphon shop, in the second-floor apartment, lived Mr. Pernos, the dentist. Though short and stocky, he had a youthful appearance, despite his grown daughter, Lica. His wife, Etty, carried herself with dignity, although age had begun to be seen, despite her platinum-toned oxygenated hair. Every day, Mr. Pernos would come down to the street, watching the pedestrians. Whenever street vendors passed, their curved wooden yokes supporting baskets of fresh fruits, vegetables, or fish, he would often buy from them and return upstairs with his groceries. A jovial man, he had a peculiar habit—jingling the coins deep inside his trouser pockets. Father once remarked:

"He's a megalomaniac—he wants everyone to know he has money."

During summer evenings, the Pernos family often dined on their kitchen balcony, overlooking the courtyard. They took a full watermelon from the icebox, sliced it in half, and each ate straight from their portion, scooping with the big soup spoon, only the heart—the sweetest center—before discarding the rest in court garbage bin. In our family, we ate our slice down to the narrow white strip beneath the skin.

It happened without warning. A group of Legionnaires stormed the Pernos' apartment in the dead of night, dragging Mr. Pernos from his bed, forcing him onto the street in his pajamas, barefoot. Shoving him into a waiting car, they sped away into the darkness. Moments later, Madam Pernos and Lica knocked frantically at our door, their nightgowns trembling against their bodies, unable to speak. We knew nothing of what had happened. But the terror etched across their faces was unmistakable—a horror that could not be erased. Mother brought them inside, wrapping them in blankets, seating them near the stove, its warmth offering what little comfort was possible. They could not return to their home. Strangers—those green-uniformed animals calling themselves Legionnaires—had ransacked the apartment, hunting for money and jewelry. They had cursed them with vile language, struck them, dragged them from their beds, and even tried to undress them—while Mr. Pernos fought desperately to protect his wife and daughter. That was when he was beaten mercilessly—

before they dragged him away. The women feared the worst. Would he even survive? Had they killed him already? Mother tended to them, reviving the fire, keeping them safe with us until morning. Before noon the next day, Mr. Pernos stumbled home, his bare feet raw against the pavement, his stained pajamas torn, his face blackened with bruises and clotted blood. For a long time after that night, he never left his house. And no one ever saw him jingling coins in his pockets again.

The other Sunday, when Father was off work, he took me across the street to Mr. Gogu's barbershop, hoping to collect the debt owed. Before Father could speak, the barber shouted from the middle of his shop:

"Get out of here, you dirty Jews! If you don't leave, I'll thrash you the way your neighbor, the dentist, was thrashed! Get out! Do you hear me? To Palestine with all of you!" Then, he slammed the door shut behind us.

Only days later, newspapers printed photographs on their front pages—images of the eminent professor, scientist, and diplomat, Nicolae Iorga, assassinated in the forests outside the capital. It was the beginning of the Legionnaire rebellion against the government. Bands of Legionnaires swept through the Dudeşti and Văcăreşti neighborhoods, breaking into Jewish homes, committing atrocities beyond belief. In the city's abattoir, Jews were hung on meat hooks, placards strung around their necks bearing the inscription: "KOSHER MEAT." At the morgue, bodies of Jews lay across the cement floor, stacked in rows of unimaginable horror. The terror spread like a plague. People avoided walking the streets—and if they had no choice, they moved along the walls, heads down, praying not to be noticed.

They say misfortune never comes alone. Whether before or after the rebellion, I cannot recall—but it was around the same time. One night, while we slept in our beds, the floor lurched violently beneath us. First, a sideways movement, shaking the shop, rattling the walls. Father rushed to our beds, pulled us from under the blankets, and gathered us beneath the wide-framed doorway. With his arms wrapped around Mother and us, we stood, clinging to his body, as the ground buzzed and creaked beneath our feet. It was dark, frightening and I could hear Mother's teeth chattering in her mouth. Then—silence. Just as we thought it had stopped, the earth roared to life again, shaking not just sideways, but now pounding up and down, hammering against itself. When it finally quieted, Father released us from his grip, turning on the light. The shop was unrecognizable. The beds sat near the wood stove; their frames shifted across the cement floor. The stove pipes had collapsed, filling the room with a thick cloud of soot. Glass and broken chinaware littered the floor, scattered in jagged piles. Outside, people ran screaming into the streets—and many were killed, crushed beneath falling walls, chimneys, and debris.

That night, one of Bucharest's most prestigious buildings, the Carlton Tower, crumbled like a house of cards. The next morning, people gathered around newspapers, studying the shocking images, unable to comprehend how such a grand structure had disintegrated in mere seconds. It was a city shaken—by violence, by fear, by the earth itself.

V

It's was well known that General Ion Antonescu, even before becoming Prime Minister, had aid Horia Sima, his second-in command, in establishing the Iron Guard - an ultra-nationalistic movement rooted in Legionnaire ideology. But soon, their partnership between Antonescu and Horia Sima unraveled. Sima's embrace of street violence and paramilitary action grew uncontrollable, making their alliance untenable. By 1941, the Legionnaires attempted an insurrection, seeking to seize key government offices and control communications. Antonescu retaliated, suppressing the movement with the force of the Romanian Army. Sima and his closest followers fled to Germany, escaping the crackdown. But Bucharest remained tense—its streets not yet safe, its people too afraid to step outside, wary of hooligans and sharp-shooters.

One evening, Father rushed into the house, turning off the room's light without a word. He sank into a chair, gesturing for us to stay silent, listening intently for any sound from outside. Only the glow of the wood stove cast flickering shadows onto the carpet.

After a long pause, he whispered to Mother:

"Keep the lights off."

Then, slowly, he explained: After stepping off the streetcar in Grivița, he noticed someone following him—heavy boots clicking against the pavement, reinforced with metal, the kind worn by the police and the military. He did not dare turn back to see who it was—nor could he run without drawing suspicion. So, he kept walking, his heartbeat racing, until he reached our house, slipping into the dark gangway, shutting the entrance door behind him.

Father had every reason to be afraid. By now, he was working at Muntenia Printing, Mr. Belizarie's typography shop on Grivița Road, just past the Buzești intersection. There, he printed highly classified documents for the Patronage Consulate, under the direct supervision of General Antonescu. The headquarters stood directly across the street from the printing shop—and if word got out that a Jew was behind the work, it would not end well for anyone involved.

One day, a security inspector entered the typography. Father had kept his unshaven beard since Grandmother's death, making it look like a polished copper brush. The moment the inspector stepped inside, he went straight to Father, poking him on the shoulder.

"What's your name, friend?"

Caught off guard, Father hesitated only briefly.

"Kimel," he answered.

Behind him, Mr. Belizarie froze, his tanned skin turning pale, as if carved from jade.

The inspector narrowed his eyes.

"All right, but what's your first name?"

"Anton," Father lied. His real name was Avram.

"And your ethnic origin?"

The air in the shop grew heavy. Without blinking, Father declared:

"I'm German, sir! Don't you see that I'm German?"

The inspector paused—then, with a satisfied nod, said:

"Very good. Very good, comrade! That's all I wanted to know."

Leaving Father, the inspector suddenly raised his voice, barking:

"Who is the Jew here? Come to me! I want to see you, and I promise—I'll do nothing to you."

No one moved. The presses hummed, undisturbed, their rhythm steady, unaffected. Everyone knew who the Jew was, but solidarity triumphed over fear.

Upstairs, in the bookbinding shop, the foreman—Marinescu—was a short man, his unshaven face, dark hair, and angular features fitting a stereotypical Jewish appearance. But Marinescu was not Jewish—not even a drop of blood in his system.

The inspector marched toward him, sizing him up.

"What's your name?"

"Marinescu," he answered.

The inspector smirked.

"Hmm. You are the Jew."

"I'm not, sir!" Marinescu protested.

"You are, but you don't want to say it."

"I'm not, sir! I swear, sir! I swear!"

The inspector's patience wore thin.

Show me your papers!" ordered the inspector.

Marinescu swallowed hard.

"I… I don't have them with me."

"So now you lie to me, eh? I've got you. Well, you can explain everything to the police. Let's go."

Only after his wife brought his documents from home, was Marinescu finally released.

The next morning, Mr. Belizarie pulled Father aside.

"Do you think the inspector didn't know you were the Jew?"

Father stiffened.

"I gave him a nice bribe to keep quiet."

The truth was—Mr. Belizarie trusted Father. He had never seen orders of such importance before, and an expert like Father was rare, expensive, and irreplaceable. His secretary, Inga, was a young blonde woman from an influential German family. Because of her high-status connections, she secured large-scale work that Mr. Belizarie had never dreamed of before. Since working with her, his refinement had transformed—his suits better tailored, his manners polished, his presence accompanied by the delicate trail of French cologne. Inga and he seemed inseparable, they came and left the company together. It was obvious to everyone—he had seduced her, despite having a wife and a son at home.

Whenever I visited the typography, Inga treated Simona and me with chocolate. For Christmas, she gave me a magnificent chocolate eagle, so exquisite I refused to eat it. For days, I admired it on my night table, proud of its size and perfect form. Until one evening, Mother decided it was time to taste it. And I cried.

One evening, after work, Mr. Belizarie turned to Father.

"Do you like this suit?"

Father nodded. "Yes, it's nice."

"Then go to my tailor tomorrow and take it."

Father never went—not the next day, not ever. Weeks passed, and finally, Mr. Belizarie asked:

"Did you pick up the suit from my tailor?"

Father smirked.

"How could I take it, if you're still wearing it?"

Mr. Belizarie laughed.

"Avram, I love you boy, but don't be stupid! Do you think I have only one suit in the same fabric? Go and take it!"

To the end of his days, Father never had a better suit. And he wore it only on the most important occasions.

VI

Uncle Aurel's tailor shop, once bustling with activity, was reopened by Mr. Nicu, a former apprentice. Determined to restore its former glory, Nicu gathered the same skilled workers, bringing along a young woman from his village to tend to the house. Yet, unlike Uncle Aurel, Mr. Nicu only rented two rooms behind the shop. The landlord, Mr. Dragomirescu, approached Father, offering him the remaining room and kitchen—now vacant and available. With this arrangement, he planned to reopen the siphon shop, which had already caught the interest of a potential tenant.

We moved again and it was much better living here. The house felt warmer, especially in the kitchen, where Father installed the bed once used by Maria. Here, Mother kept the stove fired daily, making it the heart of our home. There, on that bed of wood with a wool mattress and a blanket on top and some pillows, Simona and I spent our days inventing all kinds of games under Mother's calm and watchful presence. She rarely interfered, except when evening came and it was time for bed. Even our pleading eyes, swimming in tears of protest, failed to sway her. Ultimately, we had to obey her and go to the bedroom. The kitchen, lower than the rest of the house, looked like an addition, making it the hub of daily life, while the bedroom remained cold and rarely used. The wood stove stayed untouched for years, unless one of us was sick and had to remain in bed. At night, when Mother tucked us in, we burrowed under thick wool covers, blowing onto our hands for warmth. She would gently pound our backs, kneading us like dough, repeating:

"Nothing is healthier than sleeping in a cold room with freshly aerated sheets."

Sometimes, Father arrived home late, exhausted from work and after dinner he would let himself relax for a few minutes on this improvised bed in the kitchen. Upon seeing how tired he was, Mother covered him gently with a large scarf and let him sleep there until morning.

On bitter freezing days, when playing outside was impossible, Simona and I turned the kitchen into our playground. We transformed the chairs into trains and trolley cars, creating wagons lined up for imaginary passengers. I played the conductor, while Simona had to accept the role of the passenger or ticket seller. Many afternoons, we drew on paper at the kitchen table, illuminated by the warm glow of a gas lamp. Mr. Nicu, the tailor, fearful that we were using more bulbs than we paid for, went as far as to cut off the electricity to our rooms. When Father had free time, he took out a deck of old playing cards, teaching us funny games like Toci and Popa Prostul (The Stupid Priest).

"These will help you learn numbers," he told us.

By winter of 1941, the Romanian Army was preparing to join the Germans, readying for the Eastern Front against Russia. Mr. Dragomirescu, unable to rent his siphon shop, realized it had been requisitioned by the army. A military officer now lived there, and soon, his orderly soldiers arrived, pulling a cart full of straw into our courtyard—bringing two magnificent white horses with them. I loved those majestic creatures. On our street toward Giuleşti intersection, several horse-drawn carriages often stationed along the curb, waiting for their next fare. The carriage drivers, wrapped in long velvet coats, tightened with wide black leather belts, wore tall lamb-fur hats, making them look like figures from another time. Their devotion to their horses was palpable—like longtime friends, they talked to them, fed them oats, brushed their backs with broad strokes, and covered them with blankets in bad weather. Whenever Mother sent me to the corner grocery, I paused near the carriages, watching in admiration. The horses stomped the ground, their hooves kicking with sudden bursts, crunching oats from rugged woven sacks hanging from their napes. On some mornings, as I watched the army horses from the courtyard, I noticed something long and black flicker briefly beneath their bellies. But before I could ask about it, Mother swiftly pulled me away from the window, dismissing my curiosity without explanation.

Mother rarely visited her neighbors, but they came to us.

Aunt Fani, Mr. Fridman's wife, lived in the house across from ours. She often dropped by, sometimes bringing a fresh pot of coffee, its rich aroma curling through the kitchen air. While they sat at the table, conversing, Mother busied her hands with her work. Her husband, Mr. Fridman, had been taken with a convoy of Jews, sent outside the city to a forced labor camp. Each morning, they marched in tight formation, shovels resting on their shoulders, clearing snow from the streets, sorting rotting potatoes, or fulfilling other grueling tasks assigned to them.

Unlike many European countries, where Jews were rounded up and deported to concentration camps, Romania was never formally under German occupation. Instead, the "Jewish problem" was left to local authorities. General Antonescu's policies, though discriminatory and oppressive, were less extreme than Nazi Germany's. But for Jewish families, life was still uncertain, precarious, and deeply unjust.

Father was supposed to report for forced labor, like the others. But when the official ordinance arrived, demanding all Jews register at the recruitment offices, he stopped at the gate, hesitating. Would he step inside—sign his name, submit himself to the system? In the end, he turned back, choosing to return to his work instead. He never registered.

When Aunt Fani learned what Father had done, she shook

her curly head, covering her mouth with one trembling hand. Her voice was filled with urgency as she pleaded with Mother:

"This is a terrible mistake. If they find out, if someone tells them—because, believe me, it happens—it will be disastrous. Not just for him, but for all of us, when they'll see how many Jews lives in this place." She leaned in closer, whispering with fear:

"Tell him to surrender. It's for the best. Nothing will happen—you'll see."

That evening, when Father came home, Mother relayed Aunt Fani's warning. He listened quietly, eating without responding—his expression thoughtful, unreadable. And still, he never reported himself.

Madam Pernos rarely visited us, preferring to keep to herself, living in quiet seclusion. Her daughter, Lica, however, often came to talk with Mother, forming a close friendship. Lica had striking features—porcelain skin, dark expressive eyes, and hair like charcoal. She enjoyed playing with us, especially Simona, who adored her company during doll play. In the summer, Lica sometimes gave me money to buy ice cream from the Greek pastry shop across from the Crângași movie theatre.

"Get me a large one," she'd say, "a sandwich between two crunchy shells. And you can have a small cone."

On the way home, I devoured mine quickly, but Lica's began to melt over my fingers. Trying to save it, I first licked the dripping cream from my hands, then started on the melting ice cream itself—until little remained to deliver. Once guests left, Mother would swap seats with theirs, inspecting the house from their perspective, searching for untidy spots they might have noticed.

Of all the moments from that time, two stand out vividly in my memory. One day, an unknown man arrived, carrying a small wooden crate, no larger than a shoebox. He told Mother that her sisters in Bulgaria had found someone willing to transport a package for us. Inside, we discovered a rare treasure—chocolates, cheese, and a large tin of fish preserved in oil. Even now, I can still recall the taste of those unobtainable delicacies, a luxury beyond reaches in our household back then.

Another time, a well-dressed gentleman knocked at our door, asking if Father was home. Since Father was at work, Mother invited him in. He stepped into the kitchen, opened his leather pocketbook, and smoothed a banknote of a thousand lei onto the tablecloth. With a warm smile, he explained:

"This is a gift from your uncle—the eldest brother of your grandfather. Years ago, this uncle had immigrated to America, building a new life overseas. Now, he owns a movie studio in California. Finding you had not been easy. But now that he knows where you are, he wants to stay in touch," the gentleman explained.

After delivering his message, he left. We never heard from him—or Father's uncle—again.

Chapter 3

Storm Alert

I

It's hard for me to sort my memories in chronologically. I feel as though I'm looking at a pile of undated photographs. No matter how carefully I try to arrange them, I'm never quite sure I've got the sequence right. What the pictures do prove, beyond doubt, is that I was there: the places existed, the people existed, and every scene was real. Even if the negatives have been shuffled, the images engraved on the celluloid remain unquestionable evidence that the facts and places are true.

Through a child's eyes, between carefree days of play and moments of shattering drama, I etched on the screen of my memory a host of indelible images—images that would shape the person I would become.

We lived in the two rooms of 9 Crângași Road until the spring of 1944, when a bombing raid set the house on fire. We stayed on for a few more months there sharing the ruins, until we could find another apartment. These years marked not only our own lives but the lives of entire nation.

The white horses in our courtyard were led away a few weeks later. In their place came two yellow horses with white manes and hindquarters broader than any I had seen. The soldiers tending them didn't speak Romanian; their uniforms were green, but not the green we were used to. That winter was bitter. Now and then they would knock on our kitchen door, asking to warm themselves. They brought in with them the sting of frost mingled with the smell of stables and coarse barracks cloth. Mother offered them tea or sugarless ersatz coffee. They stood respectfully by the stove for a few minutes, thanked us in German, and went back out into the cold.

Mr. Nicu, the tailor, had been drafted, leaving the shop in the care of a young woman who lodged there. The house had passage ran from our room straight to their one all the way to the store. To give us privacy, Father blocked the French doors between our bedroom and theirs, with our massive wardrobe. Inside our bedroom we spoke in whispers so no sound would carry over there. Even so, we often heard words, moans, curses from the other side.

Spring came. We kept the door open and played in the courtyard; the horses had long since gone. The siphon-water shop reopened, run by an older man with a round belly and a neatly clipped white moustache. He had an unmarried daughter, Stela, blonde and soft-figured. When she discovered that Mother spoke fluent German, she shadowed her everywhere with a notebook, begging for translations. Each day she arrived with blank pages, a pencil, an eraser; each day she jotted down every word Mother gave her and returned with more questions. Mother answered cheerfully as she worked in the kitchen, and when a question strayed into delicate territory, she reminded Stela that a lady never spoke of such things.

I loved the shop's recent look: cool air, a constantly sluiced concrete floor, water gurgling toward the drain. A bench stood in the middle stacked with wooden crates of empty siphon bottles waiting to be refilled. In the back-room Stela sat at a small table, reciting Mother's sentences until they stuck. At dusk she emerged transformed—grey jacket, skirt slit high on the thigh, wide-brimmed hat shading her eyes, leather handbag tucked like an envelope under her arm. She wobbled on her high heels, but not before checking with Mother that the seams of her stockings were straight and that she had a few more German words for the road.

Each spring the false acacia that ruled our yard exploded into clusters of chalk-white blooms. They dangled from long branches on filament-thin stems, so heavy the limbs bowed. I would strip the strands, pile the flowers in my palm—tiny, boat-shaped sails—and eat them, filling my mouth and lungs with their honeyed perfume that lingered for hours.

One sunlit morning Mother let me run barefoot. While I

played alone in the courtyard, the stand-in tailor beckoned me into the shop. Nothing had changed since Uncle Aurel left, counters, mannequins, sewing machines, even the faces— except for a woman on a tall stool un-picking a jacket. She set her work aside, rested a hand on my shoulder, and said,

"Dorel, how are you? We'd like to see something. You don't mind, do you?"

"What?" I asked.

"We want to see your little cock. Can you show it to us?"

"No!" I shouted.

The tailor swept me onto the counter, pinned me flat, and unbuttoned my trousers. I thrashed and cried, but his elbow jammed under my chin while he yanked my underwear to my knees. The others gathered as though I were on an operating table. With a smirk he told the woman,

"See? Didn't I tell you that his is cut?" (circumcised)

When he let me down, I thought of kicking him, but bare feet against boot leather is poor revenge. I never told my parents—perhaps I'd already forced it out of mind, or my instinct told me that it was smarter to keep my mouth shut. Not long after, Mr. Nicu returned on a night in a short permission. That night shouts, crashes, and curses erupted from the other room. After that we never seen the substitute tailor and the woman.

II

Father found a beautiful wooden scooter with red-painted wheels in the storage behind our kitchen. I think it had belonged to my cousin Benu. Nothing could describe my happiness when I saw it. I would have ridden it nonstop. It wasn't just a scooter—it was a real motorcycle. First, I'd stop at the water tap under the giant tree in the courtyard to fill it with "gasoline," and then I'd race out onto the street, imitating a horn. I alerted pedestrians to my speeding as I zoomed toward the end of the block. But whenever my sister ran behind me, crying over and over to let her ride too, all the fun vanished. She wouldn't play with anything else. When she would not listen and I told her to leave me alone, she went straight to Mother, who called me back from the street. Because I refused to share the scooter, Mother pulled out the peg that connected the front and back, giving Simona the front half with the handlebars, which she could steer nicely. I was left with the back half, which wasn't fun to play with.

My joy didn't last long. A group of kids approached me at the corner and offered a handful of beer caps for a ride on the scooter. I had always wanted caps like these, but we rarely had beer at home. These caps were perfect—their flattened crimped edges made them hard for opponents to flip, which meant they were harder to lose. I'd seen how other kids played with them. It was an art to stack the caps face down and strike them with a lead coin to flip them over. Whoever flipped them won. Now I could finally have my own, and I felt proud. I waited for the kids to bring the scooter back. They never did.

I often went shopping with Mother and Simona at Piaţa Grant (Grant Market). Mother carried a reed basket, and I held Simona's hand as we walked ahead of her. In the market, Mother stopped at nearly every stall along the sidewalk, trying to bargain with the sellers. She always wanted the freshest produce and was often scolded that groceries were sold as-is, the good mixed with the bad. She had a poor purse, but she was picky about what she fed us. Eventually, she'd agree to let both herself and the seller fill the scale. When prices were too high, she'd head behind the stalls to where peasants parked their carts and buy what she needed for less.

She bought milk, cheese, and eggs from a milkwoman who came to our courtyard gate in a cabriolet pulled by a brown horse. She carried a shiny metal jug with a lid to our kitchen door. She measured the milk with a half-liter mug into Mother's vase, and then she wrote with a piece of chalk on the door frame, a line for each mug. This was her cash register version. At the end of the week, after receiving her money, she'd wipe the marks away with her licked fingers. Mother spoke Bulgarian with her, and maybe that's why she'd sometimes pour in a little extra.

Now and then, a street vendor would stop in the middle of the courtyard with baskets full of tomatoes, eggplants, or plums. Mother bargained for a full basket to use for winter preserves. Then she'd ask me to help her carry the kitchen table outside. She washed the tomatoes, split them in half with her nails, and drained their juice and seeds over the table. I'd circle around and sneak one from the pyramid, biting into it like an apple. They were juicy, sweet, and delicious. Simona always told on me, but Mother never seemed to hear—she was too busy dragging out the big copper kettle and three-legged stand from the wood storage.

The large copper kettle had been coated inside with a thin layer of tin by wonderer Gypsies who roamed the streets, calling out loudly, "Spoil tingire!" (Tin polish pots!). Mother used to trade old clothes with them for new pots and pans. Long ago, she had given them a jacket of Father's she disliked in exchange for some cookware. Not knowing it had been traded away, Father searched everywhere for it. When Mother finally told him, he was furious— he'd kept a lottery ticket in the breast pocket that still needed checking. I remember him racing around the neighborhood, asking if anyone had seen the Gypsy cart, but it was gone.

My initial excitement over the tomatoes quickly turned to misery. Mother asked me to help. First, she boiled the tomatoes in the big copper kettle by the kitchen door. Then she pulled them out, and I had to press them through a sieve until only the dry skins and seeds were left. It was the most boring job—the sieve holes were tiny, and it took ages to strain even a small batch of juice, which I had to push through with a long wooden spoon. I tried to work faster, but Mother's watchful eyes forced me to press until the pulp was bone-dry.

Next, the juice went back into the kettle to boil, and I had to stir it constantly with a long wooden paddle to keep it from sticking to the bottom of the copper basin. I heard the other kids playing in the street and would've given anything to run off and join them, but one look from Mother killed that thought. Instead, I stood in the middle of the summer heat—made worse by the wood fire—and was choked by smoke that followed me no matter where I turned. It was endless torture. I remember thinking: this must be what hell feels like.

III

When Father set a couple of pumpkins over the kitchen roof to sweeten under the first white frost; I knew that autumn had arrived. One day he came home with a graphite black slate framed in wood, a small yellow sponge dangling from a string. The next morning Mother woke me early, dressed me nicely with white long socks and black shined shoes, slipped the slate and a lined notebook into Father's old leather satchel, brought me to the door with a kiss, and let me go. Father walked with me, holding my hand. We crossed Podul Grant to the streetcar stop on Grivița Road. I was bursting with pride, and I'm sure Father was too: at last, I was about to become a student. I hoped they would pin a gold-embroidered number on my sleeve like the one Benu used to wear.

We got off the streetcar at Polizu, one stop past Gara de Nord. It was a perfect autumn morning, the clear sky and bright sun mirrored in the large shopping windows along Grivița. Shop boys sprinkled water on the pavement before sweeping so the dust wouldn't rise, and clerks hurried toward their offices. Father and I turned into a narrow street named Intrarea Poradim, lined with houses on only one side. A two-storey building on the corner held a modest, second-class hotel behind its large ground-floor windows. Hand in hand we walked the narrow street, barely wider than a car and chilled by the shadows of the houses.

White-washed facades with neat little gardens sat behind iron fences. The lane ended at a vacant lot that opened onto the grand frontage of Gara de Nord, its sweeping canopy supported by tall, round pillars, covering lines of taxis and horse-drawn carriages. Across from it, lined with Dinicu Golescu Boulevard, the new, multi-storey Railway Palace stood tall, still unfinished.

Between it and us, in the middle of the weed-choked lot, a large concrete basin full of water stood ready as an army reservoir in case incendiary bombs set the city ablaze.

The last building on the lane was large, with double wooden doors in the middle and high-set windows. A brick wall supporting a wrought-iron fence, enclosed a small, paved courtyard near the vacant yard. This was the Poradim Synagogue.

We climbed the polished concrete steps to the first floor and entered a classroom filled with boys and girls at desks larger than those in my kindergarten. A young teacher in black stood by the blackboard. She was slender, bespectacled, with shoulder-length dark hair framing her oval face; her shy demeanour melted into warmth when she smiled. I was seated beside a fair-haired boy named Marius.

The school's name was Cultura, a renowned learning center in the Jewish community for academic excellence. Its Sevastopol Street campus had been requisitioned by the army, and now the only available place for its activities was this synagogue. Poradim, the largest synagogue near Gara de Nord, had a women's horseshoe balcony above the men's hall. Women usually came to the temple only on the Sabbath or high holidays. Men come twice a day for prayers - in the morning and the evening. Some would stop at the back room near exit to share a shot of liqueur and a piece of cake, with a friendly toast "Le- Chaim!" (To life!).

The balcony entrance passed through our classroom, separated by a wall of tall windows. Opposite the stairs stood a glass display reaching from floor to ceiling, crowded with ancient Torah scrolls wrapped in velvet gowns stitched with gold, silver goblets, worn prayer books, and other ritual treasures. Older pupils were separated by classes between the right and left wings of the balcony, but most others studied on the main floor. During breaks the balcony students had to cross our room to reach the staircase.

Years earlier, on Yom Kippur—the holiest day of the year—tragedy had struck. Jewish law forbids images, sculptures or other artifacts in houses of worship, so instead of icons the synagogue's windows were filled with geometric stained-glass figures centred on the Star of David. "Thou shalt have no other gods before me. Thou shalt not make unto thee any graven image or likeness of anything that is in heaven above or that is in the earth beneath, or that is in the water under the earth," is written in the old scripture. Some cultures approved illustration of bible stories and saints in ancient times when most people could not read or understand the original words of the bible.

Above the Poradim Synagogue's staircase door, a stained-glass panel of coloured triangles formed the Star of David. By the end of the day, the sun's setting light filtered through the colored glass window onto the stairway wall flickering projections of rainbow-like colour rays. After a day of fasting and prayer, the packed sanctuary, airless with the blazing chandeliers lit only on high holidays, an elderly woman, tired of fanning the air, went to water tap to dampen her handkerchief. On her way she saw a crimson projection of sunlight on the stairwell wall and involuntarily cried:

"Fire!"

It was a deadly cry!

Panic exploded. Women stampeded toward the only exit, the narrow staircase, permitting no more than two alongside. Those at the back feared they would be trapped, pushed the ones ahead. High-heeled shoes slipped; bodies fell. The desperate crowd tumbled over them like grain before a scythe, piling higher with each second. By the time calm returned, many lay dead or injured.

The next morning newspapers ran photographs and headlines about the Poradim Synagogue disaster—a massacre born of a false alarm.

IV

After school, Father taught me to ride the streetcar alone and cross the street safely. He bought me an abonnement —a season pass with my photograph and a monthly punch card good for two rides a day. In those days you could still board a streetcar at the front door, because the ticket seller wearing a leather bag, sold tickets moving up and down the aisle checking newcomers. With my pass I was entitled to sit in first class too. Following Mother's advice, whenever I was seated and saw an elderly passenger standing, I rose and offered my place. Many thanked me; some praised my manners, and my chest swelled with pride.

Most of my classmates carried flat cardboard satchels slung across their shoulders. I lugged Father's old leather briefcase, heavy and awkward, occupying one hand the whole way home. Embarrassed, I tried to find a solution: I found one of Mother's discarded coat belts, tied the ends to the bag handle and slipping my hands through the loop like a rucksack, I had a backpack like the others.

At home Mother insisted I finish my homework the moment I'd eaten. I pulled out my slate and hurriedly filled it with row after row of big and small circles. On the reverse I drew lines of upward and downward strokes, each slightly slanted to the right and perfectly spaced. The exercise was tedious; by the time I finished, daylight had drained from the courtyard and no longer a way to go out and play. Mother cleaned the kerosene glass lamp and lit it in the middle of the kitchen table; another hung near the top frame of our bedroom door to better spread the glow.

When Father arrived, Mother served his dinner and she would tell him, as usual, the news of the day. My name came up frequently, and Father's eyes frowned to me while I prayed in silence that Mother stop talking about me.

After he ate, he asked to see my work. I stood beside his chair knowing that he would not be happy with the work I had done. He made me wipe it clean and redo every circle, every stroke, ensuring each sat perfectly between the ruled lines. If the hour grew late, he sent me to bed and finished the practice himself.

One evening Father came home with a parcel. He unwrapped layers of newspaper to reveal a sky-blue metal container. He mounted it high on the wall near the stove, attached a long copper pipe to its base, bent the pipe into the firebox, and fitted a perforated burner head. Midway down he installed a tiny valve. Finally, he filled the canister with gasoline. The contraption, he told us, had been built by an old army comrade who worked at the airport—hence the aircraft paint. Mother watched, horrified that her meals would now taste of kerosene—or worse, that the house would go up in flames.

"Avram, take that fool thing out. Take it to the garbage, please. I don't like it!"

The house never burned. Each morning Father checked the fuel, and when we rose the kitchen was already warm, Mother's dishes never smelled like gas.

A public filling station opened at the corner of Eduard Grant Street, and Mother sent me with a ten-litre can and the exact money to buy gasoline. It was a short way from home, and I went to

Giuleşti, where at the corner was Mr. Bucur's cigarette shop. The station, housed in a wooden barrack with a concrete floor, held a row of pumps whose glass cylinders filled manually as the attendant pumped the handle. Because fuel was rationed to ten litres per person, a queue formed early. In summer I left the can to keep my place and went off to play. If another child was waiting, the time passed quickly. Winter was different: play was impossible, conversation froze on my lips, and I sheltered behind the grown-ups, stamping my feet to keep the blood flowing to my toes.

Queues became a feature of life—outside Mr. Zisu's bakery for rationed bread (a quarter loaf per person) and other places. Everything was rationed: meat, cooking oil, sugar, flour, and even clothing. We had tickets for boots and shoes with wooden soles. My own pair had two slits so the soles could bend when I walked.

Marius, my bench colleague situation was different. His governess collected him sometime in bad weather in a chauffeur-driven limousine; his mother always arrived in one. She liked me and occasionally offered sweets, but Marius had to wait until after lunch. We grew close, sitting together in lessons and played together, even during our lessons. Many times, Marius would ask me to come with him home, in an elegant block on Griviţa Road beyond the Buzeşti crossroads. The entrance, a wide arcade cutting through a row of luxury shops, opened into a paved courtyard with border-planted trees and a raised terrace leading to an imposing building with a glass-covered portico. A uniformed doorman ushered us inside, and the lift carried us to a vast, light-filled hall. In the apartment a glittering Christmas tree dominated the salon. We played in Marius's room among his neatly arranged expensive toys until Father came for me. One evening Marius's mother handed him an address and made him promise to visit at the weekend.

On Sunday Father and I set out, my hair parted as Mother liked and my clothes freshly pressed. We rode the streetcar past Brâncovenesc Hospital, around the Metropolitan Seat Hill, and arrived on Calea 11 Iunie in front of a tall white building. A lady opened the door and presented us with a parcel tied with red ribbon. At home Mother untied it to reveal a blue suit, a butter-yellow silk shirt, three-quarter-length white socks, and a pair of patent-leather shoes—all for me, and all new. When she dressed me, she gazed proudly and said I looked like a prince.

V

Another relative of Mother's in Bucharest was Aunt Luți, the sister of Uncle Marius, who owned the city's Singer sewing machines dealership. Aunt Luți's husband, Uncle Mark, looked much older than she did, and they had a daughter Clara, whom we all called Cuța.

Cuţa attended same school as I did but because she was a year ahead and in a different class, I had no idea we were related. At the year-end festivities in the spring of 1942, parents, friends, and other family members were invited to the temple. There, Mother spotted Aunt Luţi, Uncle Mark, and Cuţa. Their shared delight at discovering one another after so long was touching—an outpouring of emotion only close family can evoke.

Midway through the celebration, in the hall crowded with people and bathed in light, I heard our principal, Mr. Drimer, call my name from the podium. I approached in hesitant steps, hardly able to believe my ears. Beside him stood my teacher, holding a parcel of books and a rolled-up diploma tied with a red ribbon. She handed them to me, then bent to kiss my forehead. Only when I rejoined my parents did I realise I had won second prize. Mother embraced me with tears in her eyes. After the ceremony, Aunt Luţi invited us to their home on Petru Maior Street, not far from Podul Grant. Cuţa told me she had also placed second, yet when we stepped outside to compare our prizes, I noticed her diploma had been marred by a thick stroke of ink.

In our own courtyard the old false-acacia tree had shed its white blossoms, as though a veiled bride had lifted her train. Early summer replaced the blooms with delicate, symmetrical leaflets dangling from slender green stems. Next door neighbors on the street at number 7, behind a weather-worn wooden fence, stood a black-mulberry tree. When its fruit ripened to a deep crimson, the pavement beneath was spattered with inky stains from passing feet.

I loved climbing that fence, scrambling into the upper branches, and filling a small aluminium tin—after tasting my fill first, of course. The berries hid beneath the foliage, but the hunt was rewarded by their sweetness. Their juice made me feel sticky transforming my appearance from a tidy, clean, boy, into a dirty little tramp. Back home with my shirt, face, and hands tainted by mulberries, Mother, after sharing with Simona the fruits from the aluminum can, immersed me in the white steel basin filled with water and washed me with soap and a brush, ignoring all my protests and screaming.

On weekends Giulesti Stadium overflowed with supporters who poured in from every corner of the city to cheer their beloved Rapid București. During the most dramatic moments we could hear, even from our house, the roar of thousands—cheering, whistling, or booing—echoing across the neighbourhood. During that time, the streets of Crângași and Giulești, brimmed with rows of buses stationed by the curb, waiting for the multitude of fans that would swarm the streets after the game. The buses with number 38 would form a long line from the Giulesti intersection, passing our house all the way to the end of the block.

Drivers and ticket sellers grouping on the sidewalk chat,

smoked, or played small games to pass time. One young driver squeezed the hand of a ticket-seller so hard she burst into tears, slipped away, and hid on her bus. For the first time I felt real compassion—perhaps even the first stirrings of love. For days afterward I wandered at the stop, hoping her bus would appear again. It never did, yet the image of that blonde girl in her blue cap stayed with me like a small miracle.

When Father came home for lunch, meeting his gaze filled me with terror. Mother as always served his meal and relayed the day's events, many of which now began with complaints about me. Father ate in silence, but when some nasty things were revealed, his hand would descend on the back of my neck like a thunderclap. One day, knowing for sure what will happen, I decided that it was better to hide rather than enter the house. I hid in the courtyard lavatory as Father approached. From inside I could hear every word through the open kitchen door; none of my faults were overlooked. As always, Father never said anything. Before going back to work Father came to try the lavatory's door. Finding it locked, he walked away—then returned a few minutes later and tried again. My heart pounded so fiercely I thought it would burst.

At last, he rattled the latch a third time, ready for action. "Who's in there? How long do you need?"

I stayed silent. He yanked the door; the wire hook tore free, and he found me trembling inside. Dragging me out by the ear, he left for work, and when he returned home in the evening, I was paid with interest for that. Father's memory was flawless: he never forgot a word of Mother's reproach, and he never left a debt unsettled. So, for everything done that day and the past, I received my full account in a single instalment. Only Mother, with tears in her eyes, tried to save me; Simona watched from her corner horrified and after that, regardless of my bad actions, I never hid in the toilet again.

VI

One Sunday after lunch, the four of us went to a play at a theatre on Uranus Street called Munca şi Lumina (the Work and the Light). It was my first test of live theatre. The production, *King for a Day*, left such an impression on me that even now I can picture the shoemaker's shabby apron, the courtiers' brocade, and the painted palace walls.

The story began with a poor cobbler who toiled day and night yet never earned enough to better his life. One evening, exhausted and bitter, he muttered that if he were king, the people would fare much better. A palace servant overheard him and told the monarch, who—curious—went to the cobbler's tiny shop wih hos dignitaries. Finding the shoemaker asleep on his low stool, a worn-out shoe on his knee and hammer in hand, the king ordered his courtiers to carry the man to the palace without waking him.

When the cobbler opened his eyes next morning he was dressed in fine clothes, everyone addressing him as *Your Majesty.* At first, he thought he was dreaming, but after everyone was ready to perform his wishes and he had to judge over disputes in several cases, he started to think that he truly must be king. The following dawn he awoke again on his stool, convinced the whole adventure had been a pleasant fantasy—until the real king appeared in the middle of his suite, praised his sound judgments, and invited him to remain at court as an adviser.

All the way home I chattered about this marvellous world where stories could spring to life onstage. Father promised that, if I behaved, we would attend more plays like this. For a while I truly tried—helping Mother with chores and minding my manners—yet the war soon closed most theatres, and years passed before we saw another. As it happened, we never went to a play until many years later, after the end of the war. We did see a few movies together, and some were so funny that I can never forget them.

When classes resumed for my second year, our cheerful young teacher did not followed us. In her place we were assigned an older man as severe as the synagogue benches themselves—stiff and tall for us. To stand, we had to flip up the narrow seat board.

Our class now met on the main floor, tucked into a dim corner near the rear. The teacher had neither desk nor stand; the blackboard stood in the cramped aisle between pews. Sunlight barely reached this corner and it was so cold that we often kept our overcoats on. Other classes were scattered through different parts of the sanctuary and up on the balcony. Each instructor battling to keep noise low enough that only an occasional shout escaped the partition of benches.

On the walk home I sometimes joined a quiet boy named Samulică Segal, who lived across Piața Grant. His parents ran a small market stall selling threads, ribbons, and buttons—though Mother never bought there, claiming their prices were too high. Samulică was kind and eager to have friends, but although I went sometimes to his house, he never replaced my friend Marius from the previous year. Not even Mother was happy to see us together.

Half-way down on Intrarea Poradim, a white house with a cellar had recently been transformed by the Jewish community: the mezzanine became a polyclinic, and the basement a public canteen for the needy. The canteen was in the basement, it had large windows facing the street and courtyard, and wooden picnic tables and benches aligned in rows along the walls furnished the large room.

Our neighbour Aunt Fani had a fashionable niece, Rene

involved in the operation of community, a platinum-haired young woman who smoked only Red Royal cigarettes with carton, in style then. Often, I was sent to buy them from Mr. Bucur's corner shop, and sometimes she told me to keep the change. Perhaps Aunt Fani told her niece about Mother, because one day Rene asked whether Mother might like a steady work sterilising instruments and keeping the clinic clean. Mother agreed gratefully.

From then on, most mornings we all boarded the same streetcar. Father rode two stops farther—to Muntenia, Mr. Belizarie's printing house—while Mother, Simona, and I landed at Polizu Station and walked the rest of the way. Father used to wake first, turn on the fire on the kitchen stove, and if we were slow, he would go ahead of us.

At midday Mother, Simona, and I ate at the canteen; then I carried a lunch pail with two lidded tins along Grivița Road to Father. While he slid a wide drawer of lead type from a composing frame to use as an impromptu table, I wandered among the presses. Flat-bed machines rumbled its large iron cart carrying Father's framed forms of lead going back and forth on noisy gears. Paper sheets, fed one by one from a slanted table by the machinist, were snatched by metal grippers, rolled beneath the lead forms of Father to meet the fresh kiss of print. I could have watched forever these amazing machines looking alive, trying to catch the rhythm and the sound of joy they had sung in their clanks and whistles—a hymn to mechanical perfection.

There were other machines, manually operated or energized by electrical motors with blackened leather belts running big iron wheels. Farther back stood the Linotype machines, casting whole lines of text from molten alloy. Father once set my name and Simona's in a tiny metal slug and gave it to us as a stamp; I showed it off to every child I knew.

The clinic's director, Dr Herovici, had delivered both Simona and me at Caritas Hospital; my parents were relieved to have him as our physician again, and any time we got sick, he consulted and gave us the appropriate medicine. The real reason for my parents' happiness was that Simona was born with a heart problem, and Dr. Herovici was trusted to help. When he consulted my sister, he would listen for a long time with the stethoscope over her heart, paying attention in many places to pick up the unusual beating coming from her heart.

After one consultation the very next day, Dr Herovici asked Mother to bring Simona back to the clinic. When we arrived, several physicians—one of them exceptionally old—were already waiting. One after another they laid a stethoscope to my sister's small chest, exchanging grave looks while Mother, now in a white orderly's gown, twisted her hands in a corner watching the entire scene and the doctors' grave faces.

I could not understand what was happening there, or what was wrong with my little sister. Except for a sprinkling of light-brown freckles, Simona was growing into a lovely girl with reddish wavy hair. Mother always combed her long hair in braids held by red or white ribbons that ended in nice bows. She also dressed her like a doll with printed, starched dresses. Everywhere Simona went, she would rise above other children with her effortless, straight answers, her appearance, or just her smile. I couldn't see Simona being sick because every day we played together, ran, jumped, and even beat each other. I'd never seen her suffer from anything. Why, then, were the doctors whispering so solemnly?

Mother stopped rubbing her hands nervously trying to decipher the doctors' whispers, helped Simona put on her red dress with white dots. After the consultation, Dr. Herovici came to Mother to tell her there was nothing to worry about.

That summer Simona and I made new friends at the canteen. Two of them, a brother and sister, became our friends. Anna was older than her brother, maybe about the same age as me. Her brother was a little older than Simona. They lived on a street named Frumoasă (Beautiful), in an old building near Calea Victoriei. We never went to their apartment, but Simona and I would go with them to their large cobblestone-paved courtyard, with a majestic chestnut tree shading the street, the wrought-iron fence, and most of the yard. By August the green, spiny husks began to split and glossy brown chestnuts rained onto the stones like marbles. At the clinic the nurses discarded the little serrated blades from broken ampoules. I pocketed them whenever I could; they were perfect miniature saws. Along with bits of string, bottle caps, and a forgotten cigarette holder I had found in the waiting room, those blades were my greatest treasures. When I saw the chestnuts, I started to drill into it with a blade. Then I checked the hole with the port cigarette, and it matched the size of the port cigarette and illuminated by an idea, announced a new enterprise: chestnut "pipe" heads.

I start organizing the kids to work. Under the tree we filled a basket with carefully drilled nuts—each child armed with an ampoule blade. It made us so proud to see what we'd done foreseeing big success and lots of money. Across the street on Calea Victoriei was a cigarette store. We carried the basket to the store. Inside, customers and the shopkeeper looked at us. I took the port cigarette out of my pocket and assembled it to a chestnut. They inspected the pipe, admired the skill with which each chestnut was drilled, congratulated us for our idea and enterprising spirit— but did not buy any. They gently explained that a smouldering pipe would split a chestnut in minutes. Crestfallen, we trudged home with the basket still full.

When Mother was very busy at work, she would give us

money to see a movie at one of the theatres around the clinic. Five picture houses surrounded the polyclinic. Marna, the finest, stood at the corner of Grivița and Buzești; across the street was Marconi, famous for children's programmes of Pat & Patachon, Stan și Bran (Laurel and Hardy), and Fernandel. Diana theatre lay closest to Mother's work, while two humbler halls further along Buzești tempted us less often.

We would study the lobby photographs, buy the cheapest seats, and, in the darkness, laugh with the crowd while we hunted for a place to sit. More than once, we stayed through a second showing—sometimes even a third—until we emerged into nightfall to find Mother waiting patiently outside.

One afternoon, after lunch at the canteen, on way to Anna's house, a boy waved a block of tickets outside Marna theatre and asked if we'd like to see the movie. I said yes, he ripped four tickets and they were good, or the door attendant didn't check them carefully, because he let us inside. Climbing the stairs to first balcony, I stared spellbound: it was the first colour movie I had ever seen—*Die goldene Stadt* (*The City of Gold*), a German wartime propaganda production filmed in Prague. I could not imagine anything more beautiful.

A few blocks away, on our neighbourhood, at Regie, the vast state cigarette factory, every Sunday an annex hall opened its doors for free newsreels and German war propaganda features. Crowds queued on the street in the blistering sun, the heat ricocheting off whitewashed walls until even the asphalt softened under our feet. At two o'clock sharp the doors swung wide. Inside, wooden benches stretched nearly wall to wall; attendants urged everyone to squeeze closer so that all could sit. The covered windows kept the room blissfully cool at first, but once the film started the air grew stifling and my shirt clung wet to my back. Still, I never missed a Sunday screening—each was an event in our wartime neighbourhood, a small window onto a wider, if troubled, world.

VII

The first building on Griviţa after Podul Grant heading toward the center, was the Triumph movie theatre. Next to it stood a spacious book-and-stationery shop were Father bought my schoolbooks and supplies. We did have a tiny bookstall on Crângaşi Street beside Zisu's bakery, but it was small, and from there I would buy self-glued pictures, stickers and small trinkets for decorating notebooks. The bookstore at Podul Grant by contrast, felt enormous: two wide display windows framed the doorway, and inside three walls rose all the way to a lofty ceiling, packed with shelves. Glass-topped counters held the finest drawing instruments, paints, and hobby kits—tempting boxes whose lids showed families and children laughing over brightly coloured family games, and even toys.

The owners, Mr. and Mrs. Goldștein, seemed to have stepped from one of those elegant illustrations. He was tall and broad-shouldered, with wavy black hair and a neatly clipped moustache; his grey suit and tie always carried a discreet trace of cologne. She was equally tall and slender, her dark hair framing a pale oval face lit by emerald eyes and a ready smile. Father arranged for me to help in the shop during the summer vacation—without pay, he emphasised—so I could learn a little responsibility.

On first Monday morning, Father walked me to the door, but the metal shutters were still down. He had no time to wait, so he said:

"Wait here, they'll open soon. But for my sake—behave!"

Spotting a streetcar stopped at the station, he sprinted off catching the tram. Alone on sidewalk, I start counting the open-platform trams that still in use, though most had lately been replaced by the new enclosed coaches with automatic doors.

Before long Mr. Goldștein emerged from the courtyard and rolled up the steel shutters. I stepped closer.

"Good morning, sir," I said, my voice barely above a

whisper.

He studied me with warm brown eyes.

"You must be Mr. Kimel's son."

I nodded. He unlocked the door, and we entered the cool, dim shop. He went behind the counter holding the cash machine, I stood in the centre until he drew a bright feather duster from a shelf.

"Would you start by dusting the shelves and counters?"

I took the feathered brush and began to stroke it over the shelf closest to the window. On each shelf were many hardcover books with gold printed letters gleaming under the brush. Many covers bore vivid illustrations and even inside were some with drawings that made me guess the beautiful stories and adventures inside.

Below them rows of toys beckoned, none more alluring than a red convertible whose doors opened and whose steering wheel turned the front wheels. Immersed in this new world between books and toys, I felt I had stumbled into a small paradise, and the thought that I may not be good enough, made me scared of losing this job, like when you lose the most beautiful dream in the morning. One by one I lifted each toy from its shelf, moving it to the glass counter in front of me and cleaned off the dust from the shelf. Then I wiped the toy inspecting carefully each button, hinge, and key before returning the toy back to the shelf as it was before. Shelf after shelf let me get the feeling that in this place I would never be bored.

Later, when the sun rose up to the windows, Mr. Goldştein stepped outside with a hand-crank and showed me how to lower the awning over the sidewalk.

"From now on, this will be your job," he told me.

Customers came from time to time, some asking about a particular title, others seeking a good idea for a present, a toy, or just office or school materials. Mr. Goldştein answered each question with patient courtesy, served his clients politely, and often walked with the patrons up to the door. Shortly before noon Mrs. Goldştein arrived. On learning who I was, she brushed a hand over my hair, pulled up a chair, and began chatting. Her questions were simple—about school, about Simona—but the warmth of her interest and the sparkle in her laugh put me instantly at ease. From that first moment I liked her immensely, and the long summer days ahead suddenly seemed far too short.

Although the Goldşteins were no longer young, they had never been blessed with children. Their apartment lay just beyond the shop courtyard, and each day at noon they locked the front door and led me to a dining-room where an oval table was already set. From the very first day I was treated as family. I was invited to eat with them, and they talked with me, especially Mrs. Goldştein, who told me stories about them and their friends. They let me leaf through the fairy-tale volumes on the shelves, and I was even allowed to try the toys for sale that glittered behind the glass counters.

One Sunday they invited guests for dinner and asked me to join them. Mother dressed me in my blue suit, polished my patent shoes, and parted my hair neatly to one side. The Goldştein house was full of people, and the entrance door was wide open. The dining table lengthened almost wall to wall, and I took my seat beside Mrs. Goldştein. I was presented to everyone and directly opposite sat a girl my own age, tall and pretty, her hair tied back with a white ribbon. She acknowledged me with cool indifference.

Everyone had a good time enjoying the food and the discussions around the table, especially the jokes until, midway through the second course, I accidentally moved over my chair and came from there lose, a long, nasty, mortifying *pfffft* sound that interrupted all discussions around the table. Mr. Goldştein burst into hearty laughter, launching a volley of jokes that had everyone—even the ribboned girl—wiping tears from their eyes. Burning inside-out, I bolted to their bedroom. Never had I felt the pain and humiliation of shame like I did that moment. Mrs. Goldştein soon followed, her smile gentle, her eyes full of consolation. After a quiet word and a kiss on the forehead she guided me back in time for dessert. No one mentioned the accident again, yet the sting of that moment stayed with me for years.

Some weeks later, while we were alone in the shop, Mrs. Goldştein asked softly whether I might like to be their child. Both she and her husband showered me with chocolates, small gifts, and—most precious of all—the trust to serve customers, ring up sales, and make change. I had long since lost my initial shyness and felt entirely safe with them.

That evening, after closing time, the Goldşteins walked to my parents' home with me. After a short introduction, Mr. Goldşteins told Father that they would like to adopt me. Father smiled yet declined. Mr. Goldştein prepared to a refusal, had a list of arguments to his advantage. He spoke of the love they felt, like already I was theirs. He explained about of education they could offer, the schools and teachers they would provide, and he asked:

"What's the problem, people? We are living so close that in five minutes you could see him anytime."

"I think, this argument could serve you too," responded Father smiling.

Mother listened without a word as the discussion evolved, but her mute eyes were fixed on Father.

After Father's replay, Mr. Goldştein tried to move

discussion on another topic. Using his best eloquence, he said that considering the actual economic situation, when it is so hard to stay afloat and earn an existence, would be a lot easier for Father with a child instead of two. Father remained unpersuaded in his decision.

"Not you, nor I know what will happen tomorrow. Thanks for the offer, but my son is mine."

When it became clear he would not yield, the Goldşteins expressed their regret and took their leave.

School resumed soon after, and with new homework I visited the shop less often. By winter, short days, blowing snow, and icy winds sent me straight home each afternoon, and my trips to the Goldşteins dwindled. None of us could know how swiftly events around us were about to change.

Chapter 4
The Hurricane

I

Sometimes Father sent me to buy some cigarettes. At the corner of Giulesti stood Mr. Bucur's tiny tobacco shop – a cramped narrow room that could barely hold two customers at the counter. Newspapers and magazines lay fanned across the glass display case and hung from wire racks behind the door. Cigarettes were stacked by quality in cubbyholes behind the owner, while cheaper smokes—bundles of six, eight, ten, or twelve priced at one leu, lay wrapped in paper—ready in the diamond-shaped compartments.

Mr. Bucur was middle-aged, with silver hair, a neat moustache, and thick spectacles. Many of his customers liked to linger, leaning on the counter to dissect the day's news. Perhaps that was the reason why after the communists came to power, he was arrested and shipped off to a prison camp in Russia. He returned years later: a gaunt shadow of himself, toothless and silent, the spark gone from his eyes.

Back then, knowing his clientèles, the moment I entered he would pass over a bundle of ten National cigarettes, because Father never bought a full pack. Sometimes his daughter, a striking young woman with a single thick braid of raven hair draped over one shoulder, charming and exceptionally beautiful, would take turns with her father keeping the store open from dawn until dusk. While she served me one afternoon, I drew the latest issue of *Universul Copiilor* ("The Children's Universe") from the rack. Each week the magazine printed a Haplea-and-Frosa comic strip in the centre pages, but the sheets were still uncut, pinned by a wire staple, so I could never read the ending.

Noticing my frustration, she showed me how to slit the staple with a penknife, to unfold the pages, and finally let me take the magazine home to read.

"Be very careful," she warned. "No stains—if we can't sell it afterward, you'll have to pay for it."

From that Wednesday on I slipped into the shop each week for the new issue. Back home Simona settled beside me while I read aloud and look at the cartoons inside. First both of us poring over the serial tales of Haplea's latest mischief. But the most beautiful stories were written by Moş Nae (Old man Nae), whose tales continued week after week, leaving us anxiously waiting until the next publication.

Autumn closed in. By decree the street-lamps were turned off, people had to seal every window against even a thread of light and cars on the road blinded their headlamps. Mother tacked heavy blankets over the kitchen windows; policemen prowled streets and courtyards, ready to scold any glow. Pedestrians carried pocket lanterns, and some used squeezing hand pumps to create a dim light.

After coming home one, Father was nearly bowled over in our pitch-dark gangway by a German officer stepping out of the siphon shop. The officer muttered a polite apology, but Father reached the kitchen white-faced and sweating.

Behind us at 11Crângaşi Road, back-to-back with our house, ran a modest restaurant facing the street and its owner was Mr. Iliescu. In the neighbourhood, Mr. Iliescu was known by everyone. He was a man past his prime, always in three-piece suit and tie, sitting at a table by the wall, clutching an old walking stick between arthritic hands twisted out of shape. He rarely spoke to patrons; his pastime was watching them come and go while a varnished radio murmured dance music in the corner. Some of the customers saluted him, and some just ignored this taciturn man. One day I dare ask:

"Why are your fingers twisted?"

"Because when I was a child, I wasn't a good boy and this is my punishment."

Many times, after that, I tried to figure out what kind of bad things did he as a child that made his fingers like that.

From his table, Mr. Iliescu watched absently the customers entering and leaving his restaurant as he supervised the young boys washing the glasses or serving at the counter. Most of his attention, though, followed Petrică, the nephew who now managed day-to-day business.

Sometimes, after supper, Father slipped over to Iliescu's for a shot of țuică or a beer—none kept at home—and to catch the BBC or Radio London bulletins about true war news. Many neighbours meet there.

Late in the autumn of 1943 Madam Fridman arrived in tears: her sister-in-law had been found dead that morning on Nicolae Titulescu Boulevard. Hurrying home with this camouflage darkness, the woman had stumbled into the underground stairwell of the public lavatory, right in front of her house. No one seen her, no one heard her, and she lain there until dawn. Mrs. Fridman's sister-in-law was married to a watchmaker Jean, who had a little shop in front of his house. They had no children. She was about 50 years old, and her husband, looked much older. He was heavy with a rounded belly and a white, broad moustache covering his lip.

A few weeks after the funeral Father bumped into Jean on Grivița. The man pulled him aside, and start crying:

"Mr. Kimel, can you imagine? After I lost my wife—may

God rest her soul—her relatives descended on the house and took everything I had. They emptied my home! Do you understand what I said? They took everything, everything." The man was burdened and in despair.

Some days later, the Fridmans came to us. They were middle-aged, though she had a younger-looking round face, short black hair; a plump figure covered most of the time in a floral silk dress. He, tall and skinny with rare, white hair, was a chain smoker. They sat at the table in the kitchen, and he lit a cigarette, explaining to Father:

"Just before my sister died," he began solemnly, I believe she had a premonition. She told us that if anything bad happens – you know, with all the events around us - each of us should have a something to remember her. It was her last wish, my friend. We can say that it was her last will. Don't you think the same?"

Then he went on to describe Jean, his brother-in-law, as a lazy man without value, a bum with no will, a man who did nothing good in his life.

"He's not a man, he's a piece of garbage, that's what he is." Concluded Mr. Fridman. "He does not deserve anything" added he before leaving.

When the door closed behind them, Mother asked quietly:

"What do you think?" Father didn't hesitate showing his feeling.

"Put the children to bed, douse the lamp, and leave the door open for a little fresh air."

II

The way it started that day, there wasn't anything different to notice than any other day. I walked home from school with my satchel heavy with new lessons—unaware that there would be no school the following day. The streetcar didn't come sooner or later than normal, the sun spread its April rays as usual on this warm day on which Mother made me wear the winter coat. The city's warning sirens droned their long, steady note, just as they had on countless drill days, and no one paid them any special mind.

I stepped off the tram at Podul Grant, crossed to the pedestrian walkway of wooden planks, and paused to watch the trains creeping beneath the bridge in both directions. After traversing the four curved metal spans, I started down the ramp toward Giuleşti—and caught sight of a glinting V-shaped formation of aircraft approaching from the west.

Between the bridge and Giuleşti soccer field stadium stood a broad, grey, tiered building that reminded me of a ship; the Germans had turned it into a local headquarters and field hospital. On its roof I could make out the silhouettes of soldiers manning an anti-aircraft battery. The planes—a seemingly endless parade, row on row—roared overhead, their engines beating the air like the breath of some colossal beast. Only then did people around me lift their heads.

At home Mother was preparing our lunch when she helped me out of my coat. We had taken only a few bites when a detonation strong enough to shudder the floor, rocked the house. Simona was scared and started to cry. Mother's face whitened as blood drained out. Moments later, a second blast, stronger, closer, made everything tremble. Windows blew shards out of frames. Mother sprang up, gathered us around her, looking disoriented, not knowing where to go. Thinking, she herded us out of the kitchen inside the courtyard toilet, strongly built with bricks and cement. We crowded together inside, standing, feeling safer as she locked the door behind.

Bomb after bomb crashing around, jolting the earth under us, dust drifted from the ceiling. Mother clutched us, repeating prayers in her mother tongue while we cried and embraced her like she was the only pillar of safety in the universe. These moments were endless. Each new thunder made Mother cry, "Oh, God! Oh,

God!" At last, unable to endure the deafening crashes, she flung the door open, and we sprinted to next-door neighbours at number seven, remembering that they had dug an underground bomb shelter. Mother lifted the trap-door in the grass, and we clambered one after another down the wooden ladder. Inside the dirt-walled pit neighbours and strangers crowded on the benches, crossing themselves, pounding their chests, whispering forgotten litanies. Each new explosion rattled the timbers overhead and spattered loose earth onto our hair. Some people knelt in the mud, kissing the ground.

We stood long time in that ditch – a grave for living - covered with a thick bed of dirt growing fresh grass. We remained there even after no more explosions were heard. No one had courage to go out until a volunteer announced that the planes had gone and it was safe to come out.

Moments later Father appeared, shirt dark with sweat, chest heaving. He had run home first—found us gone—then remembered the shelter. When people asked what he so, Father said:

"Grivița was bombed yard to yard. Even Podul Grant couldn't be passed now. Huge holes in the pavement, and on the wooden pedestrian's path makes it unusable."

Outside, our street couldn't be recognized. Black smoke

towers twisted into the sky from each direction. People on the street ran agitated, lamenting, tears in their eyes and desperation. Groups of two, three men carried the wounded to the stadium, hoping that they could find help.

At home, the kitchen was a jumble of broken chinaware, smashed glass, and our food scattered on the carpet. The framed pictures from the walls lay in disarray on the floor. Luckily, my grandparents' portraits were hanging on top of our beds and did not fall. In the courtyard a long section of railway rail jutted from the soil near the water tap—hurled there by some distant blast.

Father told us what happened this day. It was announced that another alarm drill would be exercised today using the familiar continuous alert tone. Those drills often repeated in expectation of the Allied forces' bombardments. Few people noticed when the signal changed to the real, intermittent wail, and so the streets were still in full activities when the American bombers released their first loads. Shop windows blew in, bricks, merchandise and debris showered onto pavements, and people darted in every direction searching for cover that no longer existed.

Yet Father thought only of reaching us. He ran entire length of Grivița road while bombs poured over aiming the railway tracks behind Gara de Nord, the most important lifeline of provision for the German front supplies.

The bombs could not stop Father from getting home. He did not stop when a tall building collapsed at his heels, nor when a man with his belly torn open begged for water. He sprinted past another on the other side of the road tried to pick up objects scattered on the street from an expensive store. The next bomb, Father no longer saw the man, nor the building.

That night we left every lamp unlit and lay on our beds fully clothed with our coats on. Mother hugged us close, whispering how blessed we were simply to be alive and together. Near midnight the sirens rose again. Father, who had been at Mr. Iliescu's restaurant listening for news, shook us awake: Russian bombers were reported inbound. Mother started shaking, and I heard her teeth chattering. Father told us to wait quietly, to see what will happen first. Mother took us to a corner of the room and asked us to pray together. With our heads aimed toward the ceiling and palms joined in front of our lips, Simona, Mother, and I prayed with tears in our eyes.

Father stood in the doorway, watching the searchlights comb the sky. When the engines drew near, the anti-aircraft batteries stitched glowing arcs overhead, punctuated by dull booms. A handful of distant bombs fell; then the noise dwindled, the sirens sounded all-clear, and night returned to its uneasy silence.

So, the summer went, raid after raid, until almost the end of

August. But nothing could erase the terror of that day—4 April 1944—one of the blackest days in Bucharest's memory.

III

That April 4th., the carefully trimmed turf of the soccer field in Giuleşti Stadium became a field hospital. The wounded lay in neat rows on the soft spring grass, while doctors in rolled-up sleeves and volunteers with bandages made from torn sheets knelt beside them. There was almost no morphine, no proper dressings, scarcely a stretcher to be found—only whatever good Samaritans hurried over in baskets and satchels. The worst cases were carried—sometimes on doors, sometimes on bits of corrugated tin—into the vaulted corridors beneath the stands.

For those who had not survived, the unclaimed bodies and limbs, people used the extinguishing water basin in front of the church on Giuleşti Road. Into that concrete deep pit, many humans recovered from the debris were buried in layers covered with soil. People soon called the place the Fourth-of-April Cemetery.

Bucharest slipped into a half-paralyzed stupor with a reduced population and non-existent activity. Whole families fled to villages or provincial towns; shops stood shuttered; trams creaked empty along buckled rails and busses died where happened to be, near the curbs. At 9 Crângaşi Road, our neighbours vanished one by one. Tailor Nicu locked his workshop and marched his people back to their native village. The Fridmans moved in with relatives downtown and Mr. Pernos found refuge with friends far in the countryside.

Father heard on Iliescu's radio that children unable to leave Bucureşti could be evacuated to camps in the safer regions of the country. Without delay, Father and Mother took us to Banu Manta City Hall, a grand building with the sweeping staircase in the front and a tower topped by a bronze lancer and flapping flag. By dawn a line of anxious parents and wide-eyed children already curled down the block.

Hours later we reached a desk where a kindly woman in a floral dress began filling out forms for Simona and me. The moment Father told her that we belong to "Mosaic" faith, her pen stopped. Visibly pained, she explained that Jewish children were not eligible. A few days later we heard whispered rumours that a trainload of evacuee children had been shelled by aircrafts outside the city.

Returning home we couldn't recognise our city. On Griviţa, near Stoica Ludescu, the back half of a multi-storey building had been sliced away as if by a giant knife; a black limousine lay wheels-down on its roof, miraculously looking as parked there. Craters pocked the road; some filled with murky rainwater that reflected broken scraps of cloud. Windowless trams stood frozen where the blast had flung them off their tracks. Busses died on spots near curbs where they been caught. Half-collapsed façades leaned over deserted pavements.

Apart from a few dazed pedestrians walking through rubble, the place felt dead. Only a handful of shops dared open in the mornings; the market attracted scarcely any peasants brave enough to bring produce. Our milk-woman never reappeared. Even Father stayed home—the printing presses silent. Those aspects increased the dramatic outlook of what was once a very dynamic city, not so long ago.

Makeshift trenches in back gardens proved no match for high-explosive bombs. Nearby Regie, a direct hit obliterated a mud bunker like the one we had once used, scattering its occupants with the splintered beams meant to protect them. Basements fared little better. Finding a safe shelter was the most important thing now.

Word spread that only two refuges were truly safe: the Telephone Palace on Calea Victoriei, near the Royal Palace, and the new, still unfinished Railway Palace in front of Gara de Nord. The latter, people swore, had concrete floors reinforced with lengths of railway track; no bomb could punch through to the multileveled construction and layers of underground floors. Queues formed day and night—many citizens preferred to sleep on the pavement rather than risk being caught at home.

Father took us once. Until the siren wailed, the line waited calmly since everyone had learnt that the bombers never reached the city before eleven. When the alarm sounded, we filed down flight after flight of concrete steps into a chill, black cavern. Veterans of earlier raids spread blankets and eiderdowns to keep warm; we came in thin cotton shirts and summer dresses, shivering. It was cold and humid, and we huddled together for warmth.

Down there we heard nothing of the raid—only the blood beating in our ears—so when all-clear finally echoed through the stairwell we bolted home, starved and exhausted.

Easter arrived, but joy did not. In kinder years Father bought new outfits and shoes, and we would run outside to proudly parade our new look to our playmates. This time there were no clothes, no shoes, no brightly dyed eggs, no walnut-rich *cozonac* from Stella or any neighbour, and Mother's own cake tins stayed cold. The sun shone, yet no-one could bring themselves to call it a holiday.

IV

May 7th, 1944. I think it was Sunday, but I'm not sure. To me every day already felt like Sunday since Father was home now instead of at the printing shop. The neighbourhood gathered, as it always did, in Iliescu's restaurant which lately became a kind of community headquarters. Old Mr. Iliescu had fled to relatives in the provinces, so his nephew Petrică kept the doors open from dawn past midnight. The battered radio on the corner shelf spat static and snippets of front-line reports. Patrons nursed tiny glasses of țuică and argued about the latest flight paths of the bombers that visited twice a day. Every morning Petrică opened the door, removed shutters and started his long day of work. Here at Iliescu's someone came with the idea to see if the snow canal that runs underground along Crângași Road could be a better refuge than the flimsy backyard trenches. Everyone knew this canal was cleaned every summer by city workers. They also knew that in winters the snow collected from city streets in big trucks, was disposed there. But no one have any idea what was inside. Its nearest access hatch lay directly in front of the siphon shop.

By mid-morning a circle of men levered up the iron cover. One volunteer clambered down the ladder-like U-shaped rungs, vanished into the gloom, then shouted back that a cavernous oval tunnel ran off beneath the street—two metres high, water trickling along its floor, cool air sighing through it like breath from the earth's lungs. Some believed that it ran under the railway tracks coming from Grivița all the way down to Roşu village outside the city, into Dâmbovița River.

Work began at once. Carpenters lowered planks and built a narrow footbridge above the water; benches were fastened along both walls, and people down the road were told to fit out their own entrances in the same way. For children they rigged a laundry basket on a rope, lowering the little ones into the dark where parents waited with candles. From now, the entire neighborhood had a safe, deep shelter.

When that very Sunday morning the siren started its rising wail, Mother's hands fluttered muffling a prayer. Father ushered us to the canal's access. She was told to go first, clutching the slimy iron rungs, her skirt brushing the damp concrete. After a few steps down, Father let Simona follow Mother, telling her to hold very carefully on to the steel bars and not to rush. Then it was my turn. When we were about halfway, it was so dark that nothing could be seen. It was cold, humid, the walls lubricious, and the steel bars seemed covered by a disgusting, slippery skin. Suddenly, I heard Mother crying from below. Simona had lost her hold on one these clamps and tumbled over Mother's head. Luckily, the distance between them was short, and Mother was able to catch her breathless but unharmed.

When we reached the wooden bridge below, a gentleman with a long candle like the ones for weddings, directed us to seat on the benches in the upper side of the tunnel, next to ones already sitting. Some brought candles flickered, gilding anxious faces in the tunnel obscurity. A few more took place on the benches next to us. The tunnel continued further dark toward Podul Grant. From there came a hollow rumble undistinguished echo. Mildew smell thickened the air; beads of water lingered around the curvatures of the concrete, leaving behind thick residual paths into the stream below.

When the first bombs landed, we knew it by the shove of air that raced through the shaft. Men who had remained topside now scrambled down—but Father did not appear. A gentleman remained hanging the upper steel clamps looking around, conveyed down what happens outside. Word travelled from mouth to mouth, like a huge wireless, broken telephone. Mother was worried about Father still outside. No long after, was transmitted that the house behind Iliescu's is on fire. Mother frightening went to ask the person with the tall candle about Father. He shrugged:

"How could I know it, Ma'am? What, can I see from here?" and told her to return to her seat.

At last, the gentleman near the hatch called down that he had seen Father alive, but after a long series of explosions the messenger admitted he could not spot him any longer.

News continued to come about more houses on fire or bombed, almost entire street burning. Then, an enormous blast from somewhere near Piața Grant punched the tunnel like a fist. Candles blew out, people tumbled from benches, babies screamed. In the pitch-dark Mother drew us to her breast and wept without a sound; I felt her tears on my hair and added my own. Voices rose—angry, desperate, praying—until hands found matches, candles caught light again, and the murmur quieted to exhausted breathing. Time stretched, it was a terrible struggle, being forced to wait indefinitely. This time, Mother and I started to fear that Father had perished in the flames, and we would never see him again.

Near sunset the sky, the noise the waiting down in darkness finally ended. We came up the shaft. The street outside was littered with rubble, fire and smoke in all directions. Directly beside the manhole a strange heap stood like an island: our bedsteads, night-tables, the vanity with its centre mirror shattered, a tumble of clothes. On the mattress springs sat Father, hair singed, face and hands black with soot and scored by cuts. He looked as though every muscle had turned to water, yet his pale-blue eyes brightened when he saw us. Mother ran to him, wrapped both arms round his shoulders, kissed the grime, then sobbed, unable to speak. Father tried to calm her patting her back, gesturing weakly over the rescued furniture.

"Look," he said, half-smiling through the ash, "that's all I could save from the fire." Mother protested:

"Who needs these? We thought that you were dead!"

The three of us embraced him there on roadway, while the sky above smouldered orange with the day's last flames.

V

Mother could see at once that Father was badly burned: his face, nose, forehead, and hands were already swelling, and we had neither water nor dressings. Our house, the yard— indeed the whole property—lay in ruins, while fires raged up and down Crângași Road. Asking for help would not benefit everyone around us nursed wounds, searched for missing kin, tending own pain and urgencies.

Without hesitation Mother left us in Father's care and headed for the German headquarters at the foot of Podul Grant. She asked to see an officer, told him she was herself German, that her husband was wounded, her children stranded in the street, and she needed help. Five German soldiers followed her back with a stretcher. They carried Father to the field hospital inside the headquarters, then returned for the furniture he had rescued, hauling it to the grassed courtyard behind the wrought-iron gate. Mother spread our mattresses there so we would have somewhere to sleep.

Before nightfall the German commandant came to speak with Mother and told her to bring us downstairs to the officer's mess for dinner. After we ate, the German officer came back to us, took Simona on his lap and gave us pieces of chocolate. He assured Mother Father's burns were superficial and insisted she fetch whatever we might need from the canteen. So, under a sky bright with stars, we slept in the open, guarded by sentries who wandered over to chat with Mother about wives, children, and the worsening front. They feared that what had befallen Bucharest would soon come upon Germany.

Two days later Father emerged from the infirmary, his hands freshly bandaged, forehead and nose raw beneath peeling skin. The next morning, he took us to see what was left of our place at 9 Crângași Road. We clambered across heaps of charred brick and buckled roofing-iron to the water tap beneath the scorched acacia. Finally, we got in the middle of our courtyard, under the tree. Only two rooms at the far end of the Fridmans' apartment— and a few green leaves high in the tree—had survived.

Father said that on 7 May, the bombers had sent incendiary bombes in dense clusters forcefully piercing roofs and starting instant fire. The first sticks punched through our attic and set the tailor shop ablaze. He dragged out the beds, the stove, anything he could, piling them under the acacia. He wanted to pool the massive wardrobe, but it needed dismantling and there was no time. Each dash inside he prayed he would make it back alive. When he saw the large, framed portraits of his parents falling and shattered on the floor, he took it as a warning and no longer put foot inside.

By that time, Pernos' upstairs rooms caught fire extending rapidly its flame across to Fridmans' apartment. Even our old acacia tree spread branches over the roofs start burning. Realising that everything he saved from fire would soon be bound to burn here in the middle of the courtyard, Father had to find a better place for his things somewhere else, and the only one safe was the street, where we later found him sitting.

Then he raced back to courtyard where the fire from Pernos' moved to Fridmans' kitchen. Soon, looked like it would extend through entire apartment. He decided to isolate the still-intact rooms not covered with an upper floor. With an axe, cut a firebreak, ripped doors from hinges, hacked through floorboards and roof timbers to isolate the two rear rooms of Aunt Fani's apartment. The bedroom and salon remained untouched; the dining room was half collapsed; its ceiling and floor half burned, and the steel roof sheets spilled into the kitchen like a frozen waterfall.

After showing all this to Mother, Father told her that he wants to sleep in the unburned rooms that night. The next day he found some neighbours to help him bring our stuff from the German headquarters. At lunch, we continued to receive food from the Germans, but by the weekend the garrison had decamped to bunkers dug into the hills near Roşu, leaving us to begin our new life amid the charred skeleton of home.

VI

We was living among ruins. In the half-burned room, its floor gaping, and part of the roof caved in— Father leaned our surviving furniture against the rear wall. Beyond it lay the front room with its wide double doors of the main entrance. Father pushed Aunt Fani's pieces back toward the walls and set our own blackened kitchen stove saved from ruins near the doorway, running the stovepipe out through a shattered window. Pots and pans salvaged from the ashes still wore their blistered enamel. Mother scoured them with wood ash, boiled water in them, and declared them safe. We slept in Aunt Fani's beds.

Summer warmth softened everything. Once Father cleared

away jagged beams, debris and broken glass, Simona and I ran barefoot in the courtyard, free to scavenge the wreckage for "building materials." Behind the siphon shop, near the wooden still intact gate, we managed to build together our own one-room palace from scorched boards and corrugated tin. Among the debris we unearthed treasures: clockworks fused by heat into fantastical sculptures of glass and metal; wind-up springs annealed into black ribbons; a pair of cast-iron stove lids that, with a bent U-shaped wire, rolled perfectly down the pavement.

From one ruin we dragged a steel sledge, its wooden seat long burned away. From another we rescued a miniature blue farm-cart miraculously untouched by flame, because there everything else, including the tree, burned. I pulled Simona home on it, like a princess returning from conquest. With mostly empty streets and few remaining people living in the city, we felt like the entire neighborhood became ours. In our little shack behind the siphon shop, sheltering us even in rain, we were absorbed in play until Mother called us to dinner, or the darkness made us stop.

The raids continued, usually twice a day. At the first wail of the siren we scuttled to the gaping manhole, clambered down the slimy U-bars into the canal, and took our accustomed places on the benches in the dark. We knew the whole routine so well that we could have done it blindfolded—which, in that blackness, we nearly did.

Between alarms, the street became a kind of public arena, especially after Iliescu's restaurant burned together tree with our house. Neighbours gathered at fences or in loose knots on the pavement, exchanging rumours, consolations, even jokes. People who had barely nodded before now spoke as if long acquainted, discovering each other's humanity in the shared ruin. Father often sat on the bench beneath the mulberry at number 7 with Mr. Jenică, whose funny stories and jokes made both laugh heartily; I never got tired of listening to them and maybe, I carried some later to my friends. Mr. Jenică wife, Aunt Maria, was much younger, slight, and wracked by a nasty cough often repeated. Because she could not manage the ladder into the canal, they waited out the raids in their shallow earth shelter in middle of their court. She wore a tiny enamel icon of the mother of God on a ribbon; whenever the siren sounded, she pressed it to her lips, crossed herself, and murmured a prayer. Her gentle fatalism soon rubbed off on Uncle Jenică, who joked that if the bombs were meant for them, the canal wouldn't help anyway.

One afternoon Mr. and Mrs. Fridman appeared, anxious to see what remained of their home. They knew that the entire neighbourhood was heavily bombarded but hadn't had any idea what had happened to their own house. Mother showed them the shards and the two rooms we now occupied.

"We'll move out the moment we'll find somewhere else to

go," she promised.

Aunt Fani moved by Mother's speech, hugged her

"What's mine is yours—stay as long as you need."

Then she asked, almost shyly: "But tell me, did you found a small metal safe box under the bed?"

Mother shook her head. "I don't know. I never looked under the bed."

Aunt Fani knelt, groped beneath the frame, and exclaimed:

, "Look, it is here! Give me something to pull it out; it's too far to reach."

She coaxed the green metallic box out with a broom handle and handed it to Mr. Fridman, waiting outside with an empty fabric bag in his hands. They also took an armful of clothes from the wardrobe and a few keepsakes from the other rooms. Laden with bundles, they thanked Mother and started for the road.

Remembering them struggle away, Mother describing to Father entire scene, asked herself:

"How will they ever carry all that home? There isn't a single taxi left in the city."

VII

It was no secret that the Germans were losing ground. Word spread daily that Soviet troops had already crossed into northern Moldavia, and the refugees pouring into Bucharest brought stories of looting, rape, and worse. The official press never denied the rumours, and everyone was worried. *Curierul de Seară* (The Evening Currier) now reduced to a single, smudged sheet, tried to steady our nerves with headlines about a miraculous German secret weapon, a flying bomb reaching long distances with heavy load of explosives. One day it ran a grainy photograph of a sleek, fin-tailed missile the caption called "the V-2 flying bomb." According to the article, it could be launched from hundreds of kilometres away and strike with the force of a small earthquake. There were, the paper hinted darkly, *other* wonders still under wraps by Germans that would turn the war to victory.

No one believed the boast outright, yet no one dismissed it, either. Hope, after all, has thin bones, but they prayed that Russian won't occupy us. In every doorway the same conversation ended the same way:

"If only the Americans reach us first!"

That single sentence seemed enough to lighten faces worn thin by sirens, fear and shortages.

On August 23[rd.], 1944, dawn broke to the growl of engines. A convoy of battered lorries rolled along Giuleşti and Crângaşi Roads. Father broke the news to us that Romania had turned arms against the Germans. At street corner in front of Bucur's cigarette store, a volunteer traffic-marshal waved cars forward with a strip of crimson cloth leading circulation coming from all directions. Camions ran with men in jumbled uniforms brandishing rifles, red pennants and patriotic songs. Somewhere nearby a few shots cracked—nobody could tell from where—or at whom. The whole scene felt tilted, like the first seconds of an earthquake, when you cannot be sure whether the floor is moving or your knees are. It was an unusual beginning of the day.

Then in the middle of all this, unmistakeable snarl of bomb diving, again we were haunted by fear of never-ending war. An escadrille of Stuka aircrafts, the black-and-white Balkenkreuz stark on their wings, dropped out of the clouds and raked the crossroads with machine-gun fire. Screams and running feet filled the street; people who just minutes earlier had been waving flags now flung themselves behind walls or flat on the cobbles.

. Father herded us like terrified chicks back to the gaping manhole. Down the greasy rungs we went, into the rank darkness we thought we had left forever. One by one the neighbours followed. joining us. For so many days and nights we been united in watchfulness, prayers and hope, always coming to same place along each of us.

From overhead came the hollow clatter of anti-aircraft guns, the heavier booms of demolition charges, the whiplash of small-arms fire echoing along the tunnel. Father climbed back up twice, returning with coats, bread crusts, and a jug of water. We passed three nights down there, candles guttering, knees drawn up against the damp, our world narrowed to the smell of mildew, sweat and fear.

Above us the city fought street by street. The Germans knew the local topography and found ways to destroy the most important quarters of the capital. Being out-numbered but disciplined—set fire to fuel depots, blew rail spurs and warehouses, tried to claw a corridor toward the west. Romanian troops, hurriedly re-badged and only half supplied, blocked them at every turn. The fighting ebbed and flared, closer, then farther, until at last even the distant thumps fell silent.

After three days and nights, everything finally calmed down, we got out hungry for fresh air, and an invigorating bath. Peace, no longer a dream; was here, real as a breath of fresh air and the clear evening sky brimming with eyes of hopeful stars.

Chapter 5

The Gloomy Clouds Scatter

I

Almost overnight everything around us began to change. The street stirred back to life filled with new animation. People returned to their homes - those who still had a home - and could freely breathe the clean air again. New newspapers appeared—*Scânteia* (*The Spark*), *România Liberă* (*Free Romania*), and several others—though they were little more than single-sheet flyers. Barefoot village boys, driven to the capital by poverty, hawked the papers on corners, shouting headlines running along the street following customers. From the sky, planes dropped sacks of leaflets that fluttered down like flocks of pigeons, spinning in the breeze.

Mr. Bucur reopened his tobacco shop at the corner, and I hurried there to see whether *Universul Copiilor*—my beloved *Children's Universe*—had returned to print. Father came home that evening with news of his own: he had been hired as a setting type for *Viitorul* (*The Future*), the National Liberal Party paper led by Gheorghe I. Brătianu. A new optimism seeped into everything, as sweet and pervasive as lilac scent after rain. Summer felt like summer again, and even the heaps of rubble around us sprouted grass and poppies.

We had not yet seen Red Army soldiers in Grant, but downtown they were everywhere. Politicians quickly staged a "welcome" stand on the main boulevard—banners, flowers, a few red flags, and speeches to a thin crowd of onlookers. By evening the soldiers spilled into taverns, drank themselves glassy-eyed, and later roamed the streets in packs, stopping passers-by for money, rings, but mostly for wristwatches scarcely existent in their country.

"*Davai ceas!*" ("Give me watch!") became the new catchphrase describing Russians.

No woman ventured out alone after dusk.

One afternoon two ragged youths, little more than skin and bone in filthy clothe, slunk into our courtyard. They hesitated at the open doorway until Mother appeared facing them.

"*Tanti* Berta?" one whispered.

Mother's hand flew to her mouth; tears welled instantly.

"Ticu? Benu? It's you? Benu, how much you've grown!"

She drew them both into her arms, then sat them at the table and piled on every scrap of food she had, puling her chair to face them. Simona and I watched, searching their faces for the cousins we dimly remembered. The food on the table practically disappeared devoured by the hungry boys, and when the plates emptied, Mother asked:

"Tell me where the others are? I mean, Mother, Father, Sergiu".

"Only Sergiu and the two of us are alive." said Ticu with tear in his eyes.

They spoke in slow fragments, taking turns, with tears and pauses interrupting the stories. Unbelievable descriptions of fear, flight, hunger, and cold made Mother and us felt sorry for them, although was hard to comprehend the depth of their suffering. Mother's eyes flooded. Now that she found out Aunt Raşela was dead, she was unable to stop her growing pain and tears. Her generous, indefatigable sister—had died. Grief closed her throat; she could barely breathe. The boys also cried.

I remember with painful clarity all the facts they mentioned about years of misery, freezing, starvation - scavenging rubbish bins for food, sleeping in derelict stables, chased like rats from village to village. Near Mogilev the whole family caught typhus; they collapsed together in an abandoned barn. Fever stole their senses. Shivering and delirious they pulled the frayed covers from each other's bodies. When recovered their consciousness, both parents were cold stiff beside them, frozen to the floorboards. Too weak to move, the children lay there for days, unaware even of the date—time itself had dissolved with everything else they once understood.

Mother wept openly, stroking their hands across the table, but the boys had no more tears. They were consumed long time ago remembering those who they had outlived.

II

From information found on the Internet, I read that in the summer of 1940, under German pressure, Romania could not avoid surrendering the regions of Bessarabia and part of Bucovina to Russia, the north side of Transylvania to Hungary, and the Dobrogea region to Bulgaria. After these concessions, the German troops did not have to invade Romania, which became a satellite of Nazi Germany.

On September 6, 1940, King Carol II abdicated his throne in favor of his 18-year-old son, Mihail, before leaving the country with his mistress for Paris. General Ion Antonescu, the former Defense Minister in Octavian Goga's government, monopolized the power of the country and was helped by most nationalist parties.

During his reign, many of the notorious Iron Guards accepted ministerial positions and pushed for institution in the country of the legionary police, following the model of the Nazi police.

On January 21, 1941, the Iron Guard, led by Horia Sima who was unsatisfied with Antonescu's resistance to his policy revolted against him and fought to seize power. They tried to defeat the army and to gain control of state organizations, simultaneously organizing a ferocious pogrom in the Bucharest Jewish neighborhood, similar to Crystal Nacht in Germany. Following the legionnaires, many hooligans joined the action as they devastated and looted Jewish homes and shops, desecrated or burned synagogues, and detained or slaughtered Jews based on lists made in advance. The Jewish bodies were found in the outskirts of the city's forests or hung on hooks from the city abattoir labelled "Kosher meat".

In the provincial cities of Romania, such atrocities never happened because the Romanian Army was very well supported by Antonescu who was in control over the situation. In Bucharest, the army was slowly gaining control as well, and it defeated the Iron Guard, arresting the leaders and organizers of the rebellion. Many of the leaders, including Horia Sima, found refuge in Germany.

On June 22, 1941, was the beginning of the war against Russia. The armies of Germany and Romania were aligned alongside the

Prut River, waiting for the order to enter Bessarabia and Bucovina. The order was received only on July 3rd, 1941. Under the encouragement of Hitler's "Final Solution" doctrine, on June 29th. the troops participated to the pogrom of Iaşi, where many Jews were killed.

At the beginning of August 1941, the Romanians started to send deportees from Bessarabia and Bucovina over the Dniester River, in an area under German occupation, named Transnistria. The Germans refused to accept the deportees and opened fire, forcing them to go back. Many Jews perished via drowning in the rivers' water or being shot by the soldiers. Of the 25,000 people who tried to pass over Dniester at Sampol, only 16,500 people succeeded in getting to the coast. Many of the survivors were killed or died of starvation and sickness on the way to deportation camps from Bessarabia and Bucovina.

Half of the Jewish population from Bessarabia, Bucovina, and Dorohoi, which numbered 320,000 people, died in the first months of the war. On September 16th, 1941, the deportation camps from Bessarabia and Bucovina started to move into Transnistria, in a zone from where the Germans withdrew, leaving control to Romania as per the Agreement of Tighina on August 30th, 1941; the deportation included 118,847 Jews. In two months, 20,000 died; some were unable to walk, and others died from sickness and starvation, but most of them were killed by the gendarmes who supervised the convoys.

Mother needed to calm herself after hearing the terrible stories told by the boys. She asked:

"Where is Sergiu?"

"Sergiu met a girl on the way back, after the Russians came. Maybe he married her. They walk slowly, so it will take some time until they'll get here."

Mother filled warmed water from her big laundry cauldron into the white basin. She took the boys one by one to the half-burned room next door, gave them what they needed, and told them to take a bath. After Father came home, he turned down our beds and let them have a good rest. The next morning when they came out for breakfast dressed in Father's clothes, clean shaved and combed, they began looking a bit closer to the way we remembered them.

III

Between the false acacia tree near the water tap, and the wall at the end of the courtyard, a long clothesline sagged with and few garments Mother scrubbed almost daily since we only had a few clothes left and she could not stand seeing us dirty. The big cauldron of water forever simmered on the stove. Yet when she left things out to dry overnight, pieces vanished—most often her hand-sewn lingerie.

One evening we had walked home from Aunt Luți and Uncle Mark's. In those days visiting was almost the only social life left: the telephones were dead, the trams still idle. We met many people there because Aunt Luți's unstoppable optimism, her ability to see everything with a touch of humour and buoyed by her unquenchable optimism—buzzed like an informal news agency with jokes, rumours, and half-reliable headlines.

The full moon lit Grivița bright as day, the bomb craters still yawning in the roadway. Streets, still not connected to electricity, streetcars were not running, and on Podul Grant, Father guided us around hazardous open holes. As we stepped into our yard, we saw a shadow behind a bedspread hanging on the line. The figure moved toward us, delighted.

"God, I've missed you so!" cried Stela—the siphon-shop owner's daughter who had vanished when the bombing began. "How happy I am to see you! How are you doing? Are you all, right?" she asked.

Mother invited her inside. At the threshold she murmured to Father to stay with us outside. Minutes later Stela burst back through the doorway, shrieking.

"But this is an outrage! I cannot believe it! To say to me that

I am a thief. Me, who loved her like a mother?" She stormed off into the moonlight, still protesting until she reached the street.

Inside, Mother shook with fury.

"Look what was stuffed in her coat."

On the table lay bras, chemises, shirts—every piece painstakingly stitched by her hand. After that night nothing else disappeared from the line, and Stela was never seen again.

Benu had been right: a few days later Sergiu arrived. Lean as a fencepost but neatly shaved, he wore a brown leather jacket and high boots, eyes glinting with their old mischief. He dodged questions about his prospects, merely saying he now lives in a fine apartment near city center, with his wife, Maricica, whom he promised to introduce soon. Ticu and Benu drifted between our house and Sergiu's, which upset Mother because she loved them and wanted to help, yet understood they needed the company of the young.

Not long after, Mr. and Mrs. Fridman returned. They hired a horse-cart, loaded their salvaged furniture and everything else, and rattled away. That was the last time we saw or heard from them.

When autumn came and each leaf spun its final pirouette to the ground, landlord Dragomirescu and his wife appeared with downcast faces. Their own home on Giuleşti Road not far from we used to live in Tabla Buți street had been flattened by bombs. Grateful to Father for saving these rooms from the fire, they nonetheless asked—apologetically, but firmly—that we find somewhere else to live.

IV

When most of the houses in our area lay gutted or flattened, hunting for a room was like searching for water in a drought. Each morning Mother left for the market and returned by way of streets she had not yet tried, pausing at shop counters or stopping strangers:

"Do you know where I could find a room for rent?"

Always the same shrug, the same weary "No idea."

At last, someone mentioned a possibility on Racoviță-Grant Street. The property belonged to Mr. Buzatu, who ran a front street restaurant. His father-in-law, the developer Mr. Shabauer, had just finished a large villa at the back of the courtyard with two small flats for rent. Mother went straight there, but Buzatu told her:

"I'm sorry ma'am, but both units are taken."

She trudged home sad and worried. Mr. Dragomirescu

would insist to vacate this house with two children in the middle of winter, and no place to go.

By luck that very afternoon, the landlord appeared. When Mother related the story about Mr. Buzatu apartments, he pricked up his ears, jotted the address, and told her:

"Do not wary anymore, Madam Kimel. I think I know what's about here. I'll take care of this!"

Near dusk a uniformed policeman knocked at the door:

"Be packed by morning," he said.

"Packed for where?" Mother asked.

"You'll see. Just find a cart and load your things. The rest is our concern."

Moments after he left, Mr. Dragomirescu arrived confirming the news. He had spoken to the district police chief, who had dispatched an officer to inspect the Racoviță-Grant apartments; they were, in fact, still empty. The chief decided that we were to be installed there at once. So, at sunrise, under a policeman's watchful eye, the lock was snapped with a chisel, and we carried our scorched furniture into a brand-new apartment. The apartment smelled fresh, walls shone chalk-white; the raw pine floor scented like mountain resin; doors and window frames had been painted a stout chocolate brown only days before.

Father placed the two oak beds side by side against the wall facing the kitchen door, warmer in winter, he said. The vanity with its broken mirror went to the wall facing window; the rescued iron stove occupied the corner between window and the kitchen door. This time we owned no carpets, so Father unfurled wide bands of heavy wrapping paper—castoffs from the printing paper rolls — across the floor to muffle the chill. In the kitchen he fashioned a cot from wooden crates and pine planks, topped with a wool mattress and a weary blanket—the very image of Maria's bed in Aunt Raşela's house.

While Mother simmered supper, Father sat cross-legged on the new cot reading the previous night's *Viitorul*. The fire gave a friendly rattle in the stove; pans hissed; steam pearled on the windowpane. For the first time in months the room felt like a promise of happiness. The promise lasted five minutes. The door burst open and a gust of cold barged in ahead of a young woman in a fur cape standing on top of cemented stairs at entrance.

"Who gave you permission to move in my house?" she shrieked.

Father rose, one handheld out as though to fend off flying glass.

"Lady, you either come inside to talk like civilised people, or leave."

She kept shouting from the landing, so he shut the door in her face. Her protests dwindled down the stairs. Only later did we learn she was Mrs. Buzatu.

I don't know when the other children started school that year, but we registered for classes the very next day. School No. 27—the former girls' school—stood on Giulești near the Regie cigarette works. The boys' building had been obliterated, so both, boys and girls, now shared this sturdy, red-tiled, two-storey construction, girls on the upper floor, boys below.

Every morning the bell called us into the schoolyard where the tricolour Romanian flag was raised on its tall mast. In the presence of the school principal, Mr. Anghelescu and all teachers, we stood in neat squares by class, reciting the Lord's Praye. Children and teachers alike crossed themselves. All but me, because I never learn to cross myself. Children elbows jabbed my ribs offended that I'm not respecting the Christian ritual. Son, they realised that simply I was different.

I entered fourth grade; Simona began first. It was beautiful; I never seen a school like this. Our classroom was spacious, brightened by tall windows spilling light onto the ink-stained desks. My bench-mate was Dinică Copescu, nicknamed Bobocică (The Bud), a year older. He and his nine years old sister Doinița were our neighbours on the street at number 56. Dinică, was wiry, forever wriggling, peppering classmates with pellets of kneaded bread. Most days he wound up facing the wall or rubbing stung palms after Mistress Angelescu—the headmaster's formidable wife—applied her ruler up to ten times depending on case. He would claim no pain, but his tears told different story. Mrs. Angelescu allowed no nonsense, hands always clasped behind backs while explaining, elbows off the desktop unless copying from the board.

During recess the courtyard echoed with shouting; girls clustered on their half, boys raced madly over the rest, tumbling in mud, ripping sleeves, collecting bruises like medals. One day, very proud of his new outfit, Dinică paraded out at school his jaunty grey peaked cap wore mostly by grown ups. Its folded crown could be lifted to resemble an SS officer's cap. He thrust his face into mine with demonstrative authority:

"Heil Hitler!" he commanded with arm outstretched.

I refused to conform. A ring of boys formed around us. Dinică's feeling his authority challenged by my refusal, urged:

"Didn't you hear? Salute! Heil Hitler!"

I stayed still; he slapped me. Tears stung but I swallowed them. He slapped again.

"What, did you not hear me? Do what I told you!"

Fury—cold and absolute—took me. I lunged, fists like

stones. I knew he was much stronger, but this time fury, humiliation, and determination had no limits. He got on top and we punched each other until Headmaster Mr. Angelescu hauled us off by the ears to his office. He listened not to my excuses; ten swats of the ruler burned our palms and we were banished to opposite corners until dismissal.

That afternoon we took different streets home—each rubbing sore hands, each tasting, perhaps for the first time, the true cost of a salute.

V

After finishing our homework on the kitchen table, Mother allowed us to play with other children on the street, because Racoviţa Grant was a quiet street and cars only seldom passed through. There were many children in the neighborhood, but at first, we made only a few friends.

Across the street, not far from us, we met a small, shy, and lonely boy named Ticuţă, the son of a carpenter. He lived in a modest cottage behind a large, old-style house with a wrought-iron fence. We became instant friends and played with the wooden toys his father made for him. Many of our games required coordination, imagination, and knowledge of the rules—but others were just play. He always came with me to Mr. Bucur's cigarette shop to pick up the latest edition of

147

The Children's Universe on Wednesdays. We would devour the magazine as we walked the street, especially the cover and centerfold. Back home, we sat on the steps by our door and read aloud, with Simona sitting next, gazing at the cartoons.

At Number 54, between Dinică's house and Mr. Buzatu's restaurant, lived a boy named Titi Bureţea, a freshman in secondary school. He had a round face like the moon and a noticeable gap between his front teeth, which gave him a peculiar look. I played mostly with him and Dinică. When the street was quiet, I'd call for Dinică; if he didn't answer, I'd knock at Titi's gate. They did the same for me.

Simona had a few girl friends who lived nearby, and many times I joined their games. One of them, Luisa, lived in the corner house at the intersection with Constantin Grant Street. She didn't play with other kids on the street, but when she rode her new bicycle, we followed her with envious eyes. Luisa was a little older than Simona. One day, she stopped her on the sidewalk and asked her name. After a few words, Luisa invited Simona to come play at her house.

"I have to ask my mother first," Simona replied, as she had been taught.

The two of them went together to ask, and Mother agreed—on the condition that I accompany them. Luisa's house was elegant. It had once been a shop, probably run by one of her grandparents, now closed. Behind it were several rooms ending in a courtyard enclosed by a high fence that blocked curious eyes. Her parents welcomed us warmly, with parental kindness. They had observed us from afar but never intervened.

They were of Italian origin, with bronze skin and ebony-black hair. Their home was handsomely furnished, with mirror-polished furniture and intricate carvings. A tall library spanned an entire wall, filled with leather-bound volumes. A large desk in the center belonged to her father, an accountant. Luisa's room opened from a short corridor, and its window faced the street. On a chest of drawers sat a collection of dolls dressed in elegant outfits, with curly hair and eyes that rolled open and shut. She also had a small writing desk, and a bookshelf filled with picture books and illustrated fairy tales—reminders of the summer I'd spent exploring the Goldştein family's library at Podul Grant. Luisa didn't go to our school; she attended a private Catholic school. But her friendship with Simona lasted all years we lived on that street.

Meanwhile, Mr. Shabauer, our landlord's father-in-law, brought in some workers from his construction site. They built a large covered shed across from our apartment, stacking thick planks of rough lumber—some still lined with bark—into neat piles that reached the rafters. It soon became our favorite place to play, sheltered from wind, rain, and snow.

One of the workers, a middle-aged peasant, wore a hempen folk shirt, white trousers, and no shoes. One day, his toenail got torn out by something on the ground. The man sat in the middle of the yard, crying and asking for help, blood trickling from his toe. Mr. Shabauer rushed to his house and came with a bottle of water and some bandages. As the poor man cleaned and wrapped his foot, the boss scolded him gently:

"Now, you see what happens when you don't cut your nails? Who's to blame for this? Can you tell me? You, only yourself! Next time, be more careful."

After that, with his foot wrapped, the man limped away, stepping only on his heel.

Later, two carpenters built a hog pen between the shed and the shared court toilet, which was used by both restaurant customers and tenants. Soon, a truck arrived with a large hog, which took several men to unload. Buckets of food were poured daily into its trough, but the animal would often knock it over, mixing food with dirt. By Christmas, it had grown so heavy it could no longer stand.

In the middle between the restaurant and the toilet, the original tenants of the property—the Niculescu family—lived in a two-room small apartment. It was an older couple with two grown sons, both unmarried and employed by the *CFR* (Romanian Railways Company). The father was retired from the same company. Mrs. Niculescu had only two front teeth left but great pride in her sons, especially Ionel, the older one, recently promoted to office supervisor.

She often came over to borrow milk, sugar, or flour. While chatting, she would stand stiffly with one hand over her chest, the other over her mouth, and lift the lids of Mother's pots on the stove, to peek at what she is taken out from the pen cooking. She talked nonstop, darting from gossip to questions and back again without waiting for answers. Mother got used to her and didn't mind her snooping or constant stories.

The other new apartment next to ours, was rented to a Transylvanian couple, older than our parents. Both were tall and stout. The man had a silver moustache and slicked-back hair; the woman was energetic and worked tirelessly. Each day she kneaded dough for bread and noodles. Noodles appeared in almost everything she cooked. One of her specialties was a sour cabbage stew with chunks of smoked bacon and noodles floating in its greasy broth, the fat forming map-like stains on the plate. Bacon was a staple, and Mother learned from her how to prepare it with paprika. She also taught her to melt lard and store it in a jar to spread on bread for our school sandwiches. And so, Mother too began making noodles.

In the evenings, before dark, the two women would sit on their doorsteps with something to keep their hands busy and chat until night fell. Before going in, Mother would call us from our games in the street.

A few days before Christmas, the hog taken out from the pen. It was so heavy, to be carried out they used a stretcher. Father said that the poor pig became quadriplegic by being fed with that dry pea mash.

Mr. Buzatu, good-natured and down-to-earth man, had called a butcher. The man laid out his arsenal of tools and knives on a table in the yard, attracting our attention. A circle of neighbors and restaurant patrons had gathered to watch. Thaen, with one precise slash, the butcher cut the hog's throat. Mother could not watch the killing and covered Simona's eyes standing in front of her. Nearby, a fire of red-hot coals was burning under a metal grate. Once ready, the butcher charred the hog's bristles, then scrubbed the skin with a stiff brush and soap. It turned white and smooth as marble. He slit the animal from neck to belly, revealing its insides. At Mr. Buzatu's request, he cut a long strip of skin, which the landlord sliced into bite-sized pieces and handed out. I tasted pork rind for the first time—warm, tender, and pleasantly chewy. Mrs. Niculescu, unable to chew hers, pocketed the piece and took it home.

Madam Shabauer, the mother of our landlord's wife, visited occasionally and spoke with Mother in German. She was warm, soft-spoken, and deeply kind. The two women would sit at the table over tea and homemade cookies—always welcomed. Overtime, they formed a kind quiet friendship sharing past stories of their life and hopes. That evening, madam Shabauer brought us a plate of sausages, meat, and a chunk of pig skin.

The next day, the hog pen was transformed into a smokehouse. Bacon, lard, and meat hung from rods while sawdust burned slowly below, flavoring the air for days.

Around midnight on Christmas, a car pulled up in front of our gate. Two men in leather coats knocked on the door of the large house at the back of the courtyard. Minutes later, they left with Mr. Shabauer. No one knew where he had been taken. Rumors spread of deportation to Russia, but there was no proof. Madam Shabauer never spoke of it, and Mother never asked.

VI

Carollers came to our house when we used to live on Crângaşi Road, and Mother always welcomed them with pretzels, fruits, or a few coins. But I never gone caroling myself. When I was very small, I remember Father buying from a street vendor, one of those decorative sticks adorned with artificial flowers—an imitation of a flowering branch that, according to an old Romanian tradition, children used to lightly tap adults with as they recited New Year's wishes

Father taught me how to chant the verses:

Sorcova, the magic wand,

Brings long life at your command,

Like an apple fresh and sweet,

Like a pear a New Year treat.

Like a rose in bloom so bright,

Strong as a hard stone, shift as a flight,

Tough as an iron, sharp as a steel,

Health and joy in all you feel!

May the year bring all things fine!

Happy New Year! More in line!

After blessing my parents, we went to Aunt Raşela and Uncle Aurel's. I received a big kiss from my aunt, but Uncle Aurel gave me money - a lot of money - I think. In the following years I no longer received a flowered stick, but Mother told me it wasn't necessary; you can recite your wishes with a simple handkerchief. She opened the cupboard, unfolded an ironed kerchief, and handed it to me to wave while saying the rhyme. I was rewarded with candies and chocolate.

This year on Christmas evening, Dinică, his sister Doiniţa, and Titi Bureţea, knocked on our door and asked if I could go caroling with them. Mother didn't want to hear such a thing, but Father gave her a quiet signal, and she relented. She wrapped me warmly in a large shawl that covered my mouth, gave me wool gloves and a cloth bag, and let me go. Just before I stepped out the door, she kissed me somewhere between the shawl and my eye and gave me a firm pat on the behind for luck. I understood that from this moment on, I was on my own.

Outside, the frost bit at our skin and the snow crunched beneath our rubber boots. Dogs barked behind fences, but we didn't mind—Dinică and Titi carried long wooden rods, and I held Doinița's hand as we followed behind. First, we'd open a gate to check for unchained dogs. Then, we'd stand before the front door of the first cottage lit window—where Christmas preparations were underway—and sing. In Romania, most houses didn't open onto the street; only shops did. Front yards were small or nonexistent, and access to homes was through fenced courtyards, often shared by several families. When we finished our song, someone would come to the door with pretzels, candy, fruits or coins. Then we moved to the next house.

We worked our way to the end of our street and continued on Niculae Filimon, and the next one over. Eventually, the cold and the late hour caught up with us. Lights in the windows were going out, and Dinică announced it was time to go home. We returned to his warm kitchen behind the main house, where we emptied our sacks full of treats—candies, pretzels, fruit, and money—and split them evenly among us.

Mrs. Copescu, Dinică's mother, was busy pulling cakes from the oven. Others were already cooling on the table—tall, golden, and fragrant. She sliced one for us. But who needed cake when the real treasure was on the far side of the room: gingerbread, chocolate, foil-wrapped candies, oranges, dried figs—sweets of every kind. Still, we eat the cake, since she ate hers first, as did the captain's orderly who'd helped her bake. When she insisted again, we couldn't say no.

Dinică's father was a career officer in the Romanian Army. His orderly, lived in a small room near the woodpile storage, behind the kitchen. His duty was to help the captain dress, shined his boots, cleaned his uniforms, and prepared his meals. But here he did handyman work, chopped firewood, and accompanied Mrs. Copescu to the market.

When I got home, my worried mother was waiting. I unloaded my haul onto the kitchen table, but she soured my joy by saying I had to split it evenly with Simona, who had stayed behind.

"But it's not fair, mommy" I riposted. "She didn't sing in freezing night with us."

"If that's so, tomorrow you'll take her with you!"

The next evening, we had to take Simona and Mother wouldn't let me go without her.

We caroled throughout the neighborhood. On the third day, Dinică emerged proudly with a beautiful star he claimed to have made himself. It had six radiant rays spreading from a lit candle in the center, surrounding an image of the Baby Jesus. Transparent paper let the candlelight shine through, and the whole star was decorated with pictures and bright colors. Dinică held it high as he walked in the middle, and the rest of us circled around him, proud of our treasure. No other star on the street looked as fine or shone so beautifully.

As before, we went door to door asking:

"Do you receive the star?"

Even if no response came, we would start to sing knowing that at end someone will reward us. In some cases, someone would come out to us, challenging our skills of singing:

"Let's see if you know how to sing it right."

To prove it to him, we'd raise our voices and sing the carol with all our heart:

New star now is rising,
Rays of hope arising,
Mysterious light it brightens.
Trust-worth news enlightens,
Trust-worth news enlightens.

.

Today Saintly dona,
Sinless pure Madonna.
The Virgin Maria
Gave birth to Messiah,
Gave birth to Messiah.

On land full of glory
Bethlehem from story
Kings followed a brightly star.
To praise Christ, the King of Stars,
To praise Christ, the King of Stars.

After the performance, we each received a coin and moved on happily. Night after night for a few days we stroll the streets with our star rewarded for effort. But one evening, a gang of older boys came toward us. They also had a star, but theirs was mounted on a long stick. When they faced us, their leader suddenly jabbed his pole at ours, smashing Dinică's beautiful star. They laughed after that and walked away.

We stood stunned. Dinică fought back tears, bent down, grabbed a chunk of ice from the side road, and hurled it after them, shouting:

"Damn you, you fucking Herrods! You'll pay for this! I'll kill you, all of you!"

Winter on Racovița Grant was more than just pleasant—it was

pure joy. On the paved side of the street, kids came out with sleds; others strapped metal skates over their boots, using keys to tighten them. Some even made their own skates from scrap iron or old stove legs from rubble, bent and fastened with rope. Simona and I had the sled we'd found among the ruins. Father repaired it with a wooden seat, secured by bolts, and added a long rope for pulling it around.

Snowdrifts were shoveled to the sides, forming mounds along sidewalks and in courtyards. After freezing overnight, they were just right for sliding. We'd drag our sled to the top and ride it down into the middle of the road. When other children came out, we often broke into full-blown snowball battles that lasted until sunset or until the opposing gang surrendered and scattered.

Sometimes Simona and I built a fort just outside our gate, cutting snow into cubes with a spade. Once our fort was ready, we stockpiled snowballs and waited for someone to dare approach. Other times, Dinică sent scouts to spy on the kids from Zoie Grant, the street behind ours, and many times we fought them—and won.

The best fun of all was sledding behind *Doamna Stanca*'s school, where a steep valley stretched from Piața Grant to Ciurel Dam. After a snowfall, we'd bring our sleds there. Kids and adults with sleds of all shapes and sizes climbed to the street level, then glided down with breathtaking speed into the white expanse below.

Lying on my belly and steering with one leg dragged in the snow, or sitting backward and pulling the rope, I flew down the slope, drunk with speed. Even when I crashed into the trampled snow, the thrill made me forget my hunger, my cold, and how soon dusk fell over the valley.

Oh, good Lord—where have those snows gone, and those glorious days that enriched these memories with joy, disappear?

VII

Every Wednesday afternoon Moş Nae, the editor of *The Children's Universe* magazine (his real name was Nae Batzaria), would meet his young readers at the *Universul* newspaper headquarters on Brezoianu Street. I went once to one of these gatherings, encouraged by a recent A+ mark received in school for a free composition written in class on theme of Mărţişor day.

Mărţişor day, celebrated yearly on first of March, is a traditional Romanian holiday somewhat like Valentine's Day, where boys give girls a small red-and-white trinket for good luck and affection. Our assignment was to write a little story symbolizing the Mărţişor. I wrote a poem—my very first—about Romanian soldiers still fighting in the Tatra Mountains, far from their families, hungry and cold, struggling through a merciless winter while facing death each day. In the poem, I gave them a golden *mărțișor* as a token of courage and gratitude.

Mrs. Angelescu, our teacher, known for her high standards never thought giving an A+ mark unless the work was exceptional. Receiving back my extemporaneous work from her with regular red-pencil corrections spread over entire page, I couldn't believe my eyes seeing at the top corner an A+ note. Then she told me to read my poem aloud to the class.

Afterward, gaining a small degree of celebrity among my colleagues. Dinică, always quick to spot an opportunity, asked me to write a love letter to a girl he liked. I did. He copied it out carefully in round calligraphic script and delivered it the very next day.

Moș Nae's office was on the first floor of a grey building with a heavy stone entrance, over which hung a huge logo sign with bold black letters reading the word UNIVERSUL. Inside, a wide cement staircase led to a dim corridor, and at its end was a glass door opening into a large office filled with desks in two rows. At the far end, near the back wall, sat Moș Nae himself.

He had an oval face framed by a white, curled-up moustache, wire-rimmed glasses, and wore a neatly tailored three-piece suit. A desk lamp cast a warm glow over the children clustered around him, eager to watch him correct their stories or drawings. Other desks were filled with kids who were quietly writing or sketching while awaiting their turn. Some had come with their mothers; whenever that happened, Moş Nae stood up, kissed the lady's hand, exchanged pleasantries, and returned to the growing stack of submissions on his desk.

No one asked who I was, or why I was there. I looked around, saw what the others were doing, and did what I still instinctively do in similar situation: I sat at an empty desk stocked with pencils and blank paper and began writing a story in the same style I admired in *The Children's Universe*. After a couple of hours, just as I was putting the final touches on my story, Moş Nae raised from his desk coming in the middle and spoke to us:

"Listen kids, is getting late. Leave your work on the desks for tomorrow. I'll take them, read and answer to you in the next magazine edition. Right? Good night my dearest."

Next Wednesday I run to Mr. Bucur shop to find out Moş Nae's review to my story in *The Children's Universe,* but it never been found.

Whenever I couldn't find children to play with on the street, I'd go to Dinică's house. His family owned one of the nicest houses in the neighborhood, with large front windows at the street and a red-brick courtyard that led to the kitchen, the woodshed, and the orderly's room. The kitchen was our favorite place in winter. It had a low ceiling, a large countryside-style brick stove with an oven, and stacks of firewood leaning against the wall. It was always warm, and the adults didn't supervise us as closely there. Mr. and Mrs. Copescu lived in the larger house in front, but the children spent their time in the kitchen, which the orderly kept clean and functional. He also spent most of his time here, washing dishes, do repairs, polishing the family's shoes, or resting on a stool until someone gave him a task to do.

Dinică was always delighted to have company. Sometimes, he'd sneak out one of his father's game sets, or—when no one was watching—he'd steal some cigarettes from the monthly carton allotted to Mr. Copescu's regiment. Once back in the kitchen, he proudly displayed his stolen treasure. When the coast was clear—his mother busy in the front house and the orderly nowhere in sight—he'd pull a glowing ember from the stove to light a cigarette. We'd crouch by the stove opening, each taking a puff, then throw open the kitchen door to let the smoke out.

One day, Dinică burst into the kitchen like a bullet, hiding something under his sweater. He had taken a magazine from his parents' bedroom—one filled with images of naked women. We gathered around the table to look, while the orderly chopped firewood outside. I never see a magazine like that. With a self-proclaimed superiority, Dinică watched my surprise seeing those pictures and asked:

"What, you've never seen naked girls?"

"No," I said. "We don't have magazines like that in our house."

"But what does your sister have between her legs? Haven't you seen?"

"How would I see? What, I'm going after her to toilet?" I felt my face burning red, embarrassed talking about my sister.

Then Dinică peeked through the door to check the yard, turned to his sister, and told her to show me. Without hesitation, Doinița leaned against the firewood and revealed herself. Dinică then stepped in front of her with his pants undone and demonstrated:

"That's how you do it." Afterward, he stood watch by the door and said, "Now, do it to her, too."

When I returned home, I carried a heavy, wordless burden. I felt as though I had witnessed and took part to something I'm forbitten to think, to speak and since I could not let go away from my mind, I'm guilty with sin. Anytime I saw Doinița, my thoughts began to unwind the images from the kitchen. Sometime, just thinking of her produced a kind of sensations I'd never knew before making me feel confused, curious, and guilty all at once.

As the weather grew warmer, our playground shifted to the timber shed in our own courtyard. Hidden between the stacked wood, we built secret forts and hideouts. Up top, near the ceiling, we could not be seen. There, we smoked more of Mr. Copescu's stolen cigarettes or pored over forbidden magazines.

Sometimes we'd sneak off to the ruined basement at the corner of our street and Scârlat Vârnav were used be a big office. Downstairs in the rubble, we discovered a toppled safe wedged between bricks and half-burnt beams. It became our hidden fortress. It was there, on top of that old safe, protected by ruin and shadow, that we repeated the strange experience from Dinică's kitchen, feeling for the first time a sensation that rushed through my body like an electric storm.

Chapter 6
Fading Horizons

I

Often the word "manifestation" kept coming up, though I didn't know what it meant. Mother grew tense whenever Father was late coming home from work. He worked the night shift at *Viitorul* (*The Future*) newspaper, but instead of returning home to sleep, he often joined groups of workers marching through the streets with banners and slogans. They were protesting the low wages that couldn't keep up with the rising cost of living. Sometimes, he barely had an hour to rest before heading back to the newsroom.

"I'm going with you next time," Mother said one day, her voice sharp with worry.

The next afternoon, when Father still hadn't come home, she left us behind and went into the city. That was why, Father told me the other day soon after we opened our eyes in the morning:

"Dorel, we'll go to manifestation, Mother and I. Be careful, take care of Simona and everything else. Understand?"

"Yes Father."

They kissed us and went. They returned late in the day, looking shaken. Mother was trembling, her face as pale as during the bombardments. Father sank silently into a chair, drained of words. Though they'd clearly argued all the way home, the discussion wasn't over.

"How can you, how can you do this? A man with two children and responsibility mix with that crowd of nobodies. What do thing helps yelling in the streets? What if they'd shot you? Hi?

 What if they'd shot both of us? Who would've taken care of the children then? Do you ever think of it?" When her frustration grew larger than she could take, she broke down and cried.

The next morning, all the newspapers ran the same story across their front pages. *The Gendarmes of General Rădescu Opened Fire on Demonstrators*, they read. The carnage had taken place on Calea Victoriei, right in front of the Royal Palace. Nine or ten were reported dead. Among them was a student from the school I was to attend in the fall. Soon after, General Rădescu resigned. On March 6, 1945, a pro-Communist government was installed, headed by Dr. Petru Groza.

In our school, there were two brothers—bright boys, the only children of their parents. One of them was in my class, and the other was two years younger. I've forgotten their names, but I can still see their faces. Their house stood at the intersection of Zoie

Grant and Constantin Grant Streets. That whole corner remains vivid in my memory. No far from it, Zoie Grant turned into a dead-end on the edge of the deep valley that reaches Piața Grant. Before the war, a tall wooden fence had enclosed the wasteland. Now, only broken stumps remained—rotted by mold or stripped for firewood during the bitter wartime winters. On this unfriendly land, people use that abandoned field as a dumping ground for rubble, garbage, the debris of bombed-out homes.

One spring day coming from school, a group of us wandered there, enjoying the warmth. Green shoots were pushing through the ruined ground, and the sun on our backs made our winter coats feel heavy. Someone stumbled across a green grenade among the debris—rust blooming beneath the paint, a curved lever held in place by a bent wire hook. It was no bigger than a goose egg.

"Let's throw it!" someone shouted.

We argued. Some thought it wasn't real. Others weren't so sure. I did remember suddenly that Mother warned me to come straight home from school for an appointment. I let Dinică know and rushed home before trouble found me.

When I arrived, Mother was almost rushing us out the door. She made me wash quickly and change my clothes. We walked all the way to Regie. As we passed through the streets, we saw groups of women gathered near fences, speaking in low voices, crossing themselves. Something had happened—something serious.

When we neared our school, the father of my classmate rushed past us, carrying my classmate in his arms toward the Giuleşti Maternity Hospital. My friend's face was drained of blood, white as wax, and yet his eyes met mine—they were still wide open, full of fear, pleading. He clutched his abdomen with both hands. Blood seeped through his fingers. That was the last time I saw him alive.

The next day, the school entered mourning. Both brothers had died—the younger was torn apart instantly by the explosion. The elder died hours later the operating table. They weren't the only ones. Several other children were wounded or killed.

In the last house at the street's end, right before the wasteland began, another classmate of mine had been hit with shrapnel. His body was riddled with fragments. For hours, surgeons fought to save him. A week later, he came home. I visited. His mother—a war widow—and his older sister received us as though we were visiting royalty. They were so grateful he had survived. I found him in bed, lying on his back, pale but smiling faintly. When he lifted the edge of his blanket, I saw rows of bloodstained bandages crisscrossing his torso. Beneath them, his skin was pocked with dark entry wounds and burns, a constellation of pain that marked the path of the grenade's iron rain. Two days later, he too was gone.

At the small neighborhood church near Piaţa Grant, funerals were held nearly every day. Sometimes whole classes from our school would attend, led by our teachers. The sanctuary overflowed with grief—parents, friends, neighbors, strangers. The entire community gathered to mourn the children we had played with, sat beside in class, shared chalk and jokes and secrets with.

Even those who had never known them came, drawn by sorrow and a sense of shared injustice. The air in the church was heavy, dark as storm clouds. But what weighed most wasn't the incense or the silence. It was the unspoken agony of the parents who had lost their only sons. Two brilliant boys, both gone in a single afternoon of April 1945. And we who survived carried their faces with us—in our sleep, in our prayers, in our silence.

II

Before the school neared its end, the talk among my classmates turned to the future—where we would go next. In our neighbourhood there was only one secondary school, Doamna Stanca, but it was for girls only. Most of the boys dreamed of Gheorghe Lazăr, located downtown near the Cişmigiu Gardens. It seemed like the best choice, not just for the school's reputation, but for its surroundings. It sat proudly on the boulevard, in the heart of the city's liveliest district, where elegant shops, cafés, and cinema houses lit up the streets, and the most glamorous people passed by in luxurious cars and carriages. Life seemed to sparkle there, pouring out in waves day and night. What could be more tempting?

But I couldn't quite share their enthusiasm. My future had already been decided. Father gave me just one option: the Ciocanul (The Hammer) Industrial School. For him, it wasn't just a school. It was a pathway to certainty, a golden ticket to a stable life. At Ciocanul, I would learn both theory and a trade. And in a world where stability was rare and jobs uncertain, a trade, he said, was like "a golden bracelet," something you could always rely on.

Mother, however, wasn't as convinced. The school was all the way across the city, and she worried what would happen to me, all alone, taking two or even three streetcars just to get there and back. When would I eat? When would I study? What if something happened? I sat quietly, listening to their debate, unsure if I should feel proud or burdened. As always, I let fate do the deciding.

One Sunday afternoon, as I was playing in the courtyard, I saw a familiar figure at our gate. It was Mr. Angelescu, our school principal. He stepped inside and asked if Father was home. We walked together into the kitchen, where Mother offered him a seat and served him and me cold water and comfiture. Father soon appeared from the bedroom, wearing an ironed shirt and tie. He shook hands with the principal and joined us at the table.

"Mr. Kimel," the principal began formally, "I've come to speak with you about your son's schooling next year. My wife, Mrs. Angelescu, and I," (even in private, they referred to each other this way) "have been closely observing David's progress. And frankly, we believe it would be a serious mistake to send him to a trade school."

He paused, then continued:

"David has a natural gift - for the arts, for poetry, for anything that demands thought, feeling, expression. He should be doing work of the mind: law, accounting, teaching, even literature. Do you agree?"

Father listened politely, his face unreadable. When the principal finished, he spoke slowly and firmly:

"I've seen what life does to people without a trade. A man who can work with his hands will never go hungry. One day, David will have a family. He needs to be able to provide for them, no matter what happens. That's why Ciocanul School is the right place for him."

Mr. Angelescu made a few more appeals, but he soon realized that Father's decision was final. He finished his comfiture, praised the hospitality, and left with a respectful goodbye.

Summer brought with it new pleasures—fresh and thrilling as if invented just for us. I tried to keep up with Dinică, who, as always, was the best at everything. Together with Titi and the others, we roamed barefoot through the lower grounds of Oatu, a patch of wild terrain that stretched from behind Piața Grant all the way to the Ciurel Dam, where we swam. When we reached the river, we threw our clothes onto the bank and ran naked into the water. The dam had long cement steps that framed the twin overflows where the water roared down in white torrents. We would climb up and brace ourselves against the churning flow, laughing as it battered us.

Afterward, we pulled on our clothes, still dripping, and made our way through the remote lower grounds toward Regie Park located next to the old brick wall of Doamna Stanca School. Here we would dry in the sun, lying down on the benches in the gazebo that served as a stage for the Sunday bands that would perform here. People gather here to enjoy the sun, the cool shade under the trees, and the music. Different bands would perform on Saturday evenings for young and old, coming with their sweethearts to dance on the grass around the gazebo, where the trees supported a constellation of coloured lamp posts.

From the gazebo, our attention was captured by the always-locked metallic door in the middle of the wall with Doamna Stanca school which had an attracting power to us. Apparently behind that door lay a mysterious tunnel - a secret passage running under the city all the way to the village of Roşu. The tales about it varied, but they all agreed on one point—behind that door lay something hidden and forbidden.

Sunlight sifted through the green canopy of grass in bright patches, and the air smelled of warm earth and temptation to sleep. On weekdays entire park was ours. As we passed by on our way home, we gave the handle a routine tug—and to our astonishment, the door opened. Inside, we found a whitewashed room, and on one wall, a narrow opening arched into darkness. The mouth of a tunnel. We stood before it, spellbound. Its curved ceiling vanished into shadow, swallowing the light.

"Let's go in," Titi whispered.

But none of us moved. We stepped just far enough to peer inside. The air was cool, damp, and faintly metallic. The darkness pressed against us like a warning. Dinică, Titi and I hesitated to step further. I didn't need to. My body already knew the answer; I had no desire to lead the crowd.

Some doors open to mysteries. Others open to fear. That one opened to show us our limits.

III

My friend Ticuţă, the carpenter's son from across the street, made a remarkable discovery in the attic of their big house. Inside an old chest that had belonged to his landlord—a man with a bald head and a grand white moustache—lay a treasure trove of forgotten books. The landlord, a passionate book lover, had collected the weekly supplements from various newspapers and had them bound into handsome volumes, each marked with gold lettering. Among them were *The Adventures of Submarine Dox*, *The Mysteries of Paris*, and the one that left the deepest impression on me: *The History of the Spanish Inquisition*.

With the old man's permission, Ticuţă lent me these volumes, one at a time. They so absorbed me that Mother had to resort to the rod just to get me to turn off the light and go to sleep. And that was how reading became my passion. Books opened doors in my mind—worlds, situations, emotions I had never known. The heroes I read about inspired me deeply. I wanted to be like them: brave, just, willing to fight for the right cause. They stirred something in me that spilled over into daydreams, even though some of the darker passages—especially the scenes in the catacombs—reminded me of my own fear when I stood before the mysterious tunnel in Regie Park.

One day in the courtyard, I was playing with my new dog, Lili. She had been given to me by a neighbour, but only after I had begged Mother in tears to let me keep her. Simona helped plead my case, and eventually, Mother relented—on one strict condition:

"You're never bringing her inside the house. Are you hearing me?"

What could I do? I made Lili a soft bed in a cardboard box. A few days later, Mr. Niculescu, the old neighbour with two sons in our courtyard, built her a beautiful wooden doghouse. Everyone loved Lili. Even Mother, who checked her carefully for fleas, often petted her and kept her water dish full and clean.

Dinică called out from the gate, tempting me to join him at the soccer field stadium. He was dressed nicely in sandals with socks, his hair combed neatly. I'd never been to a soccer match before, even though the Giuleşti Stadium was just a short walk from our home. Every Sunday, it roared with cheers, protests and songs. People came from every corner of the city, and even from the provinces, to see the matches—especially when Rapidul, the railway team, played. I was in my play clothes, barefoot, and I knew Mother wouldn't let me go if I tried to change. Sensing my hesitation, Dinică always good with persuasion, assured me:

"You're fine. Most kids are dressed like that."

From Podul Grant, a river of people surged toward the stadium, ticket stubs in hand, rushing to find the best seats. We had barely reached the electric clock on the street corner when Dinică spotted a young couple walking toward us. Without hesitation, he stepped in front of them.

"Uncle, please take me with you," he pleaded. "If I go with you, they'll let me in. I swear they won't say anything!"

The couple laughed, amused by his nerve, and agreed. I followed them until the stadium gates, where the attendant tore their tickets and let all three passes. From inside, Dinică threw me a knowing glance before darting up the stairs with his new protectors.

I was left behind, standing before the steel-barred gate, surrounded by other boys just like me—drawn there by an invisible force that refused to let us leave. Inside, from the stands, thunderous waves of sound rolled out like summer storms, stoking our curiosity and envy. Some boys begged the gatekeepers, but it did no good.

Finally, after the break in the second match, the attendants relented and let us in—with one condition:

"Cheer for Rapidul only."

From that day on, soccer became our favourite sport.

After a string of clear-skied days with the sun blazing directly above, the cherry trees began to blush red with ripeness. The glossy fruit called to us like jewels. The only problem was that none of us had a cherry tree in our courtyard. But Dinică, as always, had a plan:

"Let's go and steal some!"

"How?"

"With hoţoaice!" (thievish rods)

On our way back from swims at the Ciurel Dam, our way passed through the marshy area of Oatu's wasteland before Regie Park. In one plot, tall reeds grew so thick and high they could hide a man on horseback. Their plumed tops drooped under the weight of their seeds. With his pocketknife, Dinică cut several reeds at their base—some for us, and a few extras for the future. We carried them home under the shelter of the timber shed. There, we stripped the reeds bare, cut off the feathered crests, and carved three or four incisions at the top. Then we braced the openings with small cross-sticks. When we finished, the reeds resembled ancient spears. But we didn't fight with them—we hunted fruit. I remember that Dinică called them "thievish rods."

With these weapons in hand, we roamed the neighbourhood fences. When we spotted cherries within reach, we raised our rods over the fences, guided the open end over the fruit, and tugged until it popped free into the hollow tip.

Our most ambitious target stood behind the tall fence of the Copescu's neighbour at number 58, a notoriously grumpy old man. No one could see into his yard and nailed to the gate was a metal plate that warned: "Beware of the Dog." But behind that gate was a cherry tree unlike any other—tall, full, and bursting with cherries so round, red, and glossy they looked like something out of an advertisement.

We couldn't resist. From the street, we began poking our thievish rods over the fence, plucking cherries one by one while the dog inside barked madly, hurling himself at the barrier. At first, we ignored him. But then the gate creaked open. There, silhouetted in the doorway, stood the old man himself—pitchfork in hand, eyes blazing.

"You rascals! You sons of bitches! I'll teach you a lesson you won't forget!"

We didn't wait to see if he meant it. We ran like mad, not even daring to look back, and threw ourselves into hiding behind the timber shed in our yard. It was only later, after silence returned to the street, that we tiptoed out, shaken but exhilarated, and resumed our patrol—older, wiser, and still a little hungry for cherries.

After the soccer game at the stadium, there were no better

players in our neighbourhood than us. The only problem was—we didn't have a ball. A real soccer ball was expensive, and without one, there was no game. Fortunately, Dinică had a solution:

"Let's make our own ball. "

"What kind?" I asked surprised.

"Rags. Didn't you see a rags ball?"

He brought over some old silk stockings from Mrs. Copescu, and my task was to fill them with rags. I had to beg Mother for scraps.

"Where do you think I'm supposed to find rags, dear?" she asked, exasperated. "You don't expect me to tear up your father's shirts, do you?"

Eventually, she handed over some bits of old cloth and fabric scraps. We sat on the curb, packing the stockings with rags, twisting them tight and wrapping the material around itself until we had a rounded shape. We left just enough stocking at the end to close it up. But to do that, we needed a needle and thread—so back I went to Mother. Finally, the ball was ready, and we could get on the field.

The field was the middle of our street—the same road we used for all our games. We found stones to mark the goals, and the match began. But Dinică was bigger and faster than me, scored again and again. All I could do was run after him, barely touching the ball. Frustrated, I quit. What kind of fun was it to play barefoot on a road paved with rounded, uneven stones, always risking a stubbed or bleeding toe?

We needed change the rules. No more soccer.

Instead, we invented the *repelling game*. Each of us defended our own widened goal. The point was to throw the ball by hand and try to land it in the other player's gate. But the keeper shouldn't catch the ball—he had to repel it as far as he could. From where it landed, the attacker would try again. This new game thrilled me, because I was a better goalkeeper than Dinică. When he hurled the ball at full force, I was ready to dive onto the stones to block it. For once, I had the upper hand.

Later, when Titi Bureţea came out to the street, we switched to *The Chief in the Middle*. It was late in the afternoon, and Mother had begun calling me for dinner. Father had to leave for work. Titi was "the chief," and he was trying hard to make someone else take his place. One of Dinică's throws wasn't quite aimed at me, but I ran for it. At the same moment, Titi jumped too. He shoved me hard, and I went down—face first—onto the rough, jagged stones.

For a split second, everything went dark.

When I stood up, my face was soaked in blood. My mouth felt numb, and when I ran my tongue over my teeth, I felt the edges—broken and sharp like sawblades. Titi and Dinică helped me up and took me to a neighbour's courtyard to wash my face. But when I spoke, the air hissed strangely through the gaps in my mouth. The pain started to set in, deep and burning in my front teeth.

Mother's voice called again from the door. I wished, in that moment, that Father had already gone to work. But he was still home. When he saw me—my swollen face, my bloody shirt—he rose from his chair and asked what had happened. I opened my mouth. Mother gasped and brought her hands to her face, speechless. I tried to explain that it had been an accident, that no one was to blame. But Father didn't listen. He grabbed my hand and marched me next door, to number 54—the home of the Burețea family.

"Do you see what Titi did to my son?" he demanded. "Tell me, what would *you* do if this happened to *your* child?"

Mr. Burețea tried to apologize. Titi shrank into the corner, ashamed. Father trembling struggled to contain his rage but said no more. What could be done? My front teeth would remain permanently broken.

The next day, Mother took me to the Regie Clinic, across from the Herdan Bakery. From afar that bakery, always the air spread a warm, sweet aroma of fresh bread and pastries. The doctor numbed my pain, but there was nothing he could do about the jagged shards cutting into my tongue every time I spoke or ate.

That single, unlucky moment of hesitation—when Mother called me in and I turned too late—marked the beginning of years of self-consciousness. During my teenage years, I had to wear a cheap alloy dental crown. It gleamed with an odd metallic shine that never matched my smile. I couldn't bear the curious, inconsiderate glances of other young people. I spoke less. Smiled less. I began to turn inward.

The game had ended, but its cost stayed with me.

IV

Around this time, everyone was talking about an artist named Alexander who could ride his bicycle, eat and even lie down to sleep-on a high wire. When I first heard it, I couldn't believe it. But the stories kept spreading, and soon enough, one evening, we went to Piața Grant to see for ourselves. It must have been a Saturday or Sunday night because Father came with us.

The market square was packed. Above our heads, Alexander had stretched a cable between two towering wooden platforms. Two large headlamps pierced the dark sky as Alexander, dressed in black, walked back and forth on the nearly invisible wire. Then he rode across it on a bicycle. Then again—this time on a one-wheeled contraption like nothing I'd ever seen.

It felt impossible. I watched in awe, half-believing it was some trick. But I couldn't take my eyes off him. In that moment, Alexander became my greatest hero. From then on, whenever I walked along Giuleşti Road toward the Regie, I chose to walk the train tracks, pretending they were my tightrope.

Alexander wasn't the only performer who brought wonder to Piaţa Grant. Travelling artists often passed through, some offering circus acts, others stranger curiosities. Colorful tents promised miracles—or monstrosities. I remember the signs: *The Two-Headed Child*, *The Man with the Ox Tongue*, *The Maid with No Arms*. Long lines formed for tickets. People came out afterward shaken—crossing themselves, spitting over their shoulders, trying to drive away the devil they thought they'd glimpsed.

One time I saw the Hora Căluşarilor—the legendary horseman dance. A team of men, all in white, stomped the ground in rhythm, opinci (peasant's home-made shoes) on their feet and tricolor ribbons fluttering from their hats. The ground trembled under their steps.

Sometimes, during scorching summers when the grass

shriveled under the sun, paparudele (rain-makers dancers) would come—little Roma girls wearing skirts of white water-lily leaves. They danced and sang with tambourines, invoking rain. Patrons would douse them with buckets of water, then toss them coins. It was both ritual and show.

The bear sometimes came, too. A massive brown beast that danced on its hind legs, led by a man holding a long stick hooked to the ring in the bear's nose. For a coin, the bear would walk over a patron's back—an old cure for back pain, they said.

Behind the market, a small carousel sometimes appeared. It had chained seats or carved wooden horses that spun round and round, turned by men walking atop a circular platform. Riding one of those horses was joy itself—until the spinning slowed and came to a reluctant, ugly stop. The chained seats were mostly filled with young couples, soldiers, and maids with permission for a few hours of freedom. Afterward, they gathered around the puppet box where marionettes came alive behind a curtain. The puppeteer's hands gave them voices with funny stories and unforgettable scuffles in exchange for a coin thrown in the artist's hat at the end of the show. Even grown-ups stopped to watch on their way from their duties for a short break, standing up like everyone else as a reminder of their own childhood.

These simple joys, passed down through unmemorable

times never changed even a bit up to my own childhood. They had such a glorious past and it saddens me to see them be forgotten today because people's taste is changing, pushed in other directions by the technological revolution.

Sometimes, on warm Saturday nights, another kind of gathering happened—on the church grounds beside Piața Grant. People came with their own chairs from home and sat beneath the trees. Handwritten posters taped to the church fence announced that a film about Christ would be shown that evening. Neighbours came from across the district to watch.

At dusk, a car pulled up. A few monks in black cassocks unloaded a projector and set it on a table borrowed from the priest's house. We followed their every movement, spellbound. When the film began, it was projected onto the whitewashed wall of the church. It was silent, but the story of Christ's life and suffering unfolded in powerful images. People wept quietly. On the way home, everyone walked in silence, heads lowered, as if bearing invisible crosses of their own.

From time to time, *The Children's Universe* magazine printed a special supplement that I couldn't resist asking for money to buy it. It was a very fine puppet theatre, printed in colour on white cardboard. It had characters, backdrops, and detailed assembly instructions. All I had to do was cut the pieces and follow the steps on the back. With Simona as my assistant, I began building my own theatre.

As always, a new idea brought unsuspecting problems. This time, it was the glue. How was I supposed to assemble a theatre without any glue? I knew we had none in the house, and the instructions were clear: glue was essential. Where could I get glue from? Then, I remembered the shoemaker across the street—the one who always fixes pup our shoes. On his little worktable, there was a rusty tin can fill with bonding paste.

His shop was just a small room that opened directly onto the street, with a wooden door next to a glass window. Through the window, you could always see the shoemaker sitting low behind his bench, working with the cast-iron last cradled in his lap. Behind him, shelves overflowed with old shoes waiting to be repaired. His table was cluttered with tin cans filled with small nails, scraps of sole leather, and pieces of rubber. And there, among them, was the tin of glue.

"Uncle Costică," I greeted him as I entered. He looked up from his work, still holding the little wooden nails between his lips.

"What can I do for you, son?" The wooden tiny nails he fell in his palm before he questioned me.

"Uncle, Father sent me to get some glue."

He gave me a long look, cocking his head. "Glue, huh? What does your father need glue for?"

I shrugged. "What do I know?"

"Go home and tell your pap to put a spoonful of flour in a coffee pot, pour in some water just to cover it, and stir it over the fire until it thickens. Understood? That's the glue I use" he replied.

Back at home, I pleaded with Mother for some flour.

"What do you need flour for?" she asked.

"For my theatre," I explained.

"What for?" she asked again.

"I need it for my theatre. I have to glue the pieces together."

"Don't add too much water—and don't make a mess!" She told me while adding some flour into a small plate.

"But Uncle Costică said it should be made with the fire."

"It'll work without the fire," she assured me.

So, I took a tablespoon, added a few drops of water from the covered bucket in the corner, and stirred the flour until it turned into a kind of paste. When I felt that the paste was ready, impatiently, I start assembling the cardboard pieces—but as soon I let go off them, they fell apart. I tried again, and again, and in desperation I nearly decided to leave the entire business forgotten.

But I wanted that little theatre too much. Determined, I start looking for other solution. I got Mother's sewing box, took out a needle, some thread, and a thimble, and began sewing the connecting tabs together. At last, the structure held.

I made the stage on top of an old shoebox turned upside-down. I fixed on top of it the printed frontispiece cut-off from the magazine. For the drape, Mother gave me a piece of red cloth, but it was too stiff—it didn't open smoothly like the real theatre curtains. So, I decided to make my own: I took two pages from my notebook, on which I drew a couple of masks and folded them carefully like a concertina. I ran a thread through the folds, and by pulling it from the top or bottom, I could open and close the curtains just like I seen at theatre. Proud of my creation, assembling all other pieces and the backstage setting, everything looked perfect.

The magazine had given me four characters: the king, queen, prince, and princess. I attached long cardboard tabs to the back of each figure and used them to move the puppets onstage from the wings. The backdrop was impressive. It showed a grand stone portal, through which you could see a beautiful sunny park, trees in bloom, and a castle on a distant cliff. So proud I was, I couldn't take my eyes off it. I placed the theatre on the kitchen table, changed my voice for each character, and gave my first performance for an audience of two: Simona and Mother. That night, I think, I dreamed only of princes, queens, and enchanted kingdoms.

The next day, I invited friends and kids from the street into our courtyard. I placed the theatre outside on the entrance steps and performed a show that left them all speechless. In the days that followed, I cut out more figures—people and animals—from old magazines. I pasted them onto cardboard and made new characters for my plays. I also created fresh scenery for each new show. My audience grew. Even Lili, our little dog, never missed a performance. When I couldn't be found, children came to the gate asking Mother when I make again theatre.

Eventually, I began repeating stories. The magic faded. I grew tired of the theatre—especially once Dinică came by with new and tempting ideas for games. For a while, the little theatre sat in a corner of our bedroom like a museum relic, until one day Mother quietly threw it away. I didn't shed a tear.

V

When I was younger, I had little interest in exploring the contents of our two nigh tables—there wasn't much to find in them, anyway. But one day, I happened upon a discovery that changed everything. In the nightstand beside Father's bed, I found two photo albums filled with our family's memories. In those days, photographs were taken only on special occasions, usually at a professional photo studio. Street photography was done by itinerant photographers with box cameras mounted on wooden tripods. They could capture your image in a second, but you had to wait fifteen minutes for the print to develop and dry.

The larger album was bound in leather and brimming with sepia or black-and-white portraits: images of my grandparents, photos from my parents' wedding, and even one of myself, a baby on my grandfather's lap in Bulgaria. The second album, smaller but thicker, was filled with postcard-sized illustrations—pictures of movie stars, famous landmarks, and scenes from foreign cities.

I could spend hours with those albums and never tire of them. Simona and I would sit cross-legged on the carpet beside the bed and turn the pages slowly, absorbing every detail. Some cards showed gleaming limousines parked in front of elegant mansions. Others depicted stylish men and women playing tennis, strolling through sunlit gardens, or cruising in convertibles. They all looked like characters from the movies. The most beautiful cards were the ones with handwriting on the back—Mother's round, careful script, usually just a few words; Father's smaller, more crowded letters seemed to tremble with emotion, bursting from the narrow space meant for writing.

Looking at these images, my imagination grew wings gliding over cities, parks, and as beautiful places like the ones frozen in these photographs. I seen myself behind the wheel of one of those sleek cars or guiding a white horse through a manicured park with a grand palace rising in the background. It was so easy to be transported in the suggestive ambiance of a picture when you are only eleven year old.

In that same nightstand, tucked beside the albums, I found Father's treasured collection of Sunday literary supplements, published under the title *The Flower of Foreign Literature*. These thin, modest booklets held a universe within them. It was there I first encountered Chekhov, Tolstoy, Cronin, Maupassant, Maugham, Pearl Buck, and so many others. I read and reread those stories until the pages grew soft from wear. They awakened in me a deep and lasting love for reading—a reverence for the written word that never left me.

On Mother's side of the bed, her nightstand held a very different kind of treasure: the lump sugar box. Like many other products, sugar was also rationed, a monthly coupon per person. Before the war, Mother used to shop at the Greek cracknel shop on Crângaşi Road, Turkish delight, halvah, hard candies, and even exotic fruits. I still remembered the sugar candy—chunks of crystals that looked like shards of glass strung on a thread like beads. Sometimes the chunks were too large to pull off, and Mother had to crack them with a hammer. Simona and I adored them.

But after the war, nothing compared to the simple pleasure of lump sugar—especially when dipped briefly in a glass of water and then brought to the lips to suck the sweetness out. Every so often, we'd find a long crystal, formed by two or three cubes fused together, and the joy of those lasted even longer and lasting.

When Mother was around, the sugar box was off-limits. But the moment she stepped out to shop or chat with a neighbour, I would sneak into the bedroom and steal some sugar. Many times, I lifted the lid to see if any long cubes were left. I'd stuff my pockets with whatever I could and vanish with my treasure. I knew that soon I'd be hearing Mother lament finding the box empty:

"How did this happen? I just put that box there!"

Simona and I would exchange silent glances, trying to suppress our guilty smiles.

VI

Father told me that school would start on Monday. I could hardly believe that summer had passed so quickly. I was so taken aback I didn't know whether to feel happy or sad. That Monday, they woke me up earlier than usual. Mother's gentle coaxing had little effect, and I only managed to get out of bed when Father approached me with a stern impatience. I made my way to the washbasin, waiting for me on a chair in the kitchen. My school clothes were already laid out on another chair—fresh and neatly folded for a good first impression. My breakfast sat on the kitchen table, untouched.

Father was already at the door, hat on head, holding my schoolbag, waiting for me to finish eating. At that moment, I envied Simona, who was still fast asleep, while I was being nudged, scrubbed, and combed by Mother, who never stopped her stream of advice:

"Be polite. Listen to your teacher. Work hard. Make us proud."

With a final kiss, she sent me out the door and watched me all the way to the gate. Father and I walked together to Regie to catch streetcar number 12 or 24. It was a ten-minute walk; we never wait to take bus number 40, which ran on Giuleşti. A few years later, it would be replaced by streetcar 11. The morning was brisk and cool, and I had to stretch my legs to keep pace with Father, who always seemed to walk as if racing against time. We passed the railway barrier at Regie and climbed aboard one of the open wagons waiting at the tram terminus, which had only a few passengers in it. The ticket seller came through the aisle—a man in uniform, with an open leather satchel slung across his shoulder. Father handed him money for our fare.

At that early hour, the tram still hadn't left the station—it always waited until its scheduled departure time. From the platform, we could see latecomers sprinting to catch it, gasping for air as they climbed aboard. Once inside, they'd find a seat and wait for the ticket seller to make his rounds. At the time, only a few of the newer tramcars had fixed booths at the rear where the ticket seller sat. Most still had him walking back and forth between the two open platforms, calling out, *"Tickets, anyone?"*

Father checked his wristwatch with growing impatience. Finally, the tram lurched into motion. We rumbled through the narrow streets, past the Luther beer factory. Not long ago, people lined up there to buy liquid yeast, which was considered healthy as a daily morning tonic, even for children. At Gara de Nord—the North Central Railway Station—the tram stopped and was suddenly flooded with passengers carrying heavy bags, baskets, and burlap sacks. Through the window, I saw the Gheorghe Lazăr Lyceum, standing proudly at the corner of the beautiful Cişmigiu Gardens. Then we crossed the Dâmboviţa River at Podul Izvor and reached the Brâncovenesc Hospital station. Across the street was Piaţa Mare—the Big Market. Here, the crates and sacks from Gara de Nord were unloaded, and the tram emptied enough for Father and me to get off.

The market hall was a vast steel and glass structure painted green. Inside were butchers' stalls and a few permanent stands selling vegetables and fruit. Outside, however, a sea of wooden booths covered the paved square—rented out to small traders and peasants from the provinces, all hoping for a good sale. We had to cross this noisy bazaar to catch another tram at the opposite end of the market. We squeezed our way between booths and crowds, through the cries of vendors, haggling voices, and the general chaos of trade. Chickens clucked, eggs were weighed, cheeses sampled, and wooden carvings held aloft for inspection. Father pushed ahead through the throng, and I hurried after him.

At last, we reached tram number 16, among several others lining the street to the same stop station. Ours arrived crammed with passengers—people squeezed on the steps and clinging to the handrails. Those trying to disembark were pressed back by others trying to get on. In that tangle of elbows and frustration, Father lifted me onto the upper step of the tram and braced himself on the lower one, gripping a metal bar to keep us steady.

The streetcar travelled around the large, artesian fountain in front of the market, aligned with the majestic hill over where the Romanian Metropolitan Bishopric Seat was located. Up on there, in front of the Cathedral stood the famous statue of the she-wolf suckling the babies Rom and Remus. Continuing along Dâmbovița we passed the morgue on Căuzași Street. Its tall columns, arranged in a grim semicircle, gave me a chill every time I saw them. The tram wound its way along Dudeşti Road, past Cantemir and Vitan, and at each stop the car emptied a little more. When our station came after Vitan Road, we disembarked.

The school stood across the street, hidden behind a tall red brick wall. The double wrought-iron gates were guarded by an old man in a booth with a sliding window. He turned out to be Mr. Ştein, the school secretary's father—a thin, bespectacled man with close-cropped red hair. When he heard that it was my first day, he directed us to a barrack behind the main building to register.

We passed between two yellow-painted buildings: on the right, a structure with wide cement steps; on the left, a taller, multistory building with a basketball court in front. The classrooms were in the shorter building, whose façade was lined with large windows divided into small panes. The wooden barrack behind them had many windows and a stage at one end, facing rows of coarse wooden benches. In front of the stage, a large table had been set up where newcomers were registered.

I was assigned to Class 1-D.

Father accompanied me back toward the main building. Up a few cement steps, we entered a wide hallway with walls painted in two tones—white on top and dark green on the bottom. The floor was speckled cement, and the classroom doors, tall and black, bore large paper signs with the class numbers. My classroom was at the far end, near the street. Father walked me to the door, kissed me on the cheek, wished me good luck, and rushed off to work.

The classroom was nearly full. Most of the benches were already occupied. On the podium, at the teacher's desk, stood a young man with reddish hair and lively blue eyes. In his hand, he held a long wooden pointer, which he now used to indicate where I should sit. I was assigned a spot as the third pupil on a bench meant for only two. The boy seated at the edge stood up politely to let me slide in between him and the one at the other end. I had no choice but to place my schoolbag behind my back on the narrow bench. Around me, I noticed that many benches held three students, each one squeezed into the tightest possible space. Once the steady trickle of new students ceased, the young man stepped down, closed the door, and picked up a piece of chalk. On the blackboard—mounted on a rail so it could slide up and down—he wrote his name in clear block letters: Eşkenazi. He was our pedagogue.

He explained that his job was to maintain discipline when the teacher was absent. He was also there to support us in preparing our lessons, and we were encouraged to come to him with any school-related questions—or even personal problems. His tone was open, his eyes seeking out ours with warmth and curiosity. He spoke with ease and conviction, and something in his voice inspired confidence.

He began to describe the school's long-standing tradition of excellence: how generations of skilled professionals had been trained here, how their work was admired in the community. Then, he asked each of us to say why we had chosen this school. When it was my turn, I answered honestly:

"Because my father said so."

The class burst out laughing.

After the break, since the teachers were still in the principal's office, Mr. Eşkenazi asked what we'd like to do. No one had any suggestions, so he took the lead:

"Let's have an English lesson," he said.

Without waiting for our reaction, he turned back to the blackboard and began to write the twenty-six letters of the English alphabet, pronouncing each one clearly and slowly. Laughter erupted following nearly every letter—our ears unaccustomed to these odd, foreign sounds. What we didn't know then was that this playful, somewhat clumsy introduction To English language, would be the only proper instruction I would receive for many years—until I was forced by necessity to learn the language the way it was meant to be spoken.

The rest of the day passed in a kind of parade of teachers,

each introduced in turn. As they arrived, we were made to rise when our names were called. First came Miss Bobinger, the French teacher—an older woman, short and overweight, with thinning hair that gave her a nearly bald appearance. She moved awkwardly, and her lack of enthusiasm seemed to settle over the classroom like a fog. It was hard to imagine French as anything other than a chore.

Next was the drawing teacher, whose real name escaped me. We called him Ţăranul, (the Peasant). Yet nothing about his appearance matched the name. He was neatly dressed in a well-tailored suit and carried himself with impeccable manners. He was short and slightly round, but his attitude was firm and exact. He had us draw parallel lines freehand across the pages of our notebooks, then raise the notebooks to eye level to check the straightness. Each deviation became visible. Page after page, line after line—we trained our hands. It was from him that I learned how to draw any plan or sketch with confidence.

The math teacher, nicknamed Cioc, (the Beak), earned his moniker thanks to a pointed little goatee. He, too, was well groomed and a fine educator—an older man who maintained a steady rhythm of attention in the classroom, engaging and calm.

Then came Professor Rotblum, our music teacher, a man who looked every bit the artist. His nickname was Domnul Diapazon, (Mr. Diapason). He struggled with determination to teach us the tone and duration of each note, which he drew on the board, then had us vocalize aloud—one by one. Under his direction we formed a choir, rehearsing endlessly for the concerts held in the festivity hall inside the barrack. He had to gather over a hundred students and divide us into four voices. He worked tirelessly, coaxing harmony out of chaos. I often watched him draw on his last reserves of energy before restarting the same musical piece again.

We were allowed a ten-minute recess after each class—a novelty for many of us, who had only known a single long break at midday. At first recess, I stayed put, trying to take in the big classroom, teeming with noise and unbounded energy. Some children were bolder than others, almost like there was a silent contest for dominance. It didn't take long to identify the winner. He sat right next to me: Marcus Emil, better known by everyone as Alimănescu.

This name, Alimănescu, at the time, filled the headlines of every newspaper. In every café and street corner in Bucharest, people whispered about him. The name alone inspired fear: Alimănescu—the notorious outlaw behind robberies, break-ins, and brutal murders. Ruthless and ferocious, he left a trail of fear in his wake. Not long after school began, he made headlines again, this time for storming the Revenue Office on Giuleşti Road, near Regie. He was killed in the street, but not before several police officers lost their lives.

But before all that, Alimănescu had squeezed me like a sandwich between himself and Juju Horovici, nicknamed Jujiţiu. Both were well known among the kids, local celebrities in their own mischievous way, having shared several schools with others in the class. Our class was a fascinating blend. Some boys were small and childlike, others tall and already sporting the faint beginnings of a mustache. Some looked like miniature adults in long trousers.

Out of the fifty-six students in the class, the shortest of all was Avram Simon, a bright-eyed boy full of verve who took a seat at the front bench, directly in front of the blackboard. We later called him Piţurcă, but after a reading of Caragiale's play "A Lost Letter," Alimănescu dubbed him Agamiţă Dandanache, after one of the script's most absurd characters. The name stuck.

In time, nearly everyone earned a nickname—some clever, some silly, others harsh. Edelştein Iacob, thin as a rail, with dark skin and black-rimmed glasses, was nicknamed Răţoiul (the Duck), for the way he waddled like a metronome. Behind our bench sat Mendel Moise, a red-haired boy with a pickled-red face who quickly became Câine Roşu ("Red Dog"). As for me—I wasn't spared. I became Poetul Mazăre ("the Pea Poet"), a name that, though funny, betrayed my secret passion.

Not all my classmates were of Jewish origin, although the

school had been established by the Jewish community long before the war. Its mission was to produce generations of skilled tradesmen, educated not just in the technical aspects of their craft, but with a solid foundation of general knowledge and aesthetic sensibility. At graduation, we would receive both a diploma and a trade licence—credentials that opened doors to good jobs, or even allowed us to open our own shops, as many before us had done. The prestige of the school had endured. It was widely recognized as one of the best institutions for arts and trades in Bucharest. Generations had passed through these very benches—men of skill and character who contributed meaningfully to society.

The sweeping political changes of recent years had not diminished its stature. Even during the German occupation, the school continued to function. Many, like my father, believed that having a trade was the surest path to survival in uncertain times. After the Germans were defeated in the war, it was expected that a new democratic regime would be empowered, and the school distinguished itself like a true academy of arts and trade - with its door wide open to everyone who wanted to learn a trade, regardless of religion or social standing.

VII

After a one-hour recess for lunch, we were sent to our assigned trade shops. I was assigned to cabinet maker's shop, located on the first floor of the left-side wing, in the school's administration building. A large room stretched across the entire floor, divided into two sections. The front half was equipped with powerful machines, all operated by wide, pulley-driven belts hanging from the ceiling. In the back half—facing a wall of tall, steel-framed windows—stood several wooden benches arranged in two neat rows, with a wide passage down the centre Along the walls were smaller machines, and near the corner stood a massive wood press, nearly three meters long—like a tunnel—with thick wooden screws on top, each as wide as a man's wrist. Somewhere in the middle of this area was a big wood stove with a bucket on top, boiling bone glue.

Our shop master was Mr. Ardoş, a Transylvanian man with a small moustache and a thick Hungarian accent. He wasn't old, but he carried himself with the authority of experience. He paired us off—two students per bench—and began to demonstrate the basics: how to hold the tools, what each was called, and the materials they were made from.

Then he gave us our first task. Each of us received two pieces of machine-smooth wood. Our goal was to glue them together side by side—a simple operation, in theory. First, we had to plane the adjoining surfaces until they were perfectly straight, so that no sliver of light would pass between them when placed them one on top of the other. He showed us how to hold the plane, how to check the alignment of its blade, and how to tell whether the blade was sharp enough.

"If it's dull," he said, "instead of cutting a continuous, uniform shaving from one end to the other, the plane would break the material."

Then, without much ceremony, he returned to his own bench at the far end of the room, where he resumed his work crafting elegant Louis XIV–style chairs—assisted by a few older students. His operation was far beyond ours. Together, they glued and clamped delicate carved pieces with an ease that made the whole process look like theatre.

We, the beginners, were left alone with our raw tools and two stubborn blocks of wood.

At my workbench, I secured one piece in the vice at the end, then walked over to the cabinet where the planes were kept. Inside were dozens—some large, others small, with one or two blades. I selected one, examined its surfaces, then focused carefully on the blade. Back at my bench, I gripped the tool tightly, lined it up with the wood, and pushed. But after only a few centimetres, it dug too deeply and stopped, leaving behind a jagged, splintered coarse sliver of wood. At this point I realized that I was in trouble.

I remembered how Mr. Ardoş had tapped the plane's blade gently with a hammer to adjust it. I tried the same, but the blade wouldn't budge. It was as if it had been soldered into place. Frustrated and unsure, I approached him.

"The plane isn't working," I said.

He didn't even look up.

"Why is the plane not working?" he asked, his accent thick, his voice clipped.

"Because… well… it broke the wood."

Without a glance at either me or the tool, he lashed out with a quick, unexpected slap across my face.

"Take your fucking blade out and sharpen it!" he barked.

The heat of the slap stunned me more than the pain. I stood there, blinking, until one of the older students—thankfully—stepped in to help. He showed me how to remove the blade, separate it from the top plate, and adjust it using the screw. He brought me to the sharpening stones—one coarse, the other fine—and demonstrated the motion: smooth, even strokes, maintaining the right angle. Then he left me to finish on my own.

I worked at it as best I could, but sharpening the blade took the better part of the day. Despite all the explanations, despite my best efforts, I have to confess that even now, after all these years, I still don't truly know how to sharpen a blade on a stone. And that day, I certainly didn't succeed. I never managed to finish cleaning the edge of my board. At the end of the day, each of us signed our work with a carpenter's pencil and left the pieces in a corner, to be continued the next day.

When I finally got home, long after the usual hour—tired, hungry, and emotionally drained after the ordeal of commuting on two congested streetcars—I felt weighed down by more than fatigue. I had a sinking feeling that this was only the beginning, and nothing good would come of it.

Chapter 7

A Foggy Sunrise

I.

From now I had to get used to my new school schedule—early wakeups every morning, Mother's never-ending complaints that I'd be late, eating my breakfast in a hurry, and then racing to Regie to catch the streetcar that would get me to school on time. The tramways weren't always friendly or welcoming places—often they were so overcrowded that passengers hung on with just one foot on the platform, and it was never easy for me to navigate between these towering adults with my old, heavy leather briefcase in hand.

At school, each new hour brought a new teacher to the podium. Each had their own style and way of speaking to us. Some sparked our curiosity so completely that we sat in perfect silence, absorbing every word. Others lulled us into boredom with their flat, monotone lectures. When that happened, we'd retreat into little distractions: sketching cartoons on our notebooks, inventing quiet games, or passing written conversations back and forth with the kids nearby.

We had no standardized textbooks. Some students were lucky enough to find the ones teachers recommended in antique shops, but most of us had to rely on our notes—pages and pages of handwritten lessons scribbled onto coarse, yellowish paper, the kind on which even the pencil's graphite struggled to leave a clear mark.

Despite all this, the classroom had its own energy—vibrant, chaotic, full of youth. We played together during recesses, ran through the corridors and the big schoolyard and played games. Sometimes, we would fight, and a teacher or pedagogue would come to pull us apart. In the next recess we would be out together, run, play, or get into a new fight. We grew to know one another. We learned which classmates were brave, which were sly, which were funny, which were sensitive.

In time, we also came to know the habits of our teachers. When the brass bell rang from the wall of the administration building, we rushed back to class, pulled out our notes from previous lesson to refresh our memories, and waited. One teacher we respected deeply was Mr. Jordăchescu, our history teacher. He had a gift for storytelling, filling his lectures with rich, romantic detail. His lessons came alive with the dramas of Alexander the Great, Caesar, and Napoleon—and with the political maneuverings of Cromwell, Richelieu, and Talleyrand. As he paced the classroom, his eyes searched for ours, making sure we followed along, and when he quoted from historical speeches, he gave them life and voice. At the end of each lesson, he would write a few dates or names on the blackboard, then dictate a paragraph or two we had to copy and remember.

No one skipped his classes. There was no discipline problem, no re-examination in the fall. To our great regret, the following summer he was appointed principal of the Matei Basarab Lyceum, one of the most prestigious in Bucharest. No teacher ever matched his popularity or the respect he inspired.

Still, our school had no shortage of fine, highly respected teachers. Many others enjoyed our esteem and shared a lot of respect. One of them, I think - most admired - was Professor Ringelştein, a stocky, grey-haired engineer with a slow gait and kind eyes. We called him Moşul (Old Man). He taught us physics and materials strength in a low, calm voice. Moving in front of the blackboard, he'd write his formulas with a piece of chalk. The formulas were to stay there while he stepped back and called students forward to apply them to various problems in front of the classroom. Somehow, by the end of the class, we felt miraculously confident of that just learned lesson, was understood. I owe the Old Man the foundations of my later understanding in math and engineering. I bitterly regret having thrown away the notebooks I filled during his lessons—notes that would have spared me many headaches later in life.

What truly set him apart was his warmth. He treated us with the dignity of young adults, even when we didn't deserve it. In contrast, other teachers would scream and insult us for no reason. The Old Man's talk was slow, and he always started his lesson with an interesting story he witnesses, heard or read. He was good-hearted and trustful. When we had personal problems, he was often the first we turned to. He'd step out of class or the teachers' room to listen, then offer calm, considered advice. He seemed to understand us instinctively. He cared.

Not every teacher did.

Some were clearly in their roles because there was nothing else working to them, and their discontent spilled over into the classroom like a dark fog. These classes dragged on endlessly, and we did our best to find distractions. One of these was Professor Ionel Cohn, a math teacher past middle age who had never married and still lived with his father, also a math teacher. His name appeared often in Gazeta Matematicii (The Mathematics Magazine), and there was no doubt about his brilliance. As a classroom teacher, though, he was another story.

He always wore the same old, dark, unpressed suit and scuffed black shoes with gnawed heels. When he entered the classroom, holding the class list under his arm—never checking who was absent—we barely noticed him. Only after he lost his patience and started shouting did we pay attention. Waiting for us to take our seats on the benches, he'd walk to the blackboard and begin writing the proof of a new theorem, speaking softly to the board, never once turning around. He worked on the formulas alone absorbed by his equation, never caring who is listening or followed his demonstration. His voice dissipated somewhere over the front table, too weak to reach the end of the classroom. So, we whispered. We doodled. We stared into space.

After a while, Mr. Cohn realized that only a few students were following his explanations, mostly the ones seated in the first rows that could hear him and take notes. Therefore, he began working only with them.

At the end of each trimester, he would hand out passing grades—sometimes with a scornful look, as if he couldn't believe how ignorant we were of his subject.

We were satisfied just to pass. But later in life, those of us gifted passing marks without learning the fundamentals, would pay the price. I often found myself searching for elementary math books just to find solutions to problems I faced. I doubt I was the only one forced to learn the hard way—lessons we should have mastered under Mr. Cohn's guidance.

II

Behind school grounds, was the soccer field of the Maccabi Club, home to the first-division soccer team "Ciocanul" (the Hammer), which boasted famous players like Moisescu, Şmilovici, and the Baraş brothers. On match days, the field filled with fans who crowded the single covered tribune or stood packed along the mesh fences that enclosed the pitch.

During scheduled sports hours under the guidance of our pedagogue Eşkenazi, or our gym teacher Mr. Feller—a middle-aged man who somehow maintained his youthful energy—we'd leave the school through the main gate, loop around the block, and enter the soccer field from the far side. Once there, we'd line up for warmups on the gravel track, stretch in rows, do gymnastic training, and then play ball on the worn, yellowing turf. I usually took the goalkeeper's position—not because I was better at it than the others, but perhaps because I was less combative in the field. Still, I loved soccer and rarely missed a chance to play with my friends.

Often, I slipped away to the field during long recess—or even during French or math class. Hidden from the school building by the tall fence, I would sneak along the narrow path behind the tribune to warm up for the game. The star of our class was Şfarţman David, whom we called Şuţică. He was barely taller than Piţurcă, but fierce and tireless. He and Jujiţu, my bench mate, were the best players, and they picked their teams from the group of eager classmates.

When my name was called, I'd jog over to the goal and mark it with two stones. After a few warmup shots, Jujiţu would send me diving onto the damp grass—still wet from the morning rain. By the time I got home, my school clothes—those that Mother had so carefully pressed—were unrecognizable. She scolded me, but what could I say? That in the heat of play, when I saw Şuţică barrelling toward me, eyes scanning for an opening, the ball at his feet, I had no choice but to lunge forward, to dive at his legs without a second thought? Sometimes the ball sailed past me. Sometimes it slipped under me. But more often than not, I saved certain sure goals—and was rewarded with nothing more than my teammates' smiles and silent nods of approval.

Emil, the infamous Alimănescu, never joined our soccer games. He had a strange affinity for French and, oddly enough, he was the only one among us who seemed to retain what little Miss Bobinger managed to teach. Her classes were a kind of ordeal. When she arrived at her desk with thick glasses, elbows extended to the entire width of the desk, left the impression of being cast there like a bust on a pedestal. Once seated, she never moved.

Usually, she would call from list at random a name—

because she never learned our names—and ask the boy to read and translate a text from the book. She would let him struggle to decipher the words syllable-by-syllable without any help, translation following - mostly guessed - made time agonising slow, a monotone kind of torture, which had no sense at all. At the end of the trimester, she called us forward in alphabetical order, now alert and vindictive, demanding verb conjugations or textbook readings. This was her moment, her long-awaited victory over a class of children whose only fault was tolerating her as their teacher. With savage delight, she scribbled failing grades beside our names. She had waited all term for this. We were her captives, and she was the little tyrant with the power of judgment. It's a tragic thing to see a small-minded person pretending to be what they are not. In the theatre, a poor actor is booed off the stage. But in a classroom, an impostor becomes sovereign, and the pupils are their victims. It's even worst in everyday life to let impostors reaching power over innocent people.

During the Hebrew and religion classes, Christian students were free to leave or stay. Many stayed. One of them was a quiet boy with an uplifted-looking nose, blue eyes, and blond hair that coiled into a spiral across his forehead. His name was Mâtcă Domenic, and he was the only child of a poor couple who had worked as caregivers for a wealthy family downtown.

Over time, we became friends. I visited him often in the servant's quarters at 10 Diana Street, where he lived with his parents in two small rooms more like monk's cells than living spaces. They welcomed me with simple honesty and warm smiles that made me feel at home. They came from somewhere near Adjud, and were the very embodiment of humility, faith, and sincerity. Mâtcă or Nicuşor, as we called him, carried their spirit in everything he did.

Our Hebrew teacher, Professor Szabo, was short and severe, with no time for nonsense. He patrolled the classroom with a Hebrew book in hand—those curious volumes that opened from right to left. We struggled to learn the unfamiliar letters, though I still remembered some from my lessons at the synagogue on Poradim Street.

Mr. Szabo had no patience for ignorance. If you gave a wrong answer, you could expect a stinging ear-pull. The only one spared was Nicuşor, who sat quietly and was never asked to respond.

But when it came time for religion, Professor Szabo transformed. He became a storyteller. The old tales from the Bible came alive, and his voice—once harsh—turned rich and measured. We were spellbound. He guided us through the ancient texts with skill and reverence, drawing out their morals with a storyteller's grace. In those hours, even the most restless among us sat still.

III

Almost two years after the end of the war, little had changed across the country Food and clothes were still rationed and distributed trough tickets, though even with them, one often couldn't find the needed items due to chronic shortages. Long queues snaked in front of every store, and rumours spread that endless trains full of grain, cattle, and machinery were being sent to Russia. To make matters worse, that year we were struck by a terrible famine that claimed thousands of lives, especially in Moldova. People wandered across far-away provinces for food, and no one had enough to spare.

At school, during the ten o'clock recess, a few volunteer women would visit each classroom carrying large trays of *mămăligă*—cornmeal cubes topped with plum jam. Each student received a piece in a paper napkin, and with it in hand, we headed outside to play. At lunchtime, many of us gathered in small groups and walked to a canteen run by the Jewish community, tucked away on a narrow side street off Theodor Speranţa. Housed in what had once been a family home, the rooms were repurposed into a modest cantina for those in need. Sometimes we had to wait for the second seating, as all the tables were full. The whitewashed walls matched the white tablecloths, which were changed daily. The food, though repetitive, was good—simple dishes of cabbage, lentils, or barley, served in a rotating cycle.

I always sat flanked by Alimănescu and Jujiţu, but others often joined our group: Mendel Moise (Câine Roşu), Zilberman Marcel from the Văcăreşti neighbourhood, and the youngest of the ZML brothers, Levi, who was also in our class. At the canteen, we also met kids from other classes and even other schools, some of whom would become lifelong friends. In winter, we took a shortcut to the canteen through Strada Laptelui—Milky Street—a narrow lane that bore witness to our snowball battles, wrestling matches in the drifts, and the endless laughter over jokes and stories collected from our daily misadventures. On our return to school in Dudeşti

, we repeated the same games, until they were abruptly interrupted by the reality of our shop hours and Master Ardoş—a man capable of creating beauty from wood, but with a short fuse when things didn't go his way.

Among the old papers I've saved over the years, I recently found an article published in a Romanian newspaper—written by my dear classmate Emil, the one we all called Alimănescu. It was a personal recollection of childhood along Dudeşti Road, back when the world was very different from what it has become. I feel compelled to quote from it, lest I do a disservice to his memory—for his life was cut short by cancer some years ago.

Sentimentally or not, these words create an image of a Jewish boy's childhood, in the sorrowful years of persecution being an orphan and at the poverty limit. I did not kept notes, and I do not claim that I know to master my words, but everything was nestled in my soul. Dudeşti was a world of worried people, of tortured and persecuted people, a world of the wretched. Together lived Jews, Christians, and Gypsies, all with pallid faces, all unemployed with threadbare elbows and gnawed shoes, all continuously running after a piece of bread to secure their miserable existence. The neighbourhood was full of roadside inns and brothels, with the water tap and latrines in the courtyards, heat from a tin stove from which always came out smoke made by the sawdust or of rests of charcoal. The light in the houses came from a petroleum lamp number 8 or 11 with the glass, reduced by the black smoke build-up inside.

Emil, my dear friend—whenever I read your evocative words, I cannot help the sadness that stirs in my heart. Your memory is alive in every line. And yet, I want you to know that the world you described was not limited to only your childhood place of living, Dudeşti. It was the world of most city margins, including mine—the Grant. We all lived those same realities, and your words speak for many of us.

IV

One day, Father received a message from Uncle Rubin in Giurgiu, asking him to go to a wholesale warehouse on Bărăției Street and purchase a list of goods. Without delay, Father went to the address, bought everything as instructed, and rushed to Gara de Nord to deliver the heavy parcel to the commissionaire. But the man never showed up. The train began to roll out of the station, and Father returned home with the swollen bundle of merchandise under his arm. In the following days, no word came from Giurgiu. Father ended up paying the invoice out of his own salary, and suddenly we had no money left to buy bread. We scraped by for the rest of the week on borrowed money, but something had to be done.

On Sundays, Piața Grant filled with people. Peasants came in from the outskirts of the city with horse-drawn carts laden with fresh fruits and vegetables. The rented stalls in the centre of the market were aligned in tidy rows and taken up by licensed vendors. Small-time traders laid their goods directly on the sidewalk near the entrance to the piața, and the crowd of customers moved in endless streams, stopping to touch, haggle, and compare prices in search of a better bargain.

That night, Father slept at home because it was Sunday, and no newspaper went to press. In the morning, he drank his surrogate coffee made from cheap *Unica* packs while Mother tried to dissuade him from going alone to the market with the merchandise. She stood in front of the door, blocking his way, but Father gently pushed her aside with one hand and left, the bulky parcel tucked under his arm.

"This man will lose all his money," Mother called after him, her voice rising with frustration. "He'll be robbed! I should've gone with him." She continued to torment herself like this the entire morning. When Father failed to return in the early afternoon, Mother's anxiety grew. She couldn't focus on anything, her eyes fixed on the window, jumping at every noise from the street.

Just before sunset, around four o'clock, Father finally came home—without the bulging pack under his arm, but his hands weren't empty. His face carried a smile he could barely suppress, a quiet expression of triumph. Mother didn't know what to think. Still gripped by worry and resentment, she lashed out:

"What's wrong with you? Are you drunk?"

Without a word, Father placed his purchases on the kitchen table. A fresh loaf of bread, already missing one end. Some salami wrapped in oily paper. A small ball of butter, cold and wrapped in a grape leaf. A cube of feta cheese, its wrapper dripping whey. Mother stared at him from across the table. Simona and I leaned in close, watching, alert to every detail. The smell of warm bread, salty salami, and tangy cheese stirred a new discovered hunger in us—but under Mother's stern gaze, we knew better than to ask.

Still wearing his overcoat, Father began pulling crumpled wads of bills and coins from his pockets. Some were neatly folded, others twisted and damp. He dug into his trouser pockets, the lining of his jacket, even the inner compartments where he kept his ID papers. In the end, a mound of money lay in the centre of the table. He removed his winter coat and hat, dragged a chair over, and sat down. Carefully, he smoothed each bill and arranged them in piles by denomination. Then he asked for pencil and paper and began counting. When he was done, he subtracted the amount spent on Uncle Rubin's merchandise. All the fear, effort, and hours spent in the bitter cold had paid off.

Mother's anger faded. With fresh energy, she began clearing the table and transferring the food to plates. As she set the table for dinner, she asked if the warehouse owner from Bărăţiei Street would be willing to offer Father more goods on credit. Father thought quietly, then shrugged.

Father's salary alone wasn't enough to keep the household afloat—prices were rising by the day. Even with his night shifts, overtime, and all of Mother's careful savings, we barely managed. Inflation was tightening its grip like a vacuum, sucking the value out of every pocket. The thousand-lei bill now circulated like a one-leu note had just a year earlier. Rumours swirled that the National Bank would soon issue a one-million-lei bill. In fact, sooner than we expected, people were paying five million for a streetcar ticket.

Food was scarce. The lines in front of stores stretched endlessly. With the currency plummeting, peasants stopped bringing their produce to the markets, believing that tomorrow's prices would be better. The drought that year—devastating across the country, especially in Moldova—only made things worse. Daily bread distributed by ration (250 grams per person) was often mixed with grated potatoes or seeds from wild plants usually used to make brooms. Mălaiul (corn flour) sold was frequently musty, but we ate it anyway. On such days, mamaliga— (deep boiled maize), which many used instead of bread—was runny and thin, more like gruel than anything else.

The warehouse owner on Bărăției Street agreed to give Father a few stockings, some elastic for undergarments, spools of thread in different colours, buttons sewn onto cardboard squares, needles, and a variety of ribbons in bright shades and whimsical shapes—all on consignment. There was no question: next Sunday, Father would return to the market with his new supplies. Only this time, Mother warned, he would not go alone—and he agreed.

When Simona and I woke up that Sunday morning, we discovered that our parents had already left. Mother had prepared breakfast and left it for us on the kitchen table. After eating, we got dressed and went out to look for them.

We found them near the entrance to the piața from Constantin Grant Street. Their wares were laid out on a strip of asphalt beside many other sellers. Father stood surrounded by customers, who leaned in to inspect the goods spread out on an old tablecloth, padded underneath with layers of newspaper. Mother, too, was surrounded. Each time a customer asked for a price, she turned to Father for the answer.

Surrounding my parents were vendors selling brooms and floor brushes; others offered wooden plates, chopping boards, meat cleavers, coat hangers, clothespins, and all sorts of wooden household items. A bit farther down, a boy was selling hand-carved wooden flutes, beautifully inlaid with delicate patterns. Even more beautiful was the doina he played—a wistful tune that drifted from his flute like a sigh from the past.

There were stalls overflowing with dried fruits, honey, and sticky halvah that made my mouth water. Oh, what an exciting place it was! Gorgeous carpets and rugs—some for warming the floor, others simply for wall adorning—were on full display. Next to them, hand-made combs cut from ox horn were laid out neatly, with a raw horn set-in front as proof of authenticity. A young man crafted them on the spot, carefully cutting one tooth after another into a sliver of horn. The sliver was wedged into a groove in a long wooden cane, which he held firmly in place by pressing it between his knees as he sat cross-legged, Turkish style.

At the back corner of a building, the market widened toward Crângaşi Road, where rows of wooden stands—some on wheels, shaded by canvas awnings—lined the centre of the large, asphalted square. The space swelled with movement, voices, and a constant buzz of activity. Now and then, a loud voice would rise above the din, a vendor shouting to advertise his goods.

While Father was awkwardly measuring elastic with his shaky tailor's tape, he caught sight of me and called over, telling to run to my old friend Samulică's parents' booth and borrow their wooden measuring stick. Samulică Segal parents, my former schoolmate from Poradim, had a permanent stall in the heart of the square, open daily year-round. Their stand wasn't far, but I had to push through the crowd many times to reach it.

The Sunday market became a weekly ritual for my parents for the next two or three years. They reinvested the modest profits into more merchandise. As goods became scarcer and demand grew, they started seeking out new sources—different warehouses and new suppliers. Sometime in winter, they heard that a recently opened store on Lipscani Street named "Winter" had fabric for women's dresses—three metres per person limit.

After finishing his night shift at the printing house, Father went straight to the store. He found a lengthy line of people already there before midnight, waiting for the store to open in the morning. When he arrived home around noon, Mother was thrilled. The fabric was double-width—enough for two dresses—and had a beautiful design printed in rich colours. In the past, she would've started sewing a dress for herself and one for Simona without hesitation. But times had changed. She now calculated how much she could earn selling it—and she gave up the temptation. Still, off curiosity, she wanted to see what else the store had, but how could she leave Simona and me alone at home all night? After weighing her options and seeing no better solution, she convinced Father that the whole family should go there together. That way, they could buy not just two lengths of fabric—but four.

It was one of the rare nights when Father didn't have to work. We left home before midnight, hoping to catch one of the last streetcars. Mother had put us to sleep early, but when she came to wake us, we could barely keep our eyes open.

Outside the store, a long line already snaked around the corner. The storefront, flanked by large display windows secured by a rolling steel grille, sat at the junction of a narrow street that intersected Lipscani. Across from it stood the Sora Universal store—later known as Bucureşti.

Near the entrance, two large steel barrels had been set up with roaring fires. Smoke and tongs of flame shot into the cold air as people huddled around to warm their hands. Down the street, a few shops remained open, selling cheese pies and hot, bubbling pastries called gogoşi—plump, sugary cocoons sprinkled with powdered sugar. Some people returned to the line after a gulp of ţuică fiartă (boiled plum brandy) and maybe a few sizzling mititei.

Father told Simona and me to circle near the fire until morning. There was no point standing in line the whole time. We went toward the nearest barrel, glowing red with embers and bits of broken wood from fences long since fallen. The flames lit up the faces around it. Smoke stung our eyes, and we had to shield them with our palms and turn away—only for the wind to shift and blow it back again. People chatted to pass the time. Some told jokes to lift the mood, others shared stories—some funny, some sad. From time to time, people stamped their feet to warm their stiff limbs or blew into their cupped hands. Like us, time itself seemed frozen. I wondered how I'd endure until morning. Now and then, a police officer or night watchman would wander over to warm up at the fire. When that happened, conversations stopped abruptly, and one or two people would slip quietly into the shadows.

Simona grew tired and left the fire. She returned to Father, who held her in his arms. After a while, he propped one foot against a wall and rested her on it, tucking her inside his open winter coat to keep her warm. I stayed behind, still battling the smoky air that made my heavy eyelids sag.

At daybreak, more people poured in from all directions. The

line stretched longer and longer, curling around the building. Some latecomers tried to cut in, claiming they had been there earlier and had asked others to save their spot. But the crowd behind protested, shouting angrily. Some even pulled the impostors back by force. One scuffle broke out, but no one paid it much mind.

We stood close to Father, who held his place firmly. As the crowd thickened around us, body heat made it feel warmer than by the fire, but our feet—numb from the frozen pavement—felt like logs. Even stamping them no longer helped.

The faint morning light revealed a cloudy sky. Around us, the city stirred as crowds rushed up and down the street. Finally, someone arrived to unlock the metal grille at the store's entrance. When the doors opened and the first group was let inside, the press of bodies surged like a tide. We were pushed back and forth, nearly crushed—until Father held his arms out to protect us, bracing against the current like a rock in a river.

By noon, we emerged victorious from the store, each of us holding a coupon for fabric. They were beautiful, vibrant, and well worth the effort—but Mother looked at them with weary eyes.

"I'm not coming here again," she angrily said, brushing a strand of hair from her face. "It's not worth it. This is an ordeal—I don't need it.".

V

After the stops at Căuzaşi and Mircea Vodă, the streetcar next stop was Dimitrie Cantemir Station. Right at the corner where the two streets met stood a beautifully carved stone cross, encrusted with national motifs and letters carefully chiseled into its surface. The cross had been there for as long as anyone could remember—tall and solemn, as big as a man. I had often heard people refer to *Crucea de Piatră* (the Stone Cross), but until then I believed the name referred only to this imposing monument that stood in front of a shoe store on the corner. Soon, I would come to understand that the name evoked something else entirely.

After our practice hours at Master Ardoş's shop, when the weather was nice, I would often leave with my colleagues—who had by then become my friends—and we'd walk several streetcar stops together, laughing, chatting, and enjoying each other's company. Gradually, our walks stretched longer and longer until they covered the full distance from school to *Piaţa Mare* (the Big Market). Doing so saved me the cost of streetcar tickets, which meant extra money in my pocket. One evening, instead of taking the usual route down Dudeşti Road, we veered off along Dimitrie Cantemir Street, which ran parallel to it—just behind Crucea de

Piatră. That's where I first discovered that "love" could be bought with cash.

There was a short stretch of the street where a few old houses had been turned into brothels. Behind rusting iron gates stood young girls and women of every shape and size, dressed in tight shorts or miniskirts and low-cut tops. They welcomed passersby with flirtatious smiles and sweet calls, like the sirens from myth. As we approached, they blocked our path, beckoned us to stop, signaled with their eyes, and pretended to show us things designed to arouse curiosity, although it was forbidden by law. Once, a young woman playfully snatched my cap and ran into courtyard, where several small rooms formed a square, each with a door and a curtained window. I followed, pleading for her to return it. Only when she saw that I was on the verge of tears did she hand it back. Yet even that lesson didn't break the spell of the place. Something about the street—its forbidden magnetism—kept drawing me back.

I would pass by again, and again, my eyes wide with curiosity, watching the women leaning on fences, their voluptuous forms revealing more than I had ever seen. But I never dared speak to them. I knew my wallet would never be full enough for what they offered. Not long after those escapades, the winds of political change swept in, and the newly installed regime cracked down. The brothels of Crucea de Piatră were shut down, leaving only the scent of legend behind tales told by those who remembered them.

School filled every day of the week except Sunday, and its busy schedule gave me a new kind of freedom. I quickly learned how to make the most of it. Coming home later than usual became easily excused, given the distance and the traffic. Walking with my friends after shop practice became routine, even when the weather was bad. We would walk down Dudeşti to Mircea Vodă Street, cut toward the city centre through Anton Pann Street, pass the all-girls high school there, and continue along Domniţei Street, which led us to Regina Maria Boulevard. From there, tram 24 would take me to *Regie*. I was rarely alone—usually accompanied by one or two colleagues—and with their company, the distance felt shorter, thanks to our conversations, jokes, and gossip shared along the way. One of my regular companions was Mâtcă Domenic, who lived in the area. Often, as we passed by his house, we would pause to play another game of chess—something we did repeatedly, whenever we could.

Many of my friends had begun frequenting Zionist clubs. My cousin Cuţa attended school on Anton Pann Street, and when I happened to run into her, we often walked the same route home. She told me that many of her friends went to a club on Sevastopol Street called Ha'Shomer Ha'Tzair (Young Guardians). She liked it because there were lots of young people, interesting activities, and frequent outings. One afternoon—perhaps a Sunday—I decided to go with her and see the place for myself.

. Sevastopol Street lay between Calea Victoriei and Buzeşti Street. Halfway along it was an old Jewish graveyard, enclosed by a tall fence made of yellow brick pylons and wrought iron bars, covered from the inside with metal sheets that blocked any view of the cemetery. Not far from the fence stood a large wooden cabin about the same size of the one at our school, though this one was divided into several rooms.

The old cemetery stretched back toward *Piaţa Victoriei* (Victory Plaza). If you looked past the rows of poplar trees that lined the brick wall, you could glimpse the imposing façade of the Presidential Palace of the Ministers' Council.

Cemeteries are sad places, but people often go to visit their beautiful monuments, relaxing moments of silence, soul searching and reflection. But this one felt different—only sadness clung to it.

All the gravestones had been ripped from their places and stacked against the wall at the far end of the cemetery—no longer tributes to those who helped build the city, but a silent monument to the barbarism of those who sought to erase the past in favour of a questionable future. The moss-covered stones, chiseled with old Hebrew inscriptions, leaned in rows like fallen soldiers at the edge of a dead field. The ground itself—furrowed by the tracks of tractors lay barren of grass, as if nature itself refused to heal what had been desecrated.

Most of the club's activities took place in the wooden building near the fence. Half of it was made up of rooms with benches lining the walls and large tables in the middle. Drawings, posters, and banners in Hebrew and Romanian covered the walls. The back of the building was less furnished, with only benches along the sides. The place buzzed with groups of boys and girls, teenagers of all ages, who talked loudly. Cuţa was greeted by some girls to whom I was presented. Later she brought me to meet a young, tall boy who seemed to have a position of authority in the club. His name was Daniel, and he was responsible for the younger group of children. Soon I learned that the organization was structured by age groups: those under fourteen, called *Tzairim* (the young); the 14 to 18 group were *Benonim* (intermediates); and group over 18 were *Bogrim* (elders).

Daniel was surrounded by a flurry of younger members—some showing him things they created, others asking questions. He brought us into one of the front rooms, where I was introduced to everyone. When someone asked why I had come to the club, I had no answer and simply looked to Daniel to bail me out. He started to tell us about Ha'Shomer Ha'Tzair

He explained that our true homeland was Palestine—Israel had not yet achieved independence—and that it needed *halutzim* (young pioneers) like us to settle the land and restore its fertility, as in the days of David and Solomon.

He spoke of the war, of how the Nazis had treated the Jews

with unspeakable cruelty—driving them from their homes, stealing their belongings, locking them concentration camps, torturing and murdering them. This, he said, was why we need to create a national home for Jewish people, where no one would persecute us anymore.

"This is why we are here, to learn about our duty of creating such a country," he said.

He told us about Dr. Theodor Hertzel, who had the vision of a national state for Jews in Palestine - our ancestors' land – decades before the apparition of Hitler and the Nazis.

Then, following a review presentation, we discussed a short story by I. Peltz, a Romanian-Jewish author. The story was about a very poor man who had never sinned in his life, was run over and killed by a pair of runaway horses. In Heaven, Saint Peter not believing the man's record of innocence, went to God. The Creator checked the book Himself, checked the man, and filled with profound sympathy, told the man he could ask Him anything he wished. The poor man had no requests.

"Speak up, man," God told him. "Very little people deserve a reward, but you do!"

The man shrugged maintaining that he really didn't need anything. God's patience wearing thin, demanded:

"Do not be shy! I know that you want something but are

afraid to ask. Tell, what do you want?"

Finally, with eyes downcast and voice barely audible, he said:

"Oh Lord, if it's not much trouble, I'd like a chunk of bread with some butter on top."

The question raised was whether this modest request reflected wisdom or a tragic missed opportunity. If given the right to ask for something meaningful, why ask for something without value? The story, in a quiet way, mirrored the larger quest for a permanent Jewish homeland when many favorable voices helped the cause, why some people aren't using this chance?

Meanwhile, the other groups had finished their meetings. They gathered wood behind the cabin and lit a bonfire. We joined them, and with faces illuminated by flames, listened to stories and jokes told. There was music and sang along with the others. Eventually dusk turned to night, the fire still glowed as we played *Ha'Yeled* (The Child)—a dance in which a boy would choose a girl to dance with holding hands, and then she would choose another boy to dance, and so on. I was surprised when a girl with short pigtails and freckles—just like Simona's—took my hand to dance with her. I was pleased. On the way home with Cuţa, I wanted to find out more about that girl.

When I arrived home, Mother didn't even need to ask how it had been. She tried to make me to stop my stories, especially since school awaited me the next morning.

VI

Miss Bobinger was not the only French teacher in our school. There was another lady—her name escapes me now—but I still remember her figure clearly. Her blonde hair framed an oval face, and her scrutinizing gaze focused intently on whomever she was speaking with. Her speech was thoughtful, well-paced, and she carried herself with confidence.

One day, near the end of a lesson, she entered our classroom to recruit students for an upcoming school festival. When she asked if anyone knew a good poem, I remembered one I had found in Father's nightstand drawer. It had left a deep impression on me. The next day, I brought it to her in the teacher's office. It began with the line, *"I'm hungry, Mummy dear. Do you have bread?"* It was a long poem, heavy with feeling and dramatic ending. She read it carefully and then asked if I would like to recite it at the event.

From that day on, I met her during every long break in the barrack so she could coach me on how to recite it. With great patience, she corrected my posture, gestures, and expression. After each line, she taught me how to use my voice with nuance—when to pause, when to rise, when to soften the tone. Within a few days, I had memorized the entire poem, and as the date drew near, I started to feel the excitement of performing. In the final week before the festival, I was even excused from class for rehearsals with the full ensemble—a privilege that stirred some envy among my classmates.

The festival was scheduled for a Sunday morning. But on Friday evening, I came home unwell with a fever. On Saturday, Mother wouldn't let me out of bed. I stayed under the blankets all day, sipping tea, taking aspirin, and coughing syrup. By evening, my fever had gone down, but Mother remained cautious and continued the regimen. That night, I prayed with all my heart to be well enough for Sunday—and it seemed God heard me. The next morning, I felt in perfect health: no fever, no cough, my voice strong. I jumped out of bed ready to dress and go—but Mother was firm. She made me get back under the covers, certain that any exertion would bring the illness back. No protests or tears could change her mind. Even Father, who was often more lenient, didn't interfere.

It remains one of the heartbreaking memories of my childhood: knowing how disappointed the teacher would be, and the bitter disappointment of missing the excitement of being on that stage.

Between two and six in the afternoon, we worked in Master Ardoş's workshop. The pace was intense, especially since we often shared space with older students from whom we learned a great deal.

We continued working two to a bench, each on his own assignment. One of our first tasks was to build a carpenter's square out of hornbeam wood. It had to be constructed from two pieces, joined precisely at 90 degrees.

Master Ardoş was demanding. Every object we made had to be exact, flawless, and finished to a professional standard. He insisted on careful planning and precise execution. Beyond basic carpentry, sculpture was one of his key focuses. For him, the quality of a drawing was crucial—so he made us draw from wooden and plaster models. There were models with twisted floral motifs, leaves curling along beams, vines trailing clusters of grapes. I spent hours trying to capture these shapes in my sketchbook. No matter how much effort I put in, though, when I looked over at my classmates' pages, I felt ashamed. I couldn't yet manage to convey depth or proportion as seen in their work.

Whenever he needed help, Mr. Ardoş would call us to his bench. He was incredibly skilled, and the pieces he produced had a distinctive artistry—reminiscent of the ornate furniture you might find in the palaces of centuries past. He was a versatile sculptor too, capable of creating intricate inlays from veneers of various grains and colours—pieces admired for their imagination, finesse, and craftsmanship.

When it came time to glue furniture components together, we had to be quick. Before the hot glue cooled, we had to drop what we were doing and rush to him. Without words, he would signal with his eyes where to place the winch and in what position. The clamps had to be fastened over pads of soft wood to prevent dents in the highly polished surfaces. Heaven helps the boy who let a metal winch fall and damage one of his finished pieces—Master Ardoş's strong hand would deliver a blazing slap, and the unlucky recipient would be seeing stars for the rest of the day.

Toward the end of the year, each of us received a finely planed piece of wood on which we had to draw rows of geometric forms copied from a textbook. Once our drawings were complete, the master demonstrated how to chisel away the unwanted wood to create the raised shapes we wanted to preserve. This was our first real sculpture lesson, and he announced that these wooden panels would serve as our final examination.

Each small detail—the triangles, squares, and diamonds carved in bold relief—had to be perfectly aligned, equal, and identical to the one before. We were expected to erase all traces of the tools that shaped them. Even the slightest irregularity had to vanish beneath a surface so polished it looked almost like marble. Not all of us excelled at this task, but a few created remarkable pieces.

Among them was my classmate Bebe Şteinberg, who had a rare gift for drawing. During school hours, whenever a teacher needed a diagram or illustration on the blackboard, they would call Bebe. His talent blossomed in many directions—sculpture, theatre, even cinematography. His panel was considered the best in our entire class and was chosen for the school's annual exhibition, which was held in a hall downtown. Two years later, Bebe exhibited another wood sculpture: a scaled copy of the Soviet soldier statue holding a child, a replica of the one raised in Piaţa Victoriei in homage to the Red Army. It stood about two feet tall, and even Master Ardoş praised it as an exceptional work of art, before being sold to an art collector.

Bebe and I grew close over time. We often walked home together after shop hours. He was honest and thoughtful in conversation and never acted superior to anyone, despite his many gifts. Orphaned young, he lived in modest conditions with his mother and sister, Eva, in a rented apartment in the Nerva Traian neighbourhood. Our talks had more substance than the usual chatter I shared with others. His friendship felt like a quiet privilege. He had a strong build—taller and sturdier than most of our peers—and though he had never once been in a fight, no one dared touch me when I was with him.

In April, our principal, Mr. Walenştein, came into class and introduced us to a guest: the actor Alexe Marcovici. He was elegant, dressed in a light overcoat and a white silk scarf. Tall and slim, with slicked-back black hair that revealed a broad forehead and deep-set dark eyes, he was there to recruit students for the traditional end-of-year show.

After the principal left, Marcovici and our pedagogue, Mr. Eşkenazi, began interviewing each of us, starting with the front row. They asked whether we had ever performed in a play, whether we could declaim or improvise. After each brief conversation, Marcovici would sometimes turn to Eşkenazi and say:

"Write this one down."

When he got to me, I answered his questions as best I could. Then I overheard him tell Eşkenazi:

"Beligan's voice."

I turned to Emil beside me and whispered:

"What's that supposed to mean?"

Emil smirked: "What's what?"

"Beligan's voice."

He rolled his eyes. "Stupid. He said *găligan!*"

I jabbed Emil hard in the ribs for that one.

Radu Beligan, of course, was a famous Romanian actor known for his distinctive voice. But *găligan* just meant someone long and lanky like a lamppost.

Sitting in the first row near the door was our blond classmate, Adrian Cojocaru. Though from a wealthy family, he was a nice boy, kind to everyone. When the actor reached him, he suddenly called out:

"Class, here's Albişor! Who saw him at Baraşeum?"

The Baraşeum Theatre, during the war years, was the only stage in Bucharest where Jewish actors were allowed to perform under the German occupation. Both Cojocaru and our pedagogue Eşkenazi had acted there. Later, it would be nationalized and turned into the State Jewish Theatre, performing exclusively in Yiddish.

Despite my so-called "Beligan voice," I wasn't chosen for the play. Only a few from our class were cast, alongside Albişor and Piţurcă, who landed one of the lead roles. But the performance itself—held on a warm June evening, staged on the school's basketball court—remains unforgettable. Rows of benches and chairs stretched all the way to the brick wall that bordered the field, and even then, many students had to stand, the crowd was so large.

Even after more than sixty years, I still remember parts of the couplets, the laughter, the songs. I still see the performers' young faces, lit by the stage lights—some solemn, some exuberant, some trembling with excitement.

My only regret was that my parents and Simona weren't there with me to share in such a beautiful evening.

VII

School ended with a single "corigenţă" (a re-examination in the fall) to French. Miss Bobinger would not pardon me. This meant I would be busy over the summer, since failing the fall exam meant repeating the entire year. If I wanted to be with my friends next year, I had to learn all those verbs, declensions, and an entire vocabulary, including correct spellings. The most difficult part was pronunciation. Although Mother tried to teach me, I could never seem to get it right.

Aunt Luţi, Cuţa's mother, knew a student who was very good in French. His name was Posmantir. I had met him once at my aunt's place and found him a bit odd. He was in his twenties, with dark, wavy hair that often fell over his pale forehead, and he always carried a walking stick.

"Why do you carry that stick?" I asked one day.

"To keep the dogs away," he answered.

When he came to our home, we sat in the bedroom at the table in front of the window. With my books and notes open, I read, translated, and memorized verbs for an hour each day. When he left, I had to write a short story in French, prepare the next lesson, and learn more verbs. Oh, if only I could be free from Miss

Bobinger!

There was no time to play with my street friends. Father asked permission to bring me to the newspaper's administration office for summer practice. One morning at the start of vacation, he took me there and introduced me to everyone. I met many cheerful men and women who welcomed me with warmth and kindness. Sometimes I helped fill out forms, add numbers, or arrange blank pages. But most of the time, I played on an old typewriter, which delighted me. At lunchtime, we went to a canteen together. They sheltered me from the rain under their coats and treated me to candies and chocolate like I was their own child. Surrounded by such affection, I never regretted missing playtime with my old friends.

Sometimes, when Father worked the afternoon shift in the composing room, I would go up to visit him. I always found him the same: with wavy hair, ink-stained fingers holding a steel form, and bright blue eyes that lit up to see me. His longtime co-worker Usache would greet me with a nod. I watched the familiar workshop with interest—it always looked the same, no matter where it was: long black cupboards filled with drawers of lead letters, rubber rollers for spreading ink over the letters before making a proof sheet, strident Linotype machines, and plane presses rolling out printed sheets. This room was larger, better lit, with blue-painted walls and high ceilings. A roller table helped

Father move the heavy lead pages—a big change from when he carried them by hand.

On my way to the office on Academy Street, across from the university, I took a shortcut through Victoria Passage, where the National Theatre named Comedia (the Comedy) stood. The white building had an imposing staircase, Greek columns, and a triangular pediment. Inside, a large hall for the ticket box, led to red plush chairs guarding the main doors to theatre. Passing by gave me a thrill. The first play I saw there—with school tickets—was *Romeo and Juliet*, starring Mihail Popescu, famous for romantic roles. The play lasted nearly five hours due to the 27 scene changes. That experience was unforgettable.

From then on, I took advantage of the school encouraged theatre tickets sells, which could be paid for from our monthly scholarship grants. I saw *Othello* with Emil Botta at Sf. Sava Theatre; *O Noapte Furtunoasă* (*A Stormy Night*) with Giugaru, Birlic, and Beligan; and *O Scrisoare Pierdută* (*A Lost Letter*) with Finteşteanu, Birlic, and Elvira Popescu, all masters of their art.

A new chapter in my passion began with the opening of the Worker's Theatre CFR, housed in our neighbourhood in the building once used as a German headquarters and hospital near Podul Grant. I believe their first performance was *Uncle Tom's Cabin*, but the true premiere was the theatre's grand opening. It had a large, elegant auditorium with white walls finished in calcium-vecchio, red velvet drapes, and a wide stage with an orchestra pit. It quickly became one of the city's most beloved venues.

With a repertoire designed to attract new audiences, including plays by famous authors, this theatre played a crucial role in shaping my taste in art. It opened the world of theatre to a working-class people who would not travel to theatre district downtown to see a performance. For many, their only experience with live performance had been the short comic acts shown during movie intermissions, where performers like Titi Mihăilescu, Puiu Călinescu, and Horia Căciulescu brought joy and laughter to these audiences.

Giuleşti Theatre became a permanent temptation for me. After reading in the newspaper what was playing, especially on Saturday evenings when Father was home, I tried to convince my parents to go. Sometimes it worked, and Father would give me money to buy tickets. Other times, even Simona's and my pleas could not sway them. Then, on the day of a matinee, I'd invent a reason to leave the house and go straight to the theatre. Walking home from school had helped me save some money, though not always enough for a ticket. If I saw a side door open, I might sneak into the auditorium and sit wherever I could.

I could watch the same play over, and over, and never be bored. I even memorized some of the lines. Even today, I can rewatch a classic film with the same enthusiasm I felt the first time.

Perhaps that's why I remember so vividly productions like *Moartea Civilă* (*The Civil Death*) with Ovid Brădescu, *Vulpone* with Nicolae Sireteanu, and *Coana Chirița* with Nelly Nicolau Ștefănescu. And who could forget a comedy like *The Merry Wives of Windsor* with Otto Nicolai's sparkling overture played by a full orchestra?

VIII

My cousin Benu was the first to take advantage of the still-open border to the West, and he succeeded in arriving in Austria. Shortly after, Ticu, who continued to sleep from time to time at our place, left as well. The last thing I remember about him from that period was his hair routine. He slept in the kitchen on the wooden bed Father made, and when he woke up, he filled the white basin with water and washed his torso. On warm days, he didn't hesitate to wash himself at the courtyard tap. Then, he'd stand in front of the mirror hanging on the wall and comb his long black hair for ten minutes, in all directions.

"Why do you comb like that?" I asked him once.

"What's wrong with it?" he replied.

"You're going up and down, left and right... it's all over the place."

"Your hair needs exercise too," he said.

Sadly, that hair exercise didn't help him much. Not long after his arrival in Italy, we received a photo from his wedding to a beautiful girl he had met there—and his long black hair was gone. Like his father, he had inherited early baldness.

Sergiu rarely let us know how he was doing. His wife, Maricica, gave birth to a daughter, and they had an apartment downtown. We discovered all this by chance one day while shopping in the city. As we approached the Lafayette department store on Victoria Way, Sergiu appeared.

"Uncle Avram, Aunt Berta, what are you doing here?" he asked.

He insisted we go with him to the fourth floor, where there was a refined restaurant with starched tablecloths and silver cutlery. He seated us at a centre table and said:

"Order anything you want. Don't worry about the prices. This is my restaurant."

He wasn't exaggerating. Everyone—clients and staff alike—called him "Domn Director" (Mr. Director).

After the installation of Dr. Petru Groza's government, things in Romania didn't improve, despite new reforms. Among these were the Agricultural Reform, which redistributed land to poorer peasants, and the Universal Voting Rights Act, which included women. Still, anti-communist demonstrations erupted, followed by mass arrests, beatings, and even deaths. The Communist Party, propped up by the Soviets, gradually took control of the country, silencing opposition parties either by banning them or forcing them into submission.

The head of the Communist Party was Gheorghe Gheorghiu-Dej, a long-time prisoner at Doftana Jail during the war. He formed the Party's Central Committee with Ana Pauker, Vasile Luca, Theohary Georgescu, and Lucreţiu Pătrăşcanu. Their portraits appeared daily in the papers, especially Dej's—his stern, energetic look was meant to instill confidence in a nation drowning in confusion and poverty. When Mother saw his photo, she said he looked like Charles Boyer, her favourite actor from her youth.

During this uncertain transition, in which each change was followed by new arrests, Romania's natural resources were siphoned away by Sov-Rom (Soviet Romanian) agencies, set up to transfer Romanian goods to Russia while the population was left cold and hungry. To distract a discontented public, the communist press launched a campaign against the "Speculanţi" (Profiteers), encouraging people to report and punish merchants who hoarded goods to resell them at high prices. Newspapers proudly published photos of shopkeepers paraded through the streets with placards around their necks, hands tied behind their backs, while angry mobs spat, cursed, and beat them.

My parents continued Sundays and some holidays to go to Piaţa Grant with their merchandise. One day, a group of people stopped at their place near the curb and asked about the prices. Not yet answered the question, one started to scream:

"Speculanţi, speculanţi, let punish these speculanţi!"

People stopped on their way to see what's going on. The mob grew, everyone shouting and one came with a placard to hang around Father's neck. Without losing his head, Father pushed back and pulled out of his coat his red Union Member book. With his machine-squeezed hand from which a finger was missing he held the red Union book asking the leader of the mob covering their noise:

"What are you saying? Am I not a worker like you? What did you do last night? You slept, didn't you? Do you know what I did?" He took his paper out of his pocket and opened it to show the people. "This is what I make each night! And this is what puts food on the table to my children!" He referred to the stuff exposed on the pavement.

The crowd fell silent. Some quietly left. Mother was trembling, pale. Father, too, shook with anger. Some customers tried to make a purchase, but he packed up the goods and declared the shop closed.

Others were less fortunate. Poor Mr. Segal—the father of

my friend Samulică from Poradim School—was deformed, with a prominent hump on his back. The mob forced him through the streets with a placard around his neck, raining down fists and curses. When he collapsed, before reaching Podul Grant, kind-hearted people who knew him carried him home. He lay bedridden for weeks.

My parents kept going to the market until one day they came home empty-handed, looking as if they'd buried a loved one. The police had raided the market. Since our family's spot was close to the entrance, they were the first targeted. All their goods were confiscated. What little profit they had made was reinvested into new stock—some of it bought on credit. Now, they had lost everything. As a result, soon he was expelled from Communist Party, just short of being demise from his job at the paper where he worked.

That fall, I sat for my French re-examination with the other French teacher. The room was packed with students, many from my class. I was terrified that Miss Bobinger would appear, but to my relief, she was nowhere in sight.

When my turn came, I was asked to conjugate some verbs, answer a few questions, and read a few sentences. The teacher noted a mark of eight in my record book. With that, I was saved.

IX

I met my classmates from the previous year in a new classroom, not very different from the old one, except for its new location in the building The windows of the previous class faced the street, and now they faced the basketball field in the courtyard. Some of my old colleagues had changed classes or shops, and several new faces had appeared. Still, we were happy to meet again after a long summer break. It felt like each of us had a volume to report in response to the simple question, "What's new?"

Emil (Alimănescu) no longer leapt from bench to bench like he used to. He had grown taller and thinner, but still had the same round face, short curly hair, and the birthmark above his lip. As soon as he spotted me in the doorway, he called out:

"The Pea Poet! Here comes the poet!"

With our bags tossed over benches at random, we formed small groups, chatting, laughing, teasing—each with something to say, ask, or object to. We were so caught up in our reunion that we didn't hear the bell or notice the teacher standing patiently at the podium.

Our class master this year was Professor Ringhelştein, whom we affectionately called "Moşul" (Old Man). He cleared his throat a few times until silence settled, and we hurried to our seats. I had left my bag on the front row of benches and took a seat next to Avram Simon—also known as Piţurcă.

With his warm, fatherly voice, Moşul called the roll, then asked Bebe to copy the class schedule for the term onto the blackboard, which we each transcribed into our notebooks. As Bebe wrote, Moşul shared a little story about a new product he had recently seen, that made him think about our technical progress. An American soldier, he told us, had tossed an empty cigarette package onto the street, and a passing car ran over it. Strangely, when the car moved on, the package bounced back to its original shape—no damage, no creases.

Someone picked it up and, astonished, decided to keep it as a trophy. It was the time when the glossy nylon package of cigarettes was quoted more valuable than a real tobacco box.

"Gentleman," said the professor, "we are entering the era of plastics. Many traditional materials will be replaced by plastic—cheaper, lighter, more durable. You will witness astonishing changes in science and technology. Just wait. It won't take long."

He was right. Soon, the word "nylon" was on everyone's lips, especially young women who dreamed of owning a pair of nylon stockings. Introduced by American soldiers, they were finer, more transparent, and longer lasting than the scarce silk stockings still in use.

Another sensation of the time was the ballpoint pen—called the *pix*—which used paste instead of liquid ink. Like the nylon stockings, paste pens couldn't be found in stores and were sold on the black market at big prices. It wasn't long before some enterprising individuals began producing their own ones, crafting the barrels on lathes from aluminum with inserts received from abroad.

A whole new breed of street peddlers appeared. They roamed the busiest sidewalks—on Griviţa Road, near the Gara de Nord, or around Podul Grant—carrying small wooden crates to display their merchandises. Always on alert for police, they would stop, set up their wares, and loudly demonstrate their latest products: the best sharpening stones, miraculous stain removers, or "genuine" Russian wristwatches. At the first sight of a police cap, they would shove everything back into their pockets, grab the crate, and vanish into the crowd.

One evening, Uncle Manole from Ploieşti arrived unexpectedly with a small suitcase, claiming urgent business that would keep him in town for a day or two. As always, he brought a flood of stories and a generous bag of candies for Simona and me. Father was glad to see him and sent me to ask Mr. Buzatu for a bottle of wine on credit. I came back with a bottle of Malaga—a sweet, thick red wine that Father let us taste.

"This has *puterea ursului*," (the strength of a bear), he said.

Uncle Manole left early each morning to take care of his business. After a few days, he said that he didn't want to go back to Ploeşti, because business was better here. He said the best option was to have Father as a partner. Father declined.

"I've already had my share of failed business. I'm not doing it again."

But Uncle Manole was persistent. He jumped from his chair and began painting a grand picture of the future:

"With my contacts and your talent, we'll make millions!"

Father, unmoved, congratulated him on his ambition but said nothing more.

That's when the real reason came out—he had no money left, not even for a train ticket home. Mother, who had been wary since his arrival, now saw her fears confirmed. She had sensed something was wrong all along. She asked:

"Why don't you sell the shop in Ploieşti and use the money to start something new here?"

He looked in her eyes for a moment.

"I can't," he said. "I owe everything to creditors. They're already after me. No one's buying, business is dead. Debora's nerves are shattered. She may need to be institutionalized. Times have changed—it's not like it was."

The next day, he came home early—but went straight to Mr. Buzatu's tavern. The same happened the day after. Eventually, Mother couldn't bear it anymore.

"He has to leave," she told Father. "Do something about this!"

No one knows what was said between the brothers, or how much money changed hands, but the next morning, Uncle Manole took his suitcase, kissed us goodbye, and left.

A few days later, Mr. Buzatu appeared at our door with a bill.

"What's this?" Father asked.

"Your brother asked me to put it on your tab," said the owner.

"Did you ask me?" Father said, stepping forward.

"He's your brother, isn't he?" Buzatu shrugged.

"Well, let's be serious," Father replied. "If a stranger who sleeps under my roof asks you for money, would you give it to him without asking me first? Why would I take bread from my children's mouths to pay for his wine? I sincerely regret it, Mr. Buzatu, but I can't help you."

The landlord stood silent for a while, shrugged again, and left.

X

Was there anything more pleasant than being able to prolong your stay in bed on a holiday morning? On such a day, there was no need to jump up when the alarm rang, no walking in the dark into a freezing room, no running after a streetcar to get to school. The alarm clock usually interrupted the most beautiful dreams. With eyes still heavy from too little sleep, I'd sit on the edge of my bed, elbows on my knees, trying to piece the dream back together. If Mother didn't nudge me to get up, maybe I could sleep a little longer. But wearing her housecoat and felt slippers, she always scolded me gently—being careful not to wake Father, who had just come back from working overnight.

On holidays, though, the alarm was silent, and I could sleep until daylight crept into the room. I'd peek at the outside light through the lace of Mother's curtains and stay in bed a little longer. Often, Father would wake too. With his bright blue eyes, he would watch the room and eventually pull Simona and me toward him to tickle us.

Since we rarely lit the fire in the bedroom, we grabbed our clothes from the chair and rushed to the kitchen, where it was warm. Near the crackling stove, Mother watched a pot of milk about ready to jump over its rim. The breakfast table was already set with cups, bread, butter, and plum jam.

On that early December morning, Father told me that starting the next day I would have to go to the Coral Temple after school to begin my Bar-Mitzvah preparations. I had to be there before seven o'clock because the rabbi who would teach me to read the Torah—the Jewish holy scroll known as the Law—was tutoring other children as well.

"Don't forget," Father said. "Bar-Mitzvah means that from now on, you're a man. And a real man is always punctual and serious. Try to be there on time. If you're late once or twice, the rabbi won't work with you anymore. Understand?"

I nodded.

After finishing my shop hours, I ran to Vitan station to catch tram 19, which passed in front of the Coral Temple. I got off at Călăraşi station and walked down the short, busy street called Sfânta Vineri (Saint Friday). The temple rose behind a wrought-iron fence enclosing a small, paved courtyard. The building had three naves. The central one featured a rounded portal above which diamond-shaped stained-glass windows had been set. The side naves mirrored each other, with tall arched windows adorned with similar glasswork. The central nave sticks out forward, drawing attention to its entrance: imposing wooden doors flanked by wrought-iron lamps. The masonry frieze resembling lace stood tall above the doors. At its top, the Ten Commandments tablets centered between two turrets—symbols of the wooden rollers used to hold Torah scrolls, the centre nave seemed to emulate.

A few marble steps led to a massive carved door. Inside lay a vast and silent hall, dimly lit by a grand chandelier hanging over the central podium. The platform was low, with a large central lectern covered in rich, gold-trimmed red velvet and flanked by candlesticks. Behind it, a tall arch framed the ark of the Torah scrolls, veiled by red plush drapery. Rows of tall black benches ran down either side of a wide aisle lined with red carpet. The upper balconies—spanning three walls—rested on round columns and were decorated with ornate clusters of lamps. Though only softly lit at its centre, the hall was grand, every corner rich with artwork beyond easy description.

I stepped quietly toward the podium. In the first row, at the end of a bench, sat a man in a black overcoat and a wide-brimmed hat, reading. I stood in front of him, still wearing my cap.

"Good evening," I said.

He looked up at me through the lenses of his glasses.

"Shalom."

"I came for Bar-Mitzvah."

He held out the book.

"Can you read from this?"

I left my bag on the bench and opened the book. It was bound in leather, with golden Hebrew letters embossed on the cover. I recognized the letters from my first Hebrew classes at Poradim School, and from the weekly lessons we now had with Professor Szabo, but even so, I couldn't say I was particularly skilled at reading. I had to pause to decipher each letter carefully, analyzing the dots—because in Hebrew, the placement of these dots completely changes the vowels. Like a music student learning to read notes on a staff, a Hebrew learner needs time to build fluency. Eventually, people read without dots at all—but that takes experience. The book the rabbi gave me had no dots.

"It has no *necudot* (Hebrew for dots)," I said.

He took the book, flipped to another page, and handed it back.

"Try here."

I began to read slowly, with the emotional weight of someone taking an exam. More children arrived, filling the benches around us. Some had started earlier and were already more advanced. I was given a book to take home for practice. That evening, and in many that followed, we each took turns reading prayers aloud.

Soon, my reading became smoother, with fewer awkward pauses. By the time Hanukkah passed, we were already practicing passages from the Torah itself.

In the temple, the Torah is opened daily, and short sections are read aloud—stories of the patriarchs, familiar from the Old Testament. The text is written in vertical columns on parchment, rolled between two wooden rods. The readings are divided across the calendar year, so each holiday corresponds with a specific passage. When the scroll reaches its end, the occasion is marked by *Simchat Torah*—the celebration of the Torah—when people sing and dance in joyous ceremony. The next day, the reading begins again, from the first paragraph.

Sadly, learning to read the Torah fluently didn't mean I understood the meaning of the words. There's a world of difference between reading and understanding.

My new desk-mate, Pițurcă, was the shortest boy in class. His real name was Avram Simon, but he had many nicknames: Pițurcă, Agamiță Dandanache, the Dwarf—and more. He responded to all of them with a grin and a quick-witted comeback that often served as payback to the classmate who coined it.

What he lacked in height, he made up for in energy and humour. It was as if he had quicksilver in his veins—never still for a second. We shared the front desk, directly under the teacher's nose, yet we still managed to whisper jokes or pass each other scribbled messages. If a classmate was struggling at the blackboard, their eyes would find ours, pleading for help. Pițurcă would lower his head behind a book and whisper the answer like a prompter in a theatre.

Sometimes he got caught. The teacher would scold him or give him a failing mark. Then it was my turn to step in. I'd write the answer in oversized letters in my notebook for our desperate classmate to read. But if we gave the wrong answer, we earned not just the teacher's fury, but also the betrayed glare of the student who had followed our lead and failed.

Pițurcă lived near Văcărești Road, close to a cinema called *Izbânda* (Success). We often walked together to his house, and from there, continued alone to Piata Mare, for streetcar 12.

One evening, Clara—the neighbour's daughter—caught up with us. She occasionally showed up to share news from the neighbourhood. This time, she told us there would be auditions that night for a new amateur theatre production at the *Izbânda* cinema.

We went together. On the upper floor, a large hall was filled with young hopefuls, boys and girls, waiting for the director. When he arrived, he handed us scripts and asked us to read aloud the lines of various characters. The play was about a Black child named *Bulgăre de Zăpadă* (Snowball), set during the racial conflicts in America.

After the reading, the director announced that the leading role would go to Pițurcă. From that day on, he gained a new nickname, "Bulgăre de Zăpadă."

XI

In the first bench by the windows sat two inseparable classmates. Both were sons of wealthy families, with an upbringing and opportunities quite different from ours. It seemed the school administration had prior arrangements with their parents—one of them had even been appointed class monitor until the teacher arrived. His name was Jean Israel, and his desk partner was Carol Weldman. Jean was tall and thin, with a pallid face and jet-black hair. He always wore a grey suit made of English fabric, with long trousers and a tie. Meticulously tidy, he had a calm and conciliatory manner, often stepping in to defuse tensions when conflict seemed imminent.

Weldman was his opposite. Shorter, with a darker complexion and slick black hair. He had a quick temper, a combative attitude, and a vocabulary that wasn't entirely free of vulgarities. Not everyone accepted their authority in the classroom. Disputes sometimes erupted into shouting matches or even physical fights—especially when Jean wasn't there to mediate. None of us wanted to admit the divide between them and the rest of us, but it was always there. They kept their distance, never mingled with us or joined in our games.

At recess, we'd race to the schoolyard with plans already hatched during class. At the back fence, we gathered to play one of our favourite games, "Cal de Prinţ şi de Împărat" (*The Prince and Emperor Horse*). In the heat of the game—when nothing mattered more than how many marbles landed in the muddy hole we had dug with our fingers—neither Jean nor Weldman ever joined. And truthfully, none of us missed them. They always stayed in the classroom, where it was warm, clean, quiet and chat.

Just like the year before, once our morning classes ended, we'd head to the school canteen in groups. The route took us along Strada Ciocanul, down Strada Laptelui, and a right turn onto Theodor Speranţa brought us there. Rain or shine, our group—led by Emil— kept growing with new members from the younger grades.

The richer kids went home instead, riding bicycles, catching streetcars, or being picked up by family cars waiting inside the school gate.

Among us were many fatherless children, raised by single mothers who worked full days. These kids spent their afternoons alone or with neighbours until their mothers came home. Then, in the short time they had together, they prepared dinner, planned for the next day, and often worked late into the night on schoolwork.

I often went to Emil's house, a small one-storey home on a backstreet near our school. Their apartment had just one room and a kitchen—like most of us. I never met his mother, but I knew she had been widowed when Emil was very young. He had grown up alone and had a deep, respectful bond with his mother. Whenever we visited, he watched us closely to make sure no one touched or broke anything. He checked that we left nothing dirty behind and wouldn't rest until everything was returned exactly as it had been. That same sense of order could be seen in his notebooks, filled with carefully rounded, calligraphic handwriting—neatly written between ruled lines. And yet, there wasn't a student in the entire school noisier or funnier than Alimănescu himself.

Another classmate, Jack Cohen, lived on Strada Florilor (*Flowers Street*), near the notorious Crucea de Piatră district. He was an orphan, but that didn't stop him from excelling. After graduation, he was admitted—without entrance exams and on a full scholarship—to the Faculty of Physics and Mathematics, having completed his final school year with top marks in every subject.

Bebe Steinberg and his sister Eva, also raised without a father, carried a kind of quiet radiance and simplicity. Their understanding of life's hardships gave them inner strength, and they did their best with what they had. In doing so, they earned the respect and admiration of all.

XII

Piața Sfântul Gheorghe (the Saint George Plaza) was not only the geographic centre of the Bucharest City, but by also on its own right, the concentration point of the entire country, because all roads extended to the farthest location in cardinal directions, are born here, at kilometer zero, like sun rays. The city's oldest commercial trade was also here, and from this core it expanded, bursting across the western bank of the Dâmbovița River and beyond.

Around the Church of Saint George, the old town settled into a maze of narrow lanes, home to small craftsman shops and a handful of grocery stores. Modest single-storey homes stood side by side with the occasional two-level house or a larger warehouse stocked with goods. A few inns welcomed merchants and travellers from afar, protected by arnăuți—mercenary guards who wielded long-barrelled rifles known as *flinte* to ward off haiduci and highwaymen.

As the city grew, more churches and hospitals were built, and a large trading square took shape—where Piața Mare (Big Market) stands today. Major roads were widened to mimic those in Western cities. The old boyars and newly wealthy merchants wanted homes like the ones in Vienna or Paris. Their ladies demanded silks, brocades, and fine embroidery. Their carriages were driven by muskals in long velvet caftans. But the narrow streets of commerce remained, untouched by time—preserved through more than five centuries of history.

It was on one of those streets that the Coral Temple stood.

That day, the temple glowed as if for a high holiday, though only the front rows were filled. I wasn't the only one—several boys, all born in January, had come with family and friends to celebrate this milestone: our Bar-Mitzvah. We were dressed in our finest clothes brushed, pressed, and dusted with the perfume from our mothers' bottles. Our shoes shone like mirrors. Our hair was combed neatly. We waited, hearts racing, for the ceremony to begin.

Before we left home, Father removed his wristwatch and placed it on my arm.

"Dorel, this is your birthday gift. You're no longer a child. You're a young man now, and we have a lot of confidence in you. We hope that we'll see in your attitude that you act with maturity and are worthy of our trust. Happy birthday, Son!"and he kissed me on both cheeks.

I was overwhelmed with unspoken emotion and hugged him, then Mother and Simona. We bundled into our winter coats and set off on foot toward Regie. Simona and I walked ahead, while our parents followed, arm in arm. Father, as always, replied to Mother's remarks in brief, thoughtful phrases. He wore his old navy overcoat—the one he used for both summer and winter—which he'd recently had turned inside out by a tailor. He held Mother protectively on the curbside, his other hand cradling a cigarette. He never smoked in the house, and now he had the time to enjoy it on the way to the streetcar.

Mother barely reached Father's shoulder. She wore a printed silk scarf tied under her chin and remarked how much I had grown:

"Look" she said, "there isn't a month since I let Dorel's trousers cuffs down and now, his ankles are barely covered. He needs a new suit."

Father did not answer.

Fog rarely blanketed the city, except sometimes in autumn. But that morning, a thick mist veiled everything. We could barely see the other side of the street. When we crossed the road, it was hard to judge the traffic through the fog. After passing the Regie railway barrier and turning west toward the streetcar station, a blanket of fog hung over Plevnei Road, out of which the sun rose above, soft and red, like the flushed cheek of a baby just waking from sleep. I heard Father's voice behind me predicting:

"It's gone be a beautiful day."

With his watch on my wrist, I felt very important—like a real man. I held Simona's hand and walked carefully, chest lifted, ready to protect her if needed. She walked to my right in her blue coat with a matching hood, from which her golden curls spilled out in unruly waves like a fiery halo. Her little nose was dusted with freckles. Her red lips—usually silent but sharp when needed—made her look like an exquisite porcelain doll. I was proud of her. Though nearly four years younger than me, Simona had become not only my playmate but also my confidante in times of doubt and sadness. She had a sharp sense of perception and a gift for reading emotions. Often, I didn't even need to tell her what troubled me—she simply knew. She had humour, wit, and a gentle intelligence that made her a remarkable companion. To me, she was more than a sister—she was my friend. Perhaps that's why she was always surrounded by friends and admirers.

The rabbi who had prepared me was an elderly religious man, with grace and a lot of patience. He corrected our Torah reading word by word, until we could recognize the sacred letters at a glance. With great kindness, he saw his mission as a **mitzvah** (a good deed), especially for underprivileged children like us. He even wrote a short, personal speech for each of us, inspired by his conversations with us. We were expected to read it in front of the audience after the religious ceremony, and I had tried to memorize mine.

When my turn came, I looked from the height of the podium at the modest audience that included my parents, sister, some friends and others. Father sat still, solemn waiting to hear me speaking. Mother's eyes were locked on me, full of encouragement, as if she had stopped breathing altogether.

The hall shimmered in light like a theatre, and suddenly, everything wavered. A sudden born wave of emotion swelled in my throat, choking me. Through tears felt frozen to my lashes, I saw foggy images of my childhood—wandering with Mother and Simona from one borrowed home to another, my feet icy on the shop's cement floor, the barber who almost throw us, Father and me over the steps on street, the wartime bombings, the darkness of the sewer tunnels during air raids, all the frightening moments that marked our existence of perpetual struggle, and with them, this lump heavy in my throat that did not let me speak.

Gripping the edge of the lectern, my heart pounding, I fought to remember the words and with tears that I could not retain, finally, I began my speech. Not the one the rabbi wrote for me, but one that came from my heart like the dropping pearls slowly falling on my face. I do not remember what I said there, but I know I told my parents to not expect me to do for them what they did for me, because such struggles, sacrifices and deprivation they had to endure for me, can not be repaid.

Father stared, unblinking. Mother wept silently, her handkerchief pressed to her mouth. The room sat frozen in silence. When I finished, applause erupted. Father rose to his feet to greet me and after him the rest of the people waited to congratulate:

"Mazel Tov!" they said. "Very beautiful. Mazel Tov!"

The rabbi, family, friends, even strangers surrounded me with congratulations, handshakes and hugs. Apparently, my emotion penetrated their souls. Yet deep down, I was ashamed of myself. I had cried—cried like a baby. I had come to prove I was a man, mature and worthy of respect—and instead, I had broken down in front of everyone. What kind of man loses control like that? What kind of man cries at his own Bar-Mitzvah? I wanted to disappear.

Bravo to me, I thought bitterly. Bravo for being so brave! No, this was way too much! Never would I be forgiven for such shame!

No—I would never forgive myself for this.

PART 2
FROM AN OBSCURE YESTERDAY TO A BRIGHT TOMORROW

Chapter 1

Winds don't Stop at Stop Sign

I

Time carried me across six decades. I look back now with eyes full of melancholy on the enchanted days of my childhood, trying to recover, from the dust of the past, people and moments that once defined me. In remembering them, I feel again that warmth and love which once surrounded the child I was—without which, today, I might have grown into nothing more than a dry, wild fruit, seedless and useless to anyone.

Despite the poverty, shortages, and obstacles we faced in those difficult times, I was lucky—truly lucky—to have parents of exceptional character. They never spared themselves from sacrifice and did all they could to ensure that their children could grow up with the same chances as those from more privileged families, even in our humble corner of the city on Grant area. Perhaps that's why, on Easter, Christmas, and other holidays, when children from the neighbourhood came out in new clothes, we made sure to go out too, proudly showing off ours.

Each day brought new challenges. Soon enough, King

Mihai I was forced to abdicate, just two days before the New Year, on December 30, 1947. Earlier that same year, in August, Romania underwent a drastic monetary reform. The smallest banknote in circulation was five million lei. Only a limited amount of money could be converted, so those who had savings—whether in banks or at home—lost everything.

. The historic Romanian political parties were outlawed, and the newspaper where Father worked, *Viitorul*, was shut down. It was replaced by a new Communist newspaper, *Előre* (Hungarian for "Forward"), which operated in the same printing house. Father and his colleague Usache continued their work there.

Although the First Congress of the Labour Party—formed through the merger of the Communists and the historic Socialist Party—promised a better life for all, the reality was grim. People continued to live in poverty, deprived of necessities. Food shortages persisted, and queues stretched endlessly in front of shops.`

Housing, too, was in crisis. After the war, the bombings, and the population's migration from rural areas to the capital, there were not enough homes for everyone. Simona had turned ten, and it was no longer feasible for the whole family to share a single bedroom. Father, who had worked at *Dimineața* with Theohari Georgescu—now a major figure in the new regime and a member of the Labour Party's Central Committee—reached out to him. As a result, we were assigned a larger apartment at 13 Eduard Grant Street.

After the Education Reform of 1948, our school was renamed Şcoala Medie Tehnică de Mecanică Nr. 1 (Technical Secondary School for Mechanics No. 1). It was a vocational school now, with only a few of the former teachers and staff remaining. Mr. Ardoş's carpentry shop was dismantled entirely, and we never heard of him again.

I was placed in the Agricultural Machinery section. My former classmates were scattered across new specializations: Fine Mechanics and Optics, Machine Construction, or the Design and Fabrication of Tools and Devices. None of us knew what these specializations really meant. We hadn't been given a choice—just assignments. The school now had a new principal, new instructors, new rules, and an entirely new mission.

Still, I occasionally met my old friends at the canteen on Theodor Speranţa, though it too was soon closed—just like the Zionist youth organizations. Briefly, our Student Union was renamed UTM - Uniunea Tineretului Muncitor (Young Workers' Union) - and we were issued red membership books. New subjects became mandatory for access to higher education: Communist Doctrine, *The Short Course on the History of the Communist (Bolshevik) Party*, Political Economy, and Russian Language. Without passing marks in these courses, university admission was impossible. Selected young workers from factories were sent to the Ştefan Gheorghiu School, where they received fast-track training—

two or three years—and then assumed engineering or leadership roles in state-owned institutions.

The government also began constructing a massive new media complex, the Casa Scânteii (*The Spark House*), inspired by Moscow's Lomonosov University, a symbol of Stalinist grandeur. When it was partially completed, most of the newspapers moved their operations there, including *Előre*, where my father worked.

A massive portion of the labour used to build the Casa Scânteii came from blue-uniformed soldiers recruited from families labelled as "of unhealthy origin,". Typically, they were the sons of former landowners, merchants, office managers, and small manufacturers, whose livelihoods had been destroyed by the 1948 Nationalization Law. These young men were now repurposed as free labour on the state's biggest construction projects: the Danube–Black Sea Canal, various hydroelectric dams, and of course, the Casa Scânteii. As for the rest of us—those deemed to have a "healthy social origin"—we were recruited for weekend volunteer labour to help make up for agricultural workforce shortages, especially during the harvest on wasted nationalized land.

After finishing school in 1952, I was assigned to SMT Videle, a station for tractors and agricultural machines that served state-run farms (nationalized from boyars) and the newly formed collective farms, modeled on the Soviet kolkhoz system. Beginning in 1948, an aggressive collectivization campaign was underway. Under pressure, intimidation, and arrests, more independent farmers were forced into collective farms.

During the final months of my schooling, while researching my diploma project in the public library, I stumbled upon a literary club called cenaclu. Its weekly meetings allowed young writers, mostly high school students, some from university, one or two blue collar workers and even a couple of mature people. All were happy to read their work waiting at end to hear the critiques following. I was drawn to it immediately. Soon, I became a regular. We met, debated, read aloud—and sometimes, after heated discussion, shared a cold beer on the way home.

In September 1952, while working as a technician in Videle, I received a phone call from Bucharest. The next morning, I was to report to the Mihail Eminescu School for Literature and Literary Criticism— a fast-track program for training a new generation of ideologically correct journalists and writers. I had been nominated by my literary club. It was an immense shock for me and for SMT management. The director of SMT resisted my departure, and there was friction between the Romanian Writers' Union and the station. But in the end, permission had to be granted. That very evening, I returned home. The next morning, I presented myself at the school. It was housed in one of the grand palaces on the famous Șosea Kiseleff, right beside the Russian Embassy—an elegant white marble building originally built as a residence for Prince Carol II and his wife, Princess Helen of Greece.

In the school courtyard, while waiting for my first interview with the school board, I met young writers already known to the public: Nicolae Labiș, (a rising star of Romanian poetry, very young, not yet finishing high school, victim of an traffic accident that reclaimed his life a few years later), Gheorghe Tomozei, Rusalim Mureșan, and others who were already publishing in *Gazeta Literară* and *Tânărul Scriitor*. prime literary publications.

Living for a year among such talent and studying under the most prominent literary figures of the time—Mihail Sadoveanu, Camil Petrescu, Mihail Beniuc, and others—was the best year of my life. A beautiful dream that did not last. After the first year, not able to translate to required calls, the dream vanished—like mist in the morning air.

II

The situation in the country continued to deteriorate. The police and secret services grew more powerful, and the private lives of citizens became public matters, discussed in fabricated meetings at workplaces. Children were encouraged in school to report what their parents said at home. Informers were recruited, arrests became more frequent, and detentions without trial were common. People grew afraid to speak freely. They carried on in silence, deprived of basic necessities and forced to queue for hours just to get food.

But for a few days in 1952, one event gave the illusion of prosperity. Store shelves were suddenly filled with long-forgotten food and goods. It was the day of the monetary reform, when twenty old lei were converted into one new leu. As in 1947, people were only allowed to exchange a limited amount of money—teaching a harsh lesson: saving was dangerous. These reforms were kept secret until they were enacted, and many lost whatever savings they'd managed to hide away "for worse times." All the beautiful merchandise in the shops could only be bought for a few days only with the new currency. And although prices seemed low, almost no one had money to spend. Within days, the shelves emptied again, and the long queues returned.

After completing my studies at the literary school, I began my mandatory military service. Then, in 1955, I started work at the mechanical workshop of Casa Scânteii. In the meantime, Simona had grown into a beautiful young woman who turned heads wherever she went. Despite her modesty, admirers began to circle. For me, nothing was more flattering than walking beside her and watching strangers look back for one more glimpse of Simona.

Old friends from Ciocanul School began to visit me—friends who lived on the other side of the city. I had a feeling it wasn't me they were coming to see. Before long, Simona confided in me that of all her admirers, she had grown fond of my old schoolmate Rățoiul—Jack Edelștein. After a few months of courtship, they married and lived with us for a time on Eduard Grant Street. Eventually, they moved to a small attic apartment in the same building where his parents lived on Mircea Vodă Street.

When she became pregnant, doctors warned that due to her heart condition, natural childbirth was risky. But Simona didn't listen and gave birth to a beautiful daughter named Adina. She never complained about her health, but when she was tired or agitated, one could see the pulse in her carotid arteries beating visibly beneath her skin.

One day, we found a quiet moment to talk. She told me she wanted to have surgery at Fundeni Hospital to correct her heart problem. At that time, even in the best hospitals of the West, such surgery was considered high-risk. It wasn't urgently needed, she explained, but she was tired of living under constant medical warnings. She just wanted to live like everyone else. Then she asked me what I thought she should do. I didn't know how to answer. I couldn't tell her not to do it, but I also couldn't bring myself to encourage her either.

As for me, I had been in love a few times, but the girls I loved seemed to have dreams that didn't include me. At the Mihail

Eminescu School, I lost sight of my literary ambitions because I had fallen for a girl who consumed all my thoughts, time, and imagination. By the time I realized that all she could offer was her friendship, it was too late to salvage what I had lost that year.

Later came a girl who worked at **Casa Scânteii**, with mysterious charcoal-black eyes that burned straight into my heart. But behind her gaze was an impenetrable wall that seemed to block any emotion from surfacing. After months of courting her, she told me her parents had arranged her marriage to a promising athlete.

There were other girls who liked me, but they didn't align with what I wanted for myself. My experiences revealed to me just how many married women were unfaithful—something that made me cautious in my choices. I decided to wait for the right girl.

She appeared in 1960, during a vacation day at the **Casa** Scânteii recreation centre on the shore of Lake Herăstrău. I saw her there among a group of friends.

To my surprise, she also lived in our Grant neighbourhood, just behind the Piaţă. We walked home together that day, strolling slowly along the Şosea. Her name was Valeria, though everyone called her Vali, and she sang in the choir of the Seventh-Day Adventist Church. Her father had once been a construction contractor but was no longer employed because he refused to work on the Sabbath. As a result, the family had fallen into poverty.

Vali was the eldest of five siblings—two sisters and two younger brothers. Her mother was often overworked, managing things both at home and on construction sites, wherever her husband, **Costică Balotă**, could find occasional jobs. He would hire a small team, find materials and clients, while the mother supervised the workers.

I can never forget my first meeting with Mr. Balotă. It happened one day in early July 1961, at his home on Ştefan Plavăţ Street, behind Piaţa Grant. One of Vali's best friends, Otilia, was about to marry Mr. Manea, the pastor's eldest son, in the Grant Adventist Church.

That church, located at the corner of Eduard Grant Street, just a few proprieties apart from our house, was a lively presence in the neighbourhood. Especially in summer, when the windows were open, the sound of choral music would spill into the street. Every Friday evening and Saturday, the street filled with well-dressed people—young and old—heading to services. For a while, the air buzzed with voices and laughter before returning to its usual quiet. Simona used to attend sometimes with her best friend Cleopatra Mânzăţeanu, who often visited us. Through them, I had met many in the Adventist community—even before meeting Vali.

At that time, I was still working at Casa Scânteii, and I had been seeing Vali almost daily. Otilia's civil wedding was scheduled for July 30, and the couple invited us to join them on their honeymoon in Făgăraşi, located at the foot of tallest mountain of the country. But Vali couldn't go without her father's permission, and she believed that if Mr. Balotă met me, he might agree. I had never seen him before, and I was filled with nervous anticipation. When I entered the guest room, I saw an imposing mahogany desk, a tall glass cabinet, and the bed where Vali and her sister Zica used to sleep. The whole family had gathered when Mr. Balotă entered— freshly shaved, wearing a clean shirt and tie.

I explained that I had known Vali for over a year and that we planned to marry. We all stood there, her parents, her brothers and sisters facing one another, as if participating in a solemn pagan rite. Then Mr. Balotă began to ask questions—about my job, my family, my beliefs.

I told him that I was Jewish, though not religious, and that, in truth, I was an atheist.

At the word "atheist," Mr. Balotă's face tightened. The warmth vanished from his expression. He raised a hand gently, cutting me off.

"You've said you're a Jew, and I have no objection to that," he began, his voice steady. "Even if you told me you wanted to take Vali to Palestine, I would not stand in your way. But my daughter is a religious girl—and I will not give her to an atheist."

He stepped forward, calmly but firmly.

"With that said, please leave my house. There is nothing more for us to discuss."

He came forward to take me closer to the door.

III

I don't know what really happened after I left Mr. Balotă's house, but the next day —following the civil marriage ceremony of Otilia and Mihai Manea at City Hall—Vali and I met at Gara de Nord and boarded the train for Făgăraşi. It was a small picturesque city nestled in the heart of Romania's mountains.

When we arrived, Otilia's large family embraced us with warmth and joy. They had gathered for another wedding, this time of her cousin from the area. I remember the endless hospitality, the long nuptial table set for over thirty guests, and the joyful atmosphere that surrounded both newlyweds and visitors alike. I especially remember Mihai, who taught me how to sing along with him during the religious service. But above all, I remember Mother Victoriţa, Otilia's mother, who had a special fondness for me and sincerely wished to see Vali as my wife.

From Făgăraşi we traveled to Hărseni, a nearby village where Otilia's grandmother lived. We were given the large rooms in the guest house; with soft feather beds covered in thick wool blankets. At night, we kept the door between our rooms open so we could talk and laugh late into the evening. Behind the house was a beautiful apple orchard, its ripe fruit perfuming the air. We found one tree whose apples were so fragrant they made us giddy. We returned to it often, drawn in by its magical taste and scent.

There we began to plan our next adventure—an excursion into the Făgăraşi Mountains. But first, Mihai proposed a three-day training hike along the path used by local lumber cutters. We packed light: some canned food, changes of clothes, and a military-style water flask borrowed from our hosts. The girls carried wicker baskets to collect blackberries, and before we left, we filled them with apples from the orchard for snacking on the trail.

Laughter came easily. We swapped stories and jokes, and time flowed unnoticed, like the small mountain stream running beside our path. Otilia and Mihai were radiant in their honeymoon bliss. And Vali and I, too, began to discover new facets of each other—quirks and traits that made our connection even deeper.

On the way, Mihai described their engagement: they had known each other since childhood, but only in recent years had their friendship turned into something different. During a spring visit to Mihai's sister in Târgovişte, while the entire family sat around the table, a beautiful cake was brought out. Mihai and Otilia sliced it together and, in that moment, they became engaged with everyone's blessing.

Inspired by Mihai' story, I picked up Vali's basket of apples and, with a smile, offered one to everyone:

"Hello, kids! Eat and enjoy this apple! For this is my engagement to Vali!"

From that day on, until this moment, every year on August 15, we have celebrated our "Apple Engagement."

That vacation in Făgăraşi had a miraculous effect. Until then, I had known Vali as a serious young woman with a strong character. But here, in the wild embrace of nature, she blossomed like a child at play—enchanted by trees, birds, and flowers. Her joy was pure and contagious: she marveled at the beauty of the mornings, the chirping birds, the squirrels darting up tree trunks, and the red-spotted mushrooms on our path. She delighted in every sunbeam, every dew-speckled blade of grass, every ladybug that wandered across her hand as we lay resting. After three weeks together in the mountains, we returned home completely in love and set our wedding for December.

Never I had before felt such purpose as it grew on me coming back from Făgăraşi. I was ready to overcome any obstacle, discovering a reserve of strength and energy in myself that I didn't know existed. Not only me, but everyone saw that I was no longer the same. I was determined.

We knew we'd need a place to live, furnishings, wedding rings, a comforter—so many things. I stopped giving my salary to Mother, as I'd always done. Vali had only a modest scholarship, which she shared with her younger sister Zica. But fortune favoured us: their friend Cici had just bought a new stove and let us buy the old one in instalments. One Sunday, Vali and I went to the *Talcioc* flea market and bought some old gold to have our wedding rings made. Her mother gave us enough wool to sew two beautiful comforters. It all felt miraculous—how much we managed to accomplish with so little in such a short time.

We applied for a marriage licence at City Hall on Brezoianu Street. We chose Christmas Day, a Wednesday that year. Under the Communist regime, it was just a normal working day like any other. That night, snow fell in thick, soft flakes, blanketing the city in white. Vali dreamed of having white calla lilies in her bouquet, so we made our way to the flower shop in Piaţa Romană, reputed to be the best in the city. The streetcars were moving slowly, pushing snowploughs to clear the tracks. Snow gathered on our shoulders, and we took it as a sign—perhaps a blessing—for a marriage filled with abundance.

We got off streetcar at closer point to flower shop, and walked through the wet snow, but arrived to early. When finally, someone opened, they had no callas. We bought a bouquet of white carnations instead and rushed to City Hall, where our guests were already waiting for us at the door.

There were many friends, colleagues, and loved ones. Vali's siblings were there, and Simona came alone. But our parents didn't come. We knew they disapproved of our marriage. After returning from Făgăraşi, I'd faced daily opposition from them. Now, with our wedding finally here, their absence still hurt. I had hoped for understanding.

When I signed the marriage register, I scanned the room one last time, hoping to see them. Simona shook her head—they weren't there. The ceremony ended, with many hugs, kisses, and congratulations.

And then, they entered.

My parents stepped into the hall.

Tears filled my eyes. Their presence—though late—felt like the first true sign of acceptance. That moment meant more than words. Most of our guests returned to work afterward, as it was still a regular workday. Father had to go as well. Mother stayed with Vali and me, and we spent the rest of that snowy Christmas afternoon talking about the wedding.

IV

The weddings party was announced for January 1, 1962. Father designed and printed elegant invitations, which we mailed to friends and relatives. Mother prepared an abundance of pastries—different shapes and flavours—alongside bowls of fresh fruit and other sweets. Our house was full of people. Vali wore the same wedding dress and veil Simona used earlier, photos were taken, the girls began singing in our honour, and the boys—me included—joined in with the song Mihai had taught me in Făgăraşi.

Simona and Jack arrived later. Simona warmly embraced friends she knew from the Adventist Church at the street corner. There she met her schoolmate from Doamna Stanca, Clea Mânzăţeanu, now engaged to Costel Tolici, another member of the congregation. Jack entered with a cold "good evening." When I tried to introduce him to everyone, he declined:

"But I know all of them."

The air grew tense; I felt especially uncomfortable.

To my surprise, Mr. Balotă, Vali's father, came to the gathering, accompanied by her mother, Ecaterina, and her youngest brother, Rică. The rest of her family was already present. For the first time, our parents met. Mr. Balotă handed me an envelope with 1,500 lei as a wedding gift—an unexpected gesture that touched me deeply.

But Vali and I were, in truth, still without a home, living separately. After the wedding, we continued our daily walks from her school, ending at my parents' house where Mother prepared dinner—always with meat, knowing it was forbidden in Vali's home. Years before, Mr. Balotă had decided the family must live as vegetarians. Except for Camelia, the youngest sister, all the children loved meat and happily ate it anywhere else they were served with. After dinner, I would walk Vali home, and we'd stand talking under the lamp post near her gate until late into the night.

One night in late January, after returning from the opera, we were eating dinner in the kitchen as usual when Mother, using her most commanding tone, stopped Vali from leaving. Taking her gently by the hand, she opened the door to their bedroom and said:

"From now on, you'll live here with us."

My parents had decided to offer us their room. The existing arrangement was no longer workable. Father often worked nights, and Mother was content to sleep on my old extendable sofa in the dining room. It was a sacrifice, offered with love.

After finishing her schooling, Vali began working in the Emergency Room at Spitalul de Urgență in Bucharest. One summer evening, an elderly woman was brought in by her neighbours. Her condition was critical, and despite efforts, she passed away. Her neighbours still being there in the waiting room, told Vali that the woman had no family and had lived alone in a shared apartment on Sevastopol Street, just across from the old cemetery. I remembered that street well—from my youth when I used to attend the *Ha'Shomer Ha'Tzair* Zionist Club.

Later that evening, when I came to take Vali home, she told me about the woman and said she wanted to see the apartment. Encouraged by curiosity, we went. From the courtyard, we saw a light inside and forgotten that was late, just one hour before midnight, we knocked the door. An older man in his sixties and his much younger wife greeted us warmly. Learning we were newly married, only eight month after weeding and no place to live, they let us in and showed us the room where the old woman had lived. They told us they didn't want just anyone to move in—they wanted us. And they kept their word. When a housing inspector tried to reassign the room to others, the couple refused entry, even when threatened with the police. In the end, the apartment became ours.

Their names were Mr. Ştefan Koziac and Madam Irina. Married for many years, with no children of their own, they embraced us like family. Their home became our home. Their presence brought joy, mentorship, and a sense of rootedness we hadn't known before.

The house itself was old, built originally for an upper-class family. The basement apartment had been designed for servants. The upper four rooms, with a curved staircase leading up to a glassed-in veranda and the main entrance into a large room, probably for the dinning propose. To the left was the Koziacs' bedroom. To the right, the kitchen, and beyond that, a second bedroom—ours. We brought in my old sofa bed from my parents' home and the gas stove we had bought from Vali's friend Cici. For a year or more, we saved every penny to buy proper furniture. In the meantime, the Koziacs let us use their kitchen table and chairs, encouraged us to have guests, and offered wise counsel like loving parents.

We adored them. We still do. When cancer took them both too soon, we wept and never forgot those eight years of common living together.

Both of our children were born in that apartment on 20 Sevastopol Street: our son Marius, in June 1966, and our daughter Anca (Ancuţa), in November 1967. By the end of 1968, the state—desperate to ease the housing crisis—offered new condominiums for sale. Though modest, these apartments were quickly nicknamed "millionaire homes" for their scaring prices, fore buying one outright seemed impossible for most. In 1969, with two small children sharing a bedroom, we decided to take the leap. We bought a new apartment in one of the prefabricated buildings on Şulea Boulevard.

One quiet evening at the hospital, just before we moved, a colleague of Vali's, a believer in reading the future on a Turkish coffee grounds, looked into her empty cup and said something unexpected:

"You won't live in that new apartment for long."

"How can that be?" Vali laughed. "You buy a house to live in it your whole life."

"Maybe so," her colleague replied. "But you'll have many houses. You'll travel, see the world—and you won't stay there long."

Vali laughed again and forgot the whole exchange. I did not.

"

V

One day, Mr. Balotă showed up at my parents home door and before letting Father salute him, he said from the doorstep, loud enough for the street to hear his problem:

"Mister, you're a criminal! It's true! Why don't you go to Palestine?"

Father quickly brought him inside and shut the door. Words like that weren't meant to be shouted outdoors. Calmly, he asked what had prompted such a statement.

"Don't you see? If you go to Palestine, the children will

follow—and that way, we can leave too. What are you waiting for? What do you have here? This?" he said, waving his hand dismissively around the house. "Go! Don't wait any longer!"

When he saw that Father wouldn't budge, Mr. Balotă turned to me.

But I had never considered leaving my country. If I'd had any intention of emigrating, I wouldn't have married a Christian woman. I knew that in Israel, children were considered Jewish only if the mother was Jewish. My children would not be seen as Jews there—and I didn't want them to endure the same hardship I had experienced growing up as a Jew in a Christian country.

More than that, I loved my country. I was proud of it. I saw myself as part of it—rooted, committed, hopeful for its future. No one could make me feel otherwise. If I'd planned to leave, would I have taken out a mortgage for this new apartment—a commitment that chained my freedom for twenty-five years? So, my answer to Mr. Balotă was simple: "No."

We moved into our new apartment late that fall, on a rainy day. Despite the mud and the unfinished roads, we were happy. The apartment was warm, thanks to the heating line from the Vitan thermal plant, and the space was clean, comfortable, and bright. To help pay the mortgage, we rented out one bedroom to a young couple. I also took on a private job for Valeria's uncle in Constanţa, who commissioned me to draw plans for an automated bottle-washing machine identical to one he already used at his winery.

At that time, I was working as a technologist at *Uzinele Semănătoarea*—an Agricultural Machine Plant—where I was responsible for adapting foreign documentation to Romanian standards, materials, and technologies. My private project advanced slowly. Every evening, I worked late into the night at my drafting board, trying to find the most economical solutions to make the machine workable. for manufacturing the machine.

After nearly four months of work, I completed the project, carefully packed the ink-traced drawings, and travelled to Constanța to deliver the documentation. I was supposed to receive 10,000 lei—equivalent to an entire year's salary. But Vali's uncle refused:

"I want the machine, not the papers," he said.

I reminded him that it was impossible for anyone to build such a complex machine without precise, technical drawings. Besides, our agreement had been to provide documentation, not the machine. Manufacturing the machine would require over a ton of materials—resources that could only be obtained with ministerial approval under the rigid Five-Year Plan system. Without a powerful political connection, such approvals were out of reach.

"Here," he said, "take these demijohns of good wine. Bring them to your big boss, and you'll see—everything will get done."

That was where my tolerance ended.

"Why don't you take them to him?'

"Because this why I pay you!" he answered.

I refused the bribe and told him.

"I wouldn't be part of any dishonest dealings."

"Your call. No machine, no money!"

"You're a thief. I'm ashamed to be related to you!"

I returned home bitter, feeling as if I'd been robbed on a lonely road. That night, something broke in me. I began to think—perhaps for the first time with real seriousness—that it was no longer possible to live decently in this country. I had tried. But everywhere I turned, I found closed doors.

Overtime hours were no longer paid, still target dates required many overtime hours, sometime nights. Side jobs with other companies were banned. All outside collaborations were shut down. Salaries were dismal. Promotions were handed out by Party officials, not based on merit, but on obedience and nepotism. Loyalty was rewarded, not talent.

I began to feel that emigration—something I had long resisted—might now be the only path left to us.

My cousin Cuţa and Aunt Luţi, with whom I'd had only

sporadic contact, had grown fond of Vali. Our relationship improved after I married. Cuţa had married a road engineer, but their differences soon led to divorce. Her father, Uncle Mark, had passed long ago. After the separation, she and her mother decided to emigrate to Israel. A year later, Cuţa returned for a visit, telling stories that were hard to believe. The living conditions in Israel, freedom, dignity and opportunities they enjoy there has no comparation with our life here.

Other friends who'd travelled to Israel also came back with glowing accounts of what they'd seen. Even my mother, whose entire family in Bulgaria had relocated to Israel after the war, went to see them again. She and Father went there for a six-month visit.

That winter, after they returned, they stayed with us in our new apartment. It was hard for them to readjust to the Romanian routine—hours spent in lines, constant shortages, daily hardship. Each night, they'd share more stories from their trip. I could hardly believe it: How could such a young country, built on desert sand and constantly threatened by war, manage to be so prosperous? And why was Romania—rich in land, culture, and tradition—still struggling, decades after the war?

After Constanţa, the decision formed clearly in my mind. Emigration was no longer an abstract idea—it was the only solution. The next night, I shared my thoughts with Vali. She jumped out of bed as if touched by fire.

"How can you even think of leaving?" she cried. "To abandon my family, my friends, my job—for a place where we don't know what might happen? No! Never!"

I tried to reason with her calmly, but she was resolute and upset. For days, the subject remained closed. But slowly, perhaps with the help of friends or coworkers, she softened. Eventually, she agreed to apply for emigration—as long as I never asked her to convert to Judaism.

Less than six months after we submitted our application, I received a call from Father at work. At my request, parents agreed to go with us in Israel, to take care of children when we'll be working. Now I heard him saying:

"They have approved our file! We have to apply now for passports!"

The news struck me like lightning. My legs gave out, and I had to sit down. I knew, in that instant, that everything would change. A storm was coming—one that would turn our lives upside down.

I would be expelled from the Communist Party, where I was still a member. We would likely lose our jobs. We'd have to sell our home quickly, get rid of all our belongings, and go through the painful farewells to friends and family. There would be the exhausting bureaucracy of travel permits and passports, packing, and finally, the journey. We'll have to face the uncertainty of going with two small children to a land of strangers, with unknown language, and an undefined future.

The fortune teller first prediction at hospital had been right. Vali's coffee cup had foretold that she wouldn't stay long in our new home.

On January 4, 1972, we left Romania for good. Family, friends, and many colleagues came to Otopeni Airport that cold winter day to say goodbye. Many had taken time off work just to be with us for that final farewell.

Chapter 2
New Horizons

I

We lived in Israel for two and a half years. After several months studying Hebrew at an *ulpan*—a language school for newcomers—in Ma'alot, a northern city near the Lebanese border, we knew enough *Ivrit* (modern Hebrew) to begin looking for our own place to live and work.

Before we left the *ulpan*, Vali applied for a nursing position at Tel HaShomer Hospital in Tel Aviv, while I was hired at Ha'Argaz, a major bus and transport equipment manufacturer. Soon after, we were assigned a beautiful, brand-new apartment in Kiryat Ono, a suburb of Tel Aviv. Before the end of our first year, we had managed to buy a new car, thanks to a combination of savings and a loan from my father.

My parents had moved into a seniors' residence in Herzliya, where they received a cozy bachelor apartment just a few steps from the sea. Our own apartment came with the expectation that we would purchase it within three years. I still remember signing the purchase agreement about the prediction of the fortune teller who once read Vali's coffee grounds:

"You'll have many houses."

In just one year in Israel, we had achieved more than my parents had accomplished in an entire lifetime. And yet, peace eluded us.

Only days after our arrival, a Japanese terrorist entered the arrivals terminal at Lod Airport with a machine gun hidden under his coat and opened fire, killing many innocent people. A few months later, after we had left the *ulpan*, terrorists attacked a school in Ma'alot during the day, killing several children.

Public life in Israel carried a constant undertone of danger. At shopping centres, government offices, and even movie theatres, bags and packages were thoroughly searched before entry. On buses, the radio would broadcast the *Hadashot,* (news) every half hour, and passengers would fall silent to listen.

At her hospital, Vali saw firsthand the effects of these attacks—daily, relentless, devastating. She could never fully adapt to the tension. She was frightened for the children, for herself, for all of us. She insisted to go somewhere else.

The biggest dilemma for me was my parents. I had insisted they come to Israel with us, to help rising our children while we had to work. Now, living in separate cities, we eventually managed without their help. I seen them happy settled in Herzliya, surrounded by Mother's extended family and new friends from the residence. Still, the idea of leaving them alone behind did not feel right to me if we chose to emigrate again. After all they had done for us, how could I abandon them?

About a year after we'd settled into our apartment, my father-in-law, Mr. Balotă, came to visit. Unlike our other guests, which included Valeria's sisters and mine, he had no interest in sightseeing. While we typically arranged tours to Jerusalem, Bethlehem, Haifa, Nazareth, and the northern hills, all he wanted was help filing papers for political asylum. He didn't want to return to Romania. He hoped to stay in Israel—or emigrate elsewhere in the West.

We brought him to Jerusalem to a centre that helped emigrants and asked if they could support his request. They advised that he travel to Greece and apply for asylum there. Not long after, we received a letter from him: he had arrived safely in Athens and was now in a refugee camp in Lavrion, waiting to be accepted by another country. He told us not to worry—he was well fed, in good living conditions, and hopeful.

In March 1973, Simona and her daughter Adina came to visit us. Simona had recently undergone successful heart surgery at Fundeni Hospital and had recovered fully. She looked radiant. We travelled together throughout Israel, and she kept repeating how this was her best vacation ever.

But things were not well at home. After Adina's birth, because they were living in a cramped attic apartment with just one bedroom and her heart problems, Simona had been placed on a priority list for state housing. Jack, her husband, convinced her to move in with his parents into a larger, four-room apartment. She had never expected that this arrangement would bring such trouble.

Her mother-in-law, always home, gradually took control over the entire household. She intervened in every disagreement between Simona and Jack, dictated how Adina should be raised, and imposed her will on daily life. Simona found herself completely sidelined—excluded from decisions, isolated in her own home, without a voice in her own family. As her visit with us came closer to end, Simona told us:

"You know, I think I should try to convince Jack to come here, to Israel. I must talk to him about this. It will solve all problems."

One evening she called Jack and asked him to promise they'd apply for emigration to Israel as soon as she returned home. He refused, telling her not to think of such things. In tears, Simona told him:

"Be careful Jack; I cannot live anymore together with your parents. Understand? You better promise me now that we'll apply for immigration, otherwise I'm not coming home. It's up to you."

"Stay there! I don't care!" and he shut off the phone.

Simona enrolled in an *ulpan* in Nahariya, a small town in the north. We visited her and Adina often. With us came Cuţa, her new husband Shlomo—whom she had married in Israel—and their friend Buţu, a watchmaker from Tel Aviv.

Buţu was a quiet, gentle man in his forties, never married, with a lovely apartment in Bat Yam near the beach. He began courting Simona. For a woman with a five-year-old daughter, no possessions except the clothes on their backs, and no financial safety net, marriage to him soon seemed like the only path to stability.

After she finalized her divorce from Jack, Simona married Buţu and moved into his apartment. She was hired by one of the biggest banks in Tel Aviv, and Adina began kindergarten. We were all happy—truly happy—to see how life had turned for the better, how against the odds, her courage had led her to a new beginning. But she still suffered being separated from her first love, Jack.

II

Vali started to threaten that she would take her children and leave on her own if I continued to resist the idea of moving to another country One of her close friends from Germany, with whom she had been corresponding regularly, invited her to come live there. I tried to understand her position—I truly wanted to find the best solution for our family—but the thought of emigrating again, just when we had adjusted to life in Israel and secured good jobs, was daunting.

"Look around," I told her. "Millions of people have come here and gotten used to the war and the terror. Why can't we?"

"Because I can't. I'm depressed. Every night at hospital you don't see these young broken soldiers who cries in their sleep. I don't Marius or Anca become one of them. And I'm so tired. Coming home in the morning, take care of children, bring them to school, cook, housework, never finish. It's to much."

"Were would we go, nothing will change. We have to work different shifts until kids grow."

"I know, but there are not terrorists, no wars, no fear!"

Our conversations were brief, tense and in the little time we had together, our discussions often turned into arguments. Many of our friends—especially those in mixed marriages like ours—sided with Vali and supported her desire to leave.

But the decisive moment came with the Yom Kippur War of 1973. Surrounded on all fronts by hostile armies, with the Egyptian forces pushing through the Sinai Peninsula, I was overwhelmed by the return of old fears—the chilling sounds of sirens, the memories of hiding during wartime in Bucharest 1944. We were forced to bring our children into the shelter beneath the building, door locked and trying to keep them calm hiding our own fear.

One morning in March 1974, while working at my drafting table, I listened to Golda Meir's speech from Nahariya during a military memorial. She mentioned that over 1,500 Israeli soldiers had been killed in this war. For a country as small as Israel, the loss of those young soldiers was enormous and hurt everyone.

As I listened, my heart ached for the parents of those young men. They were heroes—not aggressors, not instigators of war— but boys thrust into battle in a fight as unbalanced as that between David and Goliath. They paid with their lives.

And what could console the poor parents of these children? Hadn't they already seen this kind of loss in the Six-Day War of 1967? Back then, those same boys buried today were just as old as my children now. They had grown up only to die as martyrs. I could not help but think: if their parents had chosen to leave Israel after that war, maybe those children would still be alive.

The thought seized me. I had to protect my children. I stood up unable to work any longer, walked out of the office, went home, and said to Vali, simply and sincerely:

"I'm ready to leave."

In our family, we had always tried to shield Mother from bad news. She tended to magnify problems and spiral into panic, and we had long learned to speak to Father first in difficult situations. He had always been more rational, wise, and quietly supportive—even helping us with extra money when we needed it.

But now, with Mother suffering from heart issues and advancing arthritis that was beginning to deform her hands, she had become more sensitive and irritable. We wanted to avoid distressing her, so I pulled Father aside one day, and told him our plans. He already knew Vali was unhappy in Israel and longed to leave. But when I told him that we had already submitted our application to immigrate to Canada, it was as if a bomb had dropped. He fell silent. His expression collapsed. He could not find a single word.

In the night before Rosh Hashanah, we gathered in Buțu's house to say farewell to everyone. Next day, we were to leave Israel and this was a last chance to be together. After dinner, Father quietly slipped away without telling anyone where he was going. When we realized he was missing, we searched for him but could not be found. It was late. The children were tired, and our packing wasn't finished. We asked the family not to come with us to the airport.

"It's better to say goodbye here, quietly," we said. "There's no need for a scene at the airport."

The truth was, we didn't want to draw attention to ourselves. If the authorities found out we were leaving the country for good, they might have tried to stop us.

Still, Father had not returned. I went out into the street to look for him. I finally found him at the far end of the block, hiding in the shadows, weeping like a child. He could barely speak. He refused to come back with me. I had to gently lead him back to the courtyard where the rest of the family waited.

Mother, to our surprise, was the one who helped calm him. She understood and supported Vali's reasons. And in that moment, I saw something clearly: for all our efforts to protect her, it was Mother who was the strongest among us. Despite our past miscommunications, she had an intuitive strength—an unspoken intelligence that allowed her to perceive even the things we tried to hide from her.

III

The same organization which helped Mr. Balotă, advised us to go to Greece and ask for refugee status. Of the eight months we spent in Greece, seven were spent with Mr. Balotă in the same refugee camp.

My father-in-law was not the easiest man to be around. He

had an uncanny ability to ask personal questions without seeming intrusive, but he never forgot a word you said—and often, when you least expected it, he would use that information against you. Not out of malice, perhaps. His heart was truly generous—he would give the coat off his back to someone in need.

Even during his modest retirement in Western Europe, living on a small social pension and knowing that Romanians were not allowed to bring money abroad, he welcomed them into his apartment and never let anyone leave empty-handed. Guests always received a meal, a gift, or some money for the road. After the fall of Ceaușescu's dictatorship, he donated his hard-earned savings to the Adventist Church in his hometown of Buzău, for computers, radios, and other equipment they needed. Few people realized that this humble, frugal man was behind such generosity. It was his way of thanking God for the love and protection shown to him and his family. Yet despite his faith and Christian outlook, he could not bear to be contradicted. When opposed, he would retaliate and use the very confidential information you had once trusted him with.

Although he rarely took advice from others, there were a few individuals whose opinions he valued deeply. His relationship with these people seemed to shape how he related to everyone else. At the Adventist Church in Grant, which he attended regularly with his family, he became increasingly critical of the youth and those who worked on Shabbat. His reproaches were so sharp and constant that, in time, many churchgoers began to avoid him.

His wife, Mrs. Balotă, was his complete opposite. —gentle as an angel, full of understanding and self-sacrifice. She could solve any problem with her pure gift of a few words. Her calming presence could soften the sting of his outbursts and restore peace. She was the one the children turned to for guidance, the one who shaped their characters and taught them the values of truth, love, and hard work. Her warmth and goodness more than compensated for his severity. She became the role model that her daughters later emulated as wives and mothers.

When my father-in-law had a task to finish a job, he always relied on his wife. She would oversee the workers, answer their questions, care for the children, and manage everything in his absence. And she never complained—not about being left alone with five children and a house full of strangers to feed, not about the looming winter or the kids needing clothes for school, and not for anything else. No one ever heard her utter a harsh word. I'm certain that it was her understanding and grace that made my marriage to Vali possible.

In Greece, our application for refugee status was submitted on political grounds—since we had left Romania, and Israel was the only country Romanians were officially permitted to emigrate to. While waiting for our case to be processed, we lived in a small hotel room in Athens for the first three weeks. After that, we've been moved into the Lavrion refugee camp. Our room there was on the first floor, just down the hall from

Mr. Balotă. The building resembled a two-storey military barracks, with a central concrete staircase and two shared bathrooms facing it—one for women, one for men.

For our children Marius and Ancuţa, their grandfather became a delightful playmate. If it hadn't been for those months in the camp, they might never have come to know him so closely. I might say the same about myself. Until then, I never had enough time to really talk to my own children, to play with them, to know them as I did in Greece. Those eight months gave us a chance to reconnect, to heal cracks that had begun to form in our relationship, and to restore the trust and love that held our family together.

One of our favourite pastimes was *Ţintar* (Target), a traditional folk game played by drawing three squares inside one another and using nine pea seeds and nine beans—or any small objects as markers. Marius and Ancuţa became skilled players, and their grandfather proudly paraded them around the camp, challenging adults to games they rarely won.

But the harmony didn't last.

The camp was filled with many people, mostly Romanians, and there were a few families like ours, some of whom had a brief experience in Israel. Every family had its own room, and we met them occasionally in the corridor, at the bathroom, or in the kitchen when we would go to receive our food and bring it home to eat.

There was a dining room used mostly by the single people. In short period of time, we'd start talking more with each other, became friends, and sometimes we would take a walk in the city together, when the sun was setting behind the port's seawater.

Mr. Balotă, who had been there long before us, began to "advise" us on whom to befriend and whom to avoid. But it was impossible to obey his instructions all the time. If someone showed us kindness, how could we turn our backs on them?

If he came to visit and saw someone of these discredited people, he would at once walk out and slam the door behind him. If such a person arrived while he was already with us, he would demonstratively get up and leave. Eventually, he warned us that if we didn't sever contact with certain families, he would stop visiting us altogether. And so, he did. For weeks, he refused to step inside our room. He avoided us in the camp, refused to greet us, and ignored our children.

One morning, it came to a head. He intercepted me in the corridor outside the bathroom and, furious, accused me of keeping him from seeing his grandchildren and daughter. He threatened to "break my head," pushed me, and kept grabbing at me. I tried to pull away, but the confrontation quickly escalated to fight. I received punches I could not avoid to defeat and he got hold of my hand to fiercely bite. Shouts drew a few people, who stepped in to break up the fight. That ended any contact between us.

Even when our papers were approved and we were ready to leave Greece, and friends and neighbours came to the bus to see us off, Mr. Balotă never left his room.

In the end, it was Vali and I who sent the children to say goodbye to him.

IV

On May 25, 1975, we arrived in Toronto after spending eight months in Greece waiting for our immigration papers. During the next five months, we were enrolled in intensive English-language courses, while the children were placed in school classes appropriate to their age.

Finding work in our professions, however, proved much harder. Language was certainly a barrier, but the real obstacle was our lack of "Canadian experience." My first job was in the maintenance department at a Ramada Inn. Every morning, I swept the area around the main entrance. The sight of myself with a broom in hand, sweeping the pavement, brought tears to my eyes. I felt a wave of shame and discouragement in those early days. Vali found a job in a jewelry factory, where she polished tiny gold amulets, pendants, and earrings with an electric machine that often burned her fingers holding the little objects.

We lived in a modest two-bedroom high-rise apartment, and with the help of our savings from Israel supplementing our wages, we managed to cover the bills, buy some furniture on installment, and enjoy the deep comfort of peaceful days. With our very first earnings, we rushed out to buy a Polaroid camera. We sent fresh photographs with every letter to our parents, family, and friends—to show them that we were well, and that they needn't worry about us.

About six months after we left Greece, Mr. Balotă was granted refugee status by Switzerland and chose to settle in Bern. Once he was established there, he went to the Romanian Embassy to request, both in writing and in person, that his remaining family members in Romania be allowed to join him. When his appeals were ignored, he began a hunger strike in front of the embassy. The local authorities intervened and demanded he stop his protest. He eventually ended the strike after receiving vague assurances—which were never honored.

His next protest took place in front of the Swiss Parliament. This time, to ensure he wouldn't be removed by force, he chained himself to a lamppost. It worked. Eventually, the entire family was granted passports.

The first to arrive in Switzerland was my mother-in-law.

She was followed by Zica and her husband, Ion Moraru, who stayed for a two-week visit before returning home. Then came Camelia, Vali's youngest sister, along with her husband, Mihail Marin, and their daughter, Cătălina.

Camelia had secretly planned to stay in Switzerland but hadn't told her husband. Only after they arrived did she tell him that she had no intention of returning to Romania. At first, Marin claimed to feel the same, but when faced with the reality of staying, he panicked and tried to persuade her to come back with him. When she refused, he turned to the Romanian authorities for help. Under pressure from the Embassy, Mr. Balotă took Camelia and Cătălina out of the country and brought them to Austria, where she applied for refugee status. She was placed in a refugee camp, and a few months later, she joined us in Toronto. Marin had no other choice but to return to Romania alone.

The youngest brother, Rică, together with his wife, Nadia, and their son, Cosmin, followed a path similar to Camelia's.

Two and a half years after we arrived in Canada, our extended family began to take root in this new and welcoming land, each of us striving to succeed through hard work, perseverance, and dedication.

A year or so, after our arrival to Canada, my parents visited us. They returned several times in the years that followed, and each time they were more pleased with our progress and the children's development. Still, it was painful to look into their eyes every time we brought them back to the airport. There was always an unspoken question hanging between us: would this be the last time we saw each other? No matter how much we encouraged them to stay hopeful, nothing could truly soften the heartbreak of those goodbyes.

When they came to visit for the first time, they saw our spacious condo in the Don Mills area, set beside a small river that bordered a golf course. Despite continuing to work in unskilled, low-paid jobs, it was our determination and faith in the future that gave us the courage to purchase the apartment—though we had no money in savings. More than once, I was laid off and had to start all over again.

I enrolled in an evening course in mechanical drafting at a local college. I needed to master the English technical terminology and the imperial measuring system, which was so different from the metric system used in Europe. That course helped me land a job as a draftsman through an agency with a consulting contract. Six months later, I secured a position as a design assistant at Mid Point Manufacturing, a division of Magna International—the largest automotive parts manufacturer in North America. Before long, I was entrusted with all major technical responsibilities: concept development, design, and tooling. I remained there for twenty fruitful years, until the plant closed in 1997 and I retired.

Vali didn't have much better luck than I did with her early

jobs. In Romania, the role of *Medical Assistant* was one of the highest-qualified positions in healthcare—overseeing registered nurses and much of the auxiliary staff. Vali had been a Medical Assistant with emergency room experience, and in Israel she had qualified as a registered nurse. But here in Canada, her diplomas were not recognized.

The first major barrier was the Test of English as a Foreign Language (TOEFL). Without passing this rigorous exam, the College of Nurses would not validate any of her credentials. Until then, working in a hospital as a nurse was out of reach.

While preparing for the TOEFL, Vali took a job at Branson Hospital, sterilizing surgical instruments. Later, when a technician position opened in the electroencephalography unit, she applied. Her practical knowledge and strong qualifications spoke for themselves, and she was hired—working there for the next twelve years. Eventually, she passed the English exam and officially became a registered nurse in Canada.

In the summer of 1981, Simona, Adina, and Buțu came to visit us. We took them on a road trip through the East Coast of the United States—exploring New Hampshire, Vermont, and New York. It was a joyful reunion, filled with laughter, teasing, and late-night conversations. We travelled together in our 1976 Chevrolet Impala, and it wasn't surprising that at some point, speeding became an issue. I received a ticket, and Simona accompanied me to dispute it in court. We arrived a little early and found ourselves sitting alone on a bench outside the judge's chambers. For the first time in many years, it was just the two of us. We sat quietly, recalling memories—the good and the bad—and drifting back into the shared landscape of our childhood.

"It was such a beautiful childhood we had, Dorel," she said. "We had so much freedom—playing outside in the middle of the street, inventing our games, making friends. No one was hovering over us. No schedules, no constraints. Nothing like the routine I'm expected to apply around my daughter's rules now. Why has the world changed so much—and so fast?"

"Maybe because you're raising a child in Israel?" I suggested.

"No," she replied. "It was the same back in Romania."

"Same thing here," I admitted.

I didn't know then that this would be the last time we would share together a meaningful conversation between just two of us.

The following spring, in 1982, we bought a house closer to our workplaces—in a quiet suburban new development on the northern edge of the city. I told Vali that, as much as I tried to ignore the fortune teller's prediction from years ago in Romania, I couldn't help but notice how many of her visions had come true, as if pieces of a puzzle were falling perfectly into place.

That summer, during the children's vacation, we took them to Florida to visit Disney World for the first time. It was a magical experience. We were captivated by the themed parks, the creativity, the atmosphere—and most of all, the joy it brought the children. We returned from that trip enchanted, not before, we purchased a one-week timeshare in a resort just a mile from the Magic Kingdom. This investment allowed us to exchange time with other resorts across the world. From that moment on, our vacations became real adventures. With modest salaries and careful planning, we managed to visit nearly all the major cities of Europe.

Later, as our curiosity and wanderlust grew, we embarked on our first ocean cruise. Traveling by sea opened new horizons—we visited art museums, ancient ruins, and historic sites across the world: the Indies, Australia, Africa, and the Orient. We experienced different cultures, deepened our understanding of history, and found ourselves filled with an insatiable desire to see more.

And with that, the unbelievable prediction once read in a coffee cup so many decades ago had come to pass—entirely and completely fulfilled:

"You'll have many houses, you'll travel a lot, and you'll see the world."

Chapter 3
The Sunset

I

In the fall of 1982, Father wrote to me that Simona had been advised by a renowned specialist from Beilinson Hospital in Petah Tikva to undergo another open-heart surgery. Before I had a chance to contact her, I learned that the operation had already taken place. The doctor had received his honorarium in a white envelope just before leaving on vacation overseas, while Simona was slowly recovering in hospital.

A few weeks later, she was involved in a minor car accident while driving through Tel Aviv. The vehicle was repaired without issue and looked as good as new. Simona appeared unharmed, but soon afterward she was rushed back to the hospital. The newly implanted valve in her heart had begun to leak, and yet another operation was required. She never woke from that surgery. After spending a week in a coma, Simona passed away at the age of 45.

Father and Buțu stayed by her side day and night. Mother knew nothing about the surgery. After Simona was quietly buried in the Holon Cemetery, Father told her that Simona had gone to

America for better treatment and would need to stay there for some time. I flew to Israel, but everything happened so quickly that I didn't arrive in time to see Simona alive—or even to attend her funeral. I stayed in Bat Yam with Buțu and Adina. Father visited us daily, coaching me on what to say to Mother about my unexpected visit. She was not to find out about Simona's death. So, we shaved and dressed as usual, in defiance of Jewish mourning tradition, and tried to appear cheerful in her presence. It was heartbreaking for each of us—especially for Father.

Our greatest concern now was Adina. She was nearing thirteen, left without her mother, and living with a stepfather we barely knew. She was too young to be left on her own, yet too vulnerable to be entrusted to chance. The only reasonable solution was to bring her to Canada, where she would be surrounded by love, care, and stability. Vali, with her noble heart and motherly instinct, offered no objection. In our home, Adina would be raised as a sister to our children—and she would be safe.

Together with Adina and Father, I went to the Kolbo-Shalom Building in Tel Aviv to apply for Adina's passport. The offices were packed beyond imagination, and it took relentless effort just to reach a clerk's window. We waited for hours, elbow to elbow in the heat and noise, but we finally managed to submit the application. We had to present a legalized death certificate for Simona and a signed statement from Buțu, confirming that he did not object to Adina leaving the country.

After a week of persistent effort, interviews, pleading, and endless lines—through which Father, as always, was instrumental—we finally obtained Adina's passport. All that remained was a simple visitor visa from the Canadian Consulate and a plane ticket.

Here what I did wrong: Adina and I went directly to the consulate, full of confidence. I felt as though I was returning to my own family where I'll find sympathy for our ordeal. I explained everything: that Adina was alone, an orphan, and in Canada she would be given the same care and love as our own children.

The officer listened politely without interruption, asked me to wait for a moment, and then invited me into the office of a superior. With genuine regret in his voice, he explained that they could not issue a visa under these circumstances. The only viable path would be for me to return to Canada alone and file adoption papers from there.

I could not believe this. If I would have asked just for a visitor visa, I think it would be granted without problems. But confessing Adina's true situation, opened a problem related to emigration that must be resolved in Canada. The lesson learned reminded me an old Romanian proverb: "to much talk, let you broke"

Before returning home, I needed to arrange two things.

Adina asked for her mother's grave to be covered with a marble plate carved in the shape of an open book, with Simona's name engraved inside. I made the sketch and placed the order. Buțu, who had been going to synagogue with me twice daily to pray, insisted on paying for it. He never remarried.

The second arrangement was to enroll Adina in a kibbutz, where she could live, study, and work with girls her age, under the guidance of teachers and family members who formed the kibbutz community. The healthy environment, the sense of collective responsibility, and the supervised independence offered a kind of structure and security we hoped would help her heal.

Back in Canada, I began gathering the adoption papers immediately. But I was told that adoptions were only possible before the child turned thirteen—and I had about a month to work on it. The most urgent requirement was her biological father's written consent. I wrote to Jack, explaining the situation and pleading with him to act quickly. I never received a reply.

I later learned that his mother had passed away. Jack and his father had since immigrated to Israel. He made some initial contact with Adina but left her to remain in the kibbutz. After completing his ulpan classes, he remarried a woman who had two adult children. Two years later, he divorced her, lost his father, and never managed to rebuild a real relationship with Adina. To her credit, Adina remained in close to him, and when he grew old and ill, she was the one who watched over him until the end.

But Adina was not left alone. Buțu, her stepfather, remained a constant figure in her life, as did Cuța, who showed such boundless love that she could be considered a second mother. My parents, especially Father, also stayed close to her, visiting often and always being there when needed.

Years passed, and still no one had told Mother the truth about Simona. On one visit to Canada, she asked me to take her to Simona's sanatorium. I claimed I was too busy with work. She said nothing, but the pain showed on her face. Next to her, Father sat in silence, staring at the ground. After nearly seven years, her younger sister, Aunt Shendy, could no longer keep the secret. One day she told her:

"What are you, stupid? Don't you see he's lying to you? Simona's been dead for seven years now. Seven years!"

Father never told me what happened after that, or how long it took to bring peace back between them. I never asked.

The last time I saw Mother was in the fall of 1985. Vali and I went to Israel and stayed with Cuța. Mother had been admitted to Kfar Saba Hospital. Father remained at her side almost constantly, only stepping away briefly to shower or tend to other urgent matters.

Vali and I sat with her, sharing the latest news about the

children. Marius was in his second year at Waterloo University, and Ancuţa was in her final year of high school. Mother, as always, was intellectually sharp—curious, perceptive, and alert. She made surprising connections, as if living inside every story we told, thousands of kilometres away.

But she had an unforgiving cancer she didn't know about. The doctors warned us gently not to hope for miracles.

Shortly after we returned home, in early December, we were told she had passed away. I returned to Israel once again, this time to be with Father, now alone. As with Simona, I arrived too late to attend the funeral.

The only consolation was that mother was buried beside Simona, the daughter she had grieved so deeply and silently for years. To know they were together—mother and daughter, forever reunited—was a balm to our sorrow.

II

I convinced Father to come with me to Toronto after Mother's death. He was always venerated by Vali and the children. Always warm, joyful, loving, and ready to help, he played with the children, told them stories, and remained a comforting presence—never intrusive, always kind. Everyone loved and appreciated him. Our friends, Vali's brothers and sisters, and all who met him enjoyed his company. Wherever he went, he left behind the impression of a gentle, unpretentious, and easygoing man. Each morning, Father and I went to the synagogue to pray. Unshaven and grey-haired, we looked so alike that many people who saw us together for the first time assumed we were brothers.

That January, for my birthday, Vali surprised me renting a video camera and filmed our first family movie. In that precious footage, I have images of my father toasting me on my fifty-second birthday—moments I now cherish. `

But in April, something changed. One of those unmistakable inner signals—passed down from his own mother—told Father that something wasn't right back home. He needed to return. Adina was nearing the end of high school at the kibbutz. As was customary in Israel, she was soon to begin her mandatory military service. During her time there, she met a persistent young man we had encountered on a previous visit. Neither of us was particularly impressed. There was nothing wrong with him—no major flaws, no visible faults—but he lacked ambition, initiative, the spark that hinted at something greater. He struck us as, "an unfinished symphony." But there was nothing to be done.

The following summer, Ancuţa and I travelled to Israel to attend Adina's wedding to Shuki. It was a beautiful celebration.

Buţu, Cuţa, and Shlomo were in high spirits, and the entire family gathered for the occasion. Adina looked radiant in her white dress, wearing a wide-brimmed hat and a veil that couldn't hide the joy shining from her eyes.

If there was a shadow over that day, it was the absence of the one person who should have led her to the chuppah: her father, Jack. In his place, my father accompanied her before the Rabbi. Simona had purchased a condominium apartment in Jaffa, and it became the couple's new home.

Adina had started working at the same bank where her mother had been employed, and in a short time, she earned a promotion to the same position Simona had once held.

After Mother's passing, Father continued to live in a senior residence in Herzliya called Beit Sirena. At eighty, he remained in good health, with a strong independent spirit that allowed him to live on his own terms. Following Simona's advice, Father had kept his savings in foreign currency to protect against inflation. This modest nest egg maintained its value over time and provided a small return.

At Beit Sirena, many of the single women took notice of him. During one of our phone conversations, Cuţa mentioned that Father had struck up a friendship with a lady doctor who lived there.

When Father later visited us in Canada, he told us that his lady friend insisted on coming together, but he won't admit it:

"What do you want to do there?"

"You took your wife there," she replied.

"True! But she was his mother. He had to take care of her!"

And with that, the matter was settled.

Still, he spoke fondly of her. She had two daughters, and they often went out together. When he decided it was time to return to Israel, he brought back presents for her and her daughters.

III

In the summer of 1989, I was able to exchange our time-share vacation for two resorts—one in Austria, at Salzbach near Zell am See, and the other in northern Italy, in Sestriere. I invited Father to come with us, and we synchronized our arrival in Zurich. With us came our 13-year-old niece Cătălina, the daughter of Vali's youngest sister, Camelia.

I believe this was one of the best vacations we ever had. Almost every day we drove the 90 kilometers distance to Salzburg, visited museums, and attended concerts. Each evening, we dined at one of the local taverns, where sizzling veal schnitzels filled the plates, beer flowed freely, and the music made us sway on the benches like palm trees in the wind. It was a joyful atmosphere, echoing the spirit of Oktoberfest with its Tyrolean tunes and dances. In the mornings, we woke to the smell of fresh bread, milk, and coffee—goodies that Father had brought back for us after walking two kilometers to the nearest dairy shop in town.

After two wonderful weeks, we stopped in Bern and booked a room at the National Hotel, right in the heart of the city. Bern had been home to Mr. Balotă, Vali's father, since 1975. At the hotel, we stayed in a large second-floor room with four beds. From our balcony, we could see the lively square below, the bustling Central Railway Station on Marktgasse, and the Parliament building rising behind the rooftops.

We awoke to sunshine, rested after the long drive from Chamonix the day before. There, we had taken a gondola up to Mont Blanc—a tour we couldn't miss. As always, Father was the first to rise. When he opened the door that morning, we saw Mr. Balotă waiting for us. While we were still in our beds, he sat at the foot of Cătălina's bed and watched us one by one head to the bathroom to wash and get dressed.

Wasting no time, Mr. Balotă took us to his home. The day flew by from morning until evening. It was already dark when we returned to the parking lot. Our rental car—used for the past three weeks—was due back the next morning at Zurich Airport.

For the first time, we met Silvia, Mr. Balotă's new wife. She was around his age, and they had married recently. My mother-in-law, Ecaterina, had passed away in Bern in 1983, worn down by a lifetime of demanding work and worry for her far-flung children.

Vali's Mother had visited Toronto once, with Mr. Balotă, but had to cut the trip short due to respiratory problems. Upon returning home, she was hospitalized and recovered briefly, but her chronic ailments proved irreversible. At her funeral, the children stood united in support of their father, who was devastated. Many came to pay their respects—especially the church community in Bern, who had admired her modesty and kindness.

More than a year later, we heard that Mr. Balotă had placed ads in a Romanian newspapers looking for a wife. He visited Canada briefly, but when he saw that his children disapproved, he returned to Switzerland. Eventually, he met Silvia, a former pharmacist and widow of an engineer. Her late husband's brother was the well-known Romanian playwright Nicolae Tăutu, author of the historical drama *Apus de Soare* (*The Setting Sun*).

Silvia was cultured and a lady in every sense of the word. She took care with her appearance, always dressed stylishly and with her hair done. But she had little experience managing a household. She didn't cook, couldn't iron a shirt, and seemed unfamiliar with where things were kept in her own kitchen. Vali had to prepare a meal for us because her stepmother didn't know where to find a pot or even a bottle of oil. This was such a stark contrast to her own mother, who had worked tirelessly until the very end—cooking, cleaning, sewing—never going to a hairdresser or buying anything nice for herself.

The next day in Zurich, we parted ways with Father. Parting is never easy, especially as the years go by and more people from one's generation begin to disappear. We never knew when, or if, we would meet again.

Still, I felt satisfied. For the first time, I had given my father a true vacation—one he had never experienced before. I hoped these memories would stay with him for a long time, though I couldn't have known that in less than two years, an even more joyful moment would come to surpass it.

IV

In December 1990, just around Christmas, we celebrated Ancuţa's engagement with Robert. They met at a Romanian wedding, where we had all been invited. Robert was the only child of a family from Cluj, and we were proud of Ancuţa's choice.

The engagement party was held in a small restaurant that

served Romanian food and featured traditional music. A Moldavian singer performed folk songs, and we danced late into the night. Father—like I had never seen him before—was radiant. He gave toasts, cracked jokes, and entertained everyone at the table. I can't recall a time when he was more joyful, and he never missed a chance to join the hora, dancing with the enthusiasm of a young man.

Sadly, Father didn't live to share in an even happier moment: Ancuţa and Robert's wedding. He passed away in January 1991, just months before the celebration that took place in August. It pains us still that God didn't grant him that final joy.

In one of first days of January, late one night, I received a phone call from Cuţa. She told me that Father had been admitted to the hospital. After the New Year, he had caught a cold and had begun to lose consciousness. She urged me to come right away.

The first thing next morning, I booked a flight for that afternoon. But while I was packing my suitcase, Cuţa called again. This time, her voice broke with sorrow: Father had passed away.

I was devastated.

I hadn't made it in time to see Simona or Mother before they passed, but I knew that my presence there was necessary to comfort the ones who endured such loss. It was my duty to support them through their pain.

But this time, it felt different.

Now, after losing Father, I had no one in need for support more than myself. It was I, that was left alone. It was I, who didn't know how to manage my pain. It was I in need to fill the void left in my soul after his death. The person for whom I cared the most, loved and admired, was gone.

Should I go there? For what?

Suddenly travelling there made no sense.

I cancelled my ticket and stayed home, with all my memories, bringing back the life of this wonderful man who was my father, my inspiration, my model.

I stayed on the floor in my living room for seven days, with all the pictures, photo albums and letters around me on the carpet to refresh my memories. I let the images speak to me—tiny paper windows that brought back the stories of our lives and the moments that had bound us together. Those quiet days gave me comfort. I cried. I laughed. I remembered. And I knew, from that moment on, that it was now my sacred duty to carry forward their stories, their love, their memory.

What do we owe to our parents for their struggle to bring us up, to instil in us their ideals of an honest living and offering their own lives as path for ours? What could we offer them in exchange for a life consumed by fighting, agitation, worry, shortcomings, and needs? What else than our unending gratitude, love, and respect for all they gave to us.

And our memory.

Through memory, we extend their lives beyond the grave, far beyond the inscription on a headstone or the annual candle lit in their honour.

As I write these words, I want to believe—and to hope—that these memories will live on in our children and grandchildren, long after we are gone, as a blueprint to comfort them through the years. That they will offer them courage to overcome the obstacles in their lives and teach them the one lesson that matter the most in life: love.

A FOGGY SUNRISE

Post-face

In this second part of memoir, I had originally planned to write only a brief epilogue, summarizing the facts and milestones that followed my Bar-Mitzvah. But as I began to write, I found those years overshadowed by profound and often dramatic realities—stories that demanded to be told.

I do not know why God chose me to report these stories etched as they are into the deepest part of my soul. I am fully aware that the events I describe are not unique. Thousands of others have lived through similar hardships and carry stories of their own. But I chose to write this for those who come after us—so they may know the truth of those times. And if Time, Geography, and Fate have gifted them with more peaceful lives, I hope these pages help them recognize how fortunate they are. Many of us—the older generations and those who came before—led very different lives. We lacked the freedoms and opportunities others might now take for granted.

Some of us arrived in the free world with wounds still open, both physical and emotional, from the countries we left behind. Romania was one such place. The war and the political upheavals of the 20th century upended not just the social fabric, but the entire economy, culture, religious life, and the simple human hope to improve one's condition in peace. Even now, more than a quarter-century since the fall of the last dictator, Nicolae Ceausescu, the scars of those regimes remain. Many Romanians continue to look for elsewhere the chances they are still denied at home. And yet, no one ever arrived in a new land to be greeted with flowers and cakes at the airport. Often, the price paid for a better life came late and through sorrowful events and sacrifice.

As for me, I was shaped with and without intention by every experience and every person I encountered along the way. I owe a great debt to all of them, for the lessons they taught me—each in their own time and place.

I know there are many whose kindness and support should have been acknowledged in these pages. To them, I offer my heartfelt apology. The limits of memory, time, and space have drawn this story to a close.

But the gratitude I feel toward them lives on, beyond these words.

David Kimel

Readers Reviews

Dear David Kimel,

Thank you for sharing **A Foggy Sunrise**, a beautiful nuanced and emotional resonant work that lingers in the heart long after the final page. From the very beginning, your prose carries a quiet weight, like morning mist that slowly lifts to reveal something both tender and true.

There is a poetic patience to the way you tell this story. You allow moments of breath, emotion to unfold naturally, and characters to speak not jut trough words but to their silences, their gestures, their longings. I felt as though I was witnessing the slow burn of awakening – whether personal, spiritual, or relational – and the fog you evoke isn't just weather; it's a metaphor, atmosphere, memory.

One of the things I admire most about your writing is you restrain. You trust your readers to sit with ambiguity, to search for meaning between the lines, and that trust pays off. The world you built feels intimate yet expansive, and your central themes – loss, hope, healing, identity – resonate with quiet power.

I also appreciate the delicate balance you struck between melancholy and light. Even in the heavier moments, there is a gentleness, a warmth, a hint of something brighter just on the horizon. It's this emotional contrast that makes **A Foggy Sunrise** feel so deeply human.

If I may offer a gentle suggestion, I would love to see you explore some of the secondary characters a bit more fully – there are hints of fascinating inner lives that I found myself to know more about. Even glimpses into their perspectives could add new layers to your already rich narrative.

David, you've crafted a meditative, graceful story that honors both complexity and beauty. **A Foggy Sunrise** is a reminder that clarity doesn't always come suddenly – it often arrives slowly, quietly, trough the mist. Thank you for guiding us through it.

With deep appreciation,

Alexis Stratton.

June 14, 2025

Writer David Kimel is a servant of the Resurrection — not of just one, but of all Resurrections. Dear readers will see for themselves how the departed loved ones come back to life, how the spirit of life returns to Simona and the others, how the old Grant neighbourhood of Bucharest and its entire quarter come alive again — with living people, with houses and gardens, and cemeteries left unchanged. How the kiosk owners, booksellers, and printers generously offer their time-honoured services. How the Stadium resounds with the roar of the matches, how the neighbourhood cinemas take note of the desperate cries of "Sound!" from viewers staring wide-eyed at the cowboys on the screen; how the apartment block on Eduard Grant fills the quarter with the music of César Franck from *Ruth* and *Rebecca*...

I was there too — in fact, I lived for decades in that Arcadia. I loved and suffered alongside Dorel. His testimonies are mine as well. Only the form of telling differs: Because only he could write with such beauty.

A Foggy Sunrise is a book full of originality in style, authenticity in content, and vitality in action. It is amusing and provocative. It has every chance of becoming a bestseller.

More than that, it lends itself beautifully to being adapted into a feature film — a historical period piece.

Mircea Valeriu Diaconescu

Germany, 2008

When I began reading **A Foggy Sunrise**, I could not have imagined it would turn out to be such a captivating read. The book is exceptionally enjoyable and equally engaging — combining all the qualities of a literary work that could easily be categorized as memoir, novel, or simply recollections. The memories, in fact, serve as a pretext for painting a broader social fresco of the interwar period leading up to the Second World War, continuing through the war years and into the early days of socialism in Romania.

The value and appeal of the text lie in the way this autobiographical journey through the various stages of a turbulent childhood is adorned with a tapestry of authentic events, described with a distinct charm that draws in the reader, awakens curiosity, and makes it hard to put the book down.

The epilogue — written in the same captivating style — inevitably leaves the reader wondering: *What happened in the six decades that followed that childhood?* And naturally, it suggests to the author the necessity of continuing with a second volume of this truly remarkable literary creation.

Prof. Dr. Tiberiu Șeicaru
Bucharest, Romania, 2008

A Foggy Sunrise was written with great sensitivity and, above all, succeeds in creating a vivid and authentic image of our lives during those times. It's a living fresco — like old photographs, it captures film-like images, frozen in both time and space. It reads like a documentary with historiographical value, from which a director could easily draw out character moments rich in emotional depth.

Each character in the writing feels alive and firmly grounded in their era, portrayed with a remarkable talent for precise description and an economy of style that sketches vivid personalities within the context of daily life.

Victoria Dimonie
Bethlehem, Pennsylvania, 2008

Clarion Review

A Foggy Sunrise by David Kimel

Autobiography & Memoire

Five stars (out of five)

This powerful memoir of wartime Romania brings back the horrors of war with the resilience of childhood.

In this beautiful, crafted memoir, *A Foggy Sunrise,* David Kimel describes his childhood growing up in Bucharest, including the lean and fearful times of World War II. He provides vivid snapshots into a time and place he witnessed but also demonstrates how he was always sustained by his strong and guiding parents.

Kimel-now in his early eighties-tells of the marriage between his mother, from a well-to-do family in Bulgaria, and his father, a Jewish man from Romania, whose own father was a native of Poland. From this melting pot of ethnicities, the author reminisces about how his extended family supported one another when times were difficult.

Kimel own family-including younger sister Simona-was forced to move from apartment to apartment over years when money from work could not be stretched to cover expenses. But the author recounts this all from a young boy's perspective, nothing that he intrigued more with a toy than his brand-new sibling.

The majority of the book chronicles his life form ages of three to thirteen, when he celebrated his Bar Mitzvah. The remaining fifty pages tell how he and various relatives emigrated from Romania to make their homes in other counties.

The author- a resident of Canada for nearly forty years-is a talented writer, creating a sense of place from his memories of Bucharest. The German army occupied Bucharest for most of the war years: Kimel relates that while some Jewish were singled out by the Legionaries-green-shirted vigilante hooligans who were similar to the brown-shirted stormtroopers-it was largely left to the local government to deal with any "Jewish problem". Bombing by the Allies and their aftermath affected the citizens, but because children are resilient, the young David looked forward to finding "treasures" in the wreckage.

Conscious of his audience, he translates Romanian words for easier understanding, placing the English terms in parenthesis, such as *Piaţa Mare* (the Big Market) and *Podul Izvor* (Izvor Bridge). He expands on cultural customs, recalling that it normal to address all elderly people as Aunt and Uncle, whether or not they were relatives.

Using vivid descriptions and most minute of details to depict the places and people his past, Kimel recalls this about his school: "A double wrought iron gate door was guarded by an old man sitting inside a little booth that had a sliding window." He describes the man inside, the father of the school secretary as "A little, thin man with glasses, and hair cut short."

Many figures from his past are brought to life: teachers at his all-boy vocational school who earned nicknames from students; his many relatives (and their many peccadilloes) who resided in nearby towns; playmates, both good and bad; and even one or two adults who took advantage of unsupervised children.

The most memorable, however, are Kimel's parents. He recounts how he missed being with them and Simona prior to their death, and so spread out photos on the floor to remember "The little images imprinted on paper brought back the stories of our lives, the precious moments that bonded each of us together…and I knew that from now I alone, I have the duty to preserve their lives and their memories." These photos would have been a great addition to such a personal story.

This powerful memoir leaves a lasting impression as a glimpse of a time and place that is no more.

Robin Farrell Edmunds

2014

Glossary

Pronunciation. In Romanian Language:

a: a is pronounce like **a** in **a**dd, m**a**p.

e: is pronounce like **e** in **e**nd, p**e**t.

i: is pronounce like **i** in **i**t, g**i**ve.

o: is pronounce like **o** in **o**dd, h**o**t.

u: is pronounce like **oo** in p**oo**l, f**oo**d.

ă: is pronounce like **a** in **a** dollar, **a**bout.

â: is pronounce like **i** in g**i**rl, g**i**rdle.

ș: is pronounce like **sh** in **sh**ore, **sh**ould.

ț: is pronounce like **tz** in **tz**ar, **tz**igane.

ce: is pronounce like **ch** in **ch**erry, **ch**ain.

ci: is pronounce like **ch** in **ch**icken, **ch**in.

chi: is pronounce like **k** in **k**ing, **k**ill.

che: is pronounce like **k** in **k**eg, **k**ernel.

ge: is pronounce like **g** in **g**el, **g**em.

gi: is pronounce like **g** in **g**ee, **g**in.

ghe: is pronounce like **g** in **g**et, **g**eyser.

ghi: is pronounce like **g** in **g**ift, **g**ive.